LEE BROOK

The West Yorkshire Ripper

For Eric—
It's been ten years, Grandad, and I still miss you.
You would have loved this novel.

Contents

Chapter One

The Leeds Organised Crime Group, an assemblage of seasoned officers, was bracing for a pivotal operation. Detective Inspector George Beaumont, his heart thudding with anxiety and resolve, studied the intricate plans sprawled before him.

Detective Superintendent Jim Smith, a figure of commanding presence, broke the silence. "Focus, everyone. Our target: Piers Keaton, right-hand man to the notorious Schmidt. Today, he's moving a significant drug haul into Leeds."

The room's attention shifted to the detailed motorway map Smith was pointing at. "DCI Atkinson will initiate a rolling roadblock on the M62. Keaton's going to walk right into our trap."

George, accustomed to the rush and risks of high-stakes operations, felt a surge of determination. His team, well-trained under his vigilant eye, was about to strike a critical blow to Schmidt's criminal network.

The team, now fully briefed, dispersed to their unmarked vehicles. George's mind raced with strategies as the sirens wailed, cutting through the quiet of the motorway. They were on the cusp of cornering Schmidt's empire.

The setup was impeccable. Up ahead, officers, under the guise of a road accident, had staged the roadblock. Then, like a scene from a thriller, a black SUV, driven with reckless abandon, hurtled towards them. It was Keaton, unmistakable in his audacity.

DCI Atkinson's voice, strained with urgency, crackled over the radio. "All units, engage. He's not stopping!"

What followed was a maelstrom of screeching tires and strategic manoeuvrers. Keaton, desperate to escape, rammed into the police cars with a ferocity that sent some spinning out of control. George, maintaining a cool head amidst the chaos, directed his team with precision.

The climax was as swift as it was dramatic. Their quarry's vehicle, clipped skilfully by one of the units, spiralled out of control, crashing through the barriers and flipping dramatically.

George was the first out of his car, his weapon drawn and pointed at the overturned SUV. "Armed police! Surrender now!"

Defiance in the face of defeat, Keaton emerged, battered but not yet broken, attempting a futile escape. George, adrenaline and training in perfect synchrony, tackled him to the ground, a swift and decisive end to the chase.

"It's over, Keaton," George declared, the satisfaction of the moment marred by the weight of what was still to come.

Back at the station, the buzz of the day's success had faded, leaving George in a contemplative silence. Keaton's arrest was a victory, yet the elusive Schmidt remained a looming threat. The fight against the cartel was far from over, each victory a step in a much larger, more perilous game.

His thoughts were abruptly interrupted by DSU Smith. "George, we have another situation. A new Ripper killing in Chapeltown."

The words hit George like a cold wave. The past, it seemed, was not content with being a mere shadow. New horrors were unfolding on the streets he vowed to protect.

"You want me to lead the investigation?" George asked, already knowing the answer.

Smith nodded solemnly. "If you're ready."

George stood, a mix of resolve and grim determination in his eyes. "I'm ready." The criminal underworld of Leeds, with its cartels and now a Ripper imitator, was a dark labyrinth. But George Beaumont was no stranger to darkness. He would bring light to it, one case at a time.

With a heavy heart but unwavering spirit, George donned his coat, stepping out into the night that held both his city's demons and his resolve to face them.

Chapter Two

The rain fell in relentless sheets over the darkened streets of Chapeltown. Detective Inspector George Beaumont pulled his trench coat tighter against the chill as he ducked under the police tape cordoning off the latest gruesome crime scene. Even with over a decade on the force, the sight before him turned his stomach.

The victim lay broken and bloodied in the filthy alley, her matted blonde hair obscuring her face. As George circled the body, the rigidity of the limbs told him she had been dead for some time. Bloody lacerations criss-crossed her torso and legs, precise and deliberate in their cruelty.

The Yorkshire Ripper's signature.

"Four decades since his last kill, and some bastard decides to copy him," George muttered. Leeds had enjoyed a long reprieve from fear since the original 1970s murders. But this eviscerated body was proof the Ripper now stalked these streets once more.

Recently promoted DC Candy Nichols appeared at George's side. "The victim's name is Abigail Trent, 25 years old. She left a friend's flat after a house party around midnight last night." She frowned. "Never made it home."

George knelt down, taking in Abigail's face. In death, her

features had taken on a doll-like fragility, accentuating her youth. Far too young to become prey to such evil. Anger and regret roiled in his gut. If only they had caught this monster sooner.

"The lacerations are new, aren't they, sir?" Candy asked.

George nodded. "The bastard's copying Sutcliffe now." He shook his head. To kill in Chapeltown was already an insult, but to kill and eviscerate his victim was completely bang out of order.

Candy added, "Forensics is sweeping the scene now, but it doesn't look like he left us anything useful."

Dead ends and false trails had plagued the original investigation. This killer was always a phantom, a shadow. Even now, his copycat was the same and raised more questions than answers. Why Leeds after attacking Bradford? Why copy the Ripper? What sparked the bloodlust?

George studied the alley, imagining the attack as it unfolded. Abigail's last moments were filled with terror and agony as the Ripper tore into her vulnerable flesh again and again. Closing his eyes, George murmured a quiet prayer for her lost soul—another innocent lamb slaughtered by a lion in sheep's clothing.

He opened his eyes with renewed purpose. "Increase patrols in the area and set up roadblocks around Chapeltown. Canvass for witnesses. Someone must have seen or heard something useful."

Candy nodded, then paused, uncertainty in her eyes. "Do you think he will kill again, sir?"

The same question plagued George since he'd heard about the first murder in Bradford three weeks ago. George looked at Abigail Trent. He thought he'd captured the Ripper copycat when he caught Freddie Harman, but clearly, they had the wrong guy.

"Yes," George replied. His mate, criminologist Mark Finch, had warned him, but he hadn't listened. "Unfortunately, I think he's just getting started."

As Candy coordinated with the PCs milling about, George let his gaze wander the crumbling row of houses lining the alley. Most sat dark and abandoned, windows boarded up and condemned. But in one dingy basement flat, a torn curtain shifted. George tensed.

Was it a witness or the killer himself?

The curtain stilled as quickly as it moved.

"Candy," George said and nodded towards the curtain.

She nodded and followed as George approached the basement entrance, senses alert. The wooden door stood slightly ajar. George nudged it open with his foot. The hinges creaked but revealed only inky darkness within.

Torch raised, George swept the beam around the cramped interior—no furniture or personal effects. Layers of grime and peeling paint told him no one lived here.

Moving farther inside, George scrutinised every corner. He found a smear of blood on the wall. Fresh. He motioned Candy over.

"He was here. Watching us." George's jaw clenched. The Ripper had the audacity to observe right under their noses.

Candy shot him a worried look. "Do you think he's still nearby?"

"No. But he will be back. This flat gives him a perfect vantage point." George could almost feel the Ripper's lingering presence like a venomous spider retreating deeper into its web. But he would find the light eventually and force the monster into the open.

George stepped back into the rain, surveying the tapestry of tragedy before him once more. Abigail Trent deserved justice. All the Ripper's victims did, both past and still to come, because George knew with absolute certainty that Abigail would not be the last to suffer the Ripper's wrath.

Not if the Ripper could help it.

This was no mindless spree. The Ripper followed his own perverse design, killing and then vanishing only to reappear when the fervour died down—a patient predator with intelligence and cunning on his side.

But George had something stronger: conviction. However long it took, he would unravel the secrets that shrouded this ghostly killer in shadow. He would dig into the dark core of this man's twisted psyche, understand his motivations, and decode the symbolism behind his brutal methods.

The Ripper craved power over his victims. Such evil could never be satisfied. It would drive him to kill again and again. And one day soon, he would slip up. Leave the evidence George needed.

When that crucial moment came, George would be ready. He would descend like lightning, ripping away the Ripper's shroud and exposing the fetid truth beneath. There would be justice. For Abigail. For the dead. For the city living on borrowed time before the next murder.

George had lived in Leeds most of his life and had spent his early policing years on the beat. He knew its neighbourhoods and pubs, its pride and flaws.

He also knew about the pall of fear cast over Leeds during the original Ripper murders. Parents were afraid to let their children walk home from school alone. Women were warned to avoid the streets after dark—daily life ruptured by panic.

Things were different now. He understood this killer's twisted psyche better than anyone in Yorkshire. The Ripper copycat had crafted his own mythology as an untouchable bogeyman. A myth George intended to destroy.

This was his city to protect. His streets. His people. All those years ago, the Ripper carved himself a place in Leeds' history through violence and terror. Now, the bastard thought he could simply take up where Sutcliffe left off. Resume Sutcliffe's grisly work as if those lost decades meant nothing.

But George would never let that happen. George would prove once and for all that even monsters could be brought to justice.

The Ripper had returned from the past to haunt this city again.

Chapter Three

The sombre silence in the briefing room was shattered by the metallic clang of Detective Sergeant Luke Mason slamming his fist on the table. "Bloody hell, I haven't seen carnage like this since my days as a beat cop back during the Ripper's reign."

Detective Superintendent Jim Smith didn't blame Luke for the outburst. The gruesome photos from the latest murder scene were enough to rattle even the most hardened officer. "I know, Luke. It's like we've stepped back in time to a nightmare we thought was over."

Mason ran a shaky hand through his thinning silver hair as he examined the images again. The precise slashes across the torso, the ritualistic posing of the body, the look of abject horror still etched on the victim's lifeless face—all of it pointed to a sinister mimicry of Yorkshire's most infamous killer.

Except this was no historic case file. The glossy Polaroids strewn across the table offered ghastly proof that a new Ripper now stalked northern England's streets.

"Four decades gone by, and some mad bastard decides to dredge it all up again," Smith muttered.

Luke nodded. Though only a rookie on foot patrol back then, the original Ripper murders left deep scars on his psyche that hadn't faded with time. The terror and helplessness he witnessed in Leeds simmered under the surface and never fully healed.

Until now.

This new spree wasn't just a horrific crime wave. For Mason, it was a reckoning—a second chance to snare the elusive monster that traumatised his adopted home town and got away.

George recognised that steely glint in the older man's eye. It mirrored his own simmering urge to settle the score for good.

George turned his focus to the evidence board mounted on the far wall. Mason had worked the earliest Ripper murders back in '75, but this killing spree truly kicked off for the West Yorkshire Police nearly two months ago in Bradford with the body of a young prostitute, Cosima Winfrey. That brutal murder scene was when George first feared the Ripper's twisted spirit had been resurrected.

Sadly, he'd been right. Cosima was only the first. Since then, two more slain women had been left displayed after nocturnal stalkings, though they knew Freddie Harman was responsible for one of them.

George added the newest images to the Big Board—Abigail Trent, a university student, found in an alley in Chapeltown just hours ago. That meant they had three they could attribute to the Ripper copycat: Cosima Winfrey and Tabitha Arrand from Bradford and Abigail Trent from Leeds.

Seeing the growing patchwork of victims staring back at him, George's jaw clenched with resolve. "Three women dead so far by his hand. And those are just the ones we've found. If we don't catch this maniac soon, the number will only climb."

Mason leaned back, looking every bit his age as the weight of still-raw memories bore down. "You weren't even thought of back then, son," he said to George. "You didn't see the bloody panic. My missus was too scared to leave the house after dark. Folks rushed home before sundown, avoiding shadows. And the hate toward any single man who dared walk the streets."

"And the hate us coppers got," said Jim Smith.

"Don't I bloody know it." Mason shook his head bitterly. "I saw mobs accuse innocent blokes just because they resembled the vague suspect sketch. I even shaved off my beard." He shrugged. "Nearly started riots over fear and anger. It poisoned the whole city until people didn't trust their own neighbours any more. Became a ghost town after dark. Can't imagine going through all that madness again."

George absorbed the haunting recollections and understood the deeper fear fuelling Mason's reaction. This wasn't just a serial killer they were chasing. It was a ghost from the past with an insatiable hunger to watch women suffer and die. To feed on the public's paranoia like a ravenous vampire. To achieve the mythical infamy of Yorkshire's bogeyman.

George laid a steadying hand on Mason's shoulder. "It won't come to that, Luke. You're not the same rookie. You've learned. Hell, we've all learned." He gestured at the Big Board's grisly tableau. "It won't come to that, I promise you."

"Don't say stuff like that, son. It's not worth—"

"This murdering bastard wants to be the next Peter Sutcliffe," George interrupted. "He wants to carry on that bloody legacy and make Leeds fear the Ripper's shadow again. But we won't give him the satisfaction." George's voice hardened, carrying the weight of oath. "We'll figure out who this pretender is, why he's picked up the Ripper mantle again after all this time. And we'll put him in the fucking ground where he belongs."

Mason studied his DI's granite expression and nodded slowly, a fragile hope dawning in his eyes. Maybe this time could be different.

Chapter Four

The modest brick semi-detached house was silent except for the muffled sobs coming from the living room. Detective Inspector George Beaumont stood awkwardly in the hallway, preparing himself for the devastating grief awaiting within. In front of him was Family Liaison Officer Cathy Hoskins.

Taking a deep breath, he stepped inside. The Trents were huddled together on the faded sofa, clutching each other for solace. A box of tissues sat on the coffee table, damp and nearly empty.

At the soft creak of the floorboards, Abigail Trent's mother, Carol, raised her head. Her eyes were raw and puffy behind a veil of dishevelled blonde hair, so much like her daughter's. She studied Beaumont for a moment before recognition set in.

"Inspector...did you find him? The Ripper?" The faintest flicker of hope in her broken voice.

Beaumont's heart twisted, wishing he could offer closure. "Not yet, Mrs Trent. But we will keep chasing every lead without rest until we do. You have my word."

Carol nodded numbly before a fresh sob escaped her throat. She reached for the framed photo, sitting amidst the wilted flower arrangements and clutching it to her chest like a lifeline. It showed Abigail on graduation day, smiling brightly with her whole future ahead. Now destined to be forever young, 25 years old for all eternity.

"My baby girl...she was so beautiful, so full of life," Carol choked out. "Studying to be a teacher, you know. Wanted to shape young minds. Had a passion for it. She would've been brilliant..."

Unable to continue, she broke down again. Abigail's father, Donald, wrapped a comforting arm around his wife, though the profound grief carved into his features showed he was just as shattered. When he finally spoke, his voice was hollow. Defeated.

"We already lost our eldest, Anna, two years back to leukaemia. To have Abigail taken from us this way, too...it's not right. No parents should have to bury their children." His words dissolved into anguished weeping.

George stood awkwardly, wishing he could offer more than empty condolences, hoping to give them the one thing they truly wanted: their precious daughter back. A young life cruelly cut short by a monster's thirst for blood. He despised feeling so powerless.

After a period of unrestrained mourning, Carol Trent composed herself enough to meet Beaumont's eyes again. "Inspector...please, you have to find who did this. Who took our little girl from us. Please make him suffer for what he's done. Swear to me you'll find him!"

Her raw desperation carved into George's soul. He moved closer, kneeling by the sofa so they were at eye level. "Mrs Trent, I give you my word that I will not rest until Abigail's killer is brought to justice. Your daughter deserves nothing less, OK? This Ripper copycat may think he can hide, but he will find no refuge in Yorkshire."

George hesitated, then continued. "And though it brings little comfort, please know that Abigail did not suffer. The actual..." He faltered, not wanting to revisit grisly details. "It was over quickly. She did not suffer, OK. I swear to you." It was a small mercy but the only one he could offer.

Carol seemed to take fragile solace in this, fresh tears trailing down her cheeks as she clung to the photo. "Bless you, Inspector. I know you'll do everything possible to find this fiend. Our Abby deserves justice. She deserves to rest peacefully."

Donald Trent spoke up again, voice taut with sorrow and simmering rage. "Find him, Inspector. Don't let him take more daughters from more families. It's your duty to end his evil before he rips apart other homes like ours." His fists were clenched, his body shuddering with grief and impotent fury over his slain child.

George rose solemnly. "You have the full commitment of myself and the police, Mr and Mrs Trent. What was done to Abigail will be answered for, no matter how long it takes. Her death will not be meaningless. I promise."

Exiting the house, Beaumont took a moment in the brisk night air to steady himself. Seeing the Trents' raw anguish only deepened his resolve.

* * *

The Incident Room was abuzz with the team poring over the intricate details of the Ripper's history. George stood at the centre, orchestrating the flow of information like a conductor. His team, a mix of seasoned veterans and eager young detectives, hung on every word.

"As we know, Sutcliffe's reign was marked by brutality and precision," George began, his voice steady. "But there's more to his story, layers we've yet to fully understand."

Candy Nichols, her eyes scanning a dossier, looked up. "What about his personal life? There were always gaps in what the public knew, sir."

George nodded, a thoughtful expression on his face. "Indeed. Rumours and unconfirmed reports suggested there was more to Sutcliffe than met the eye. Hints of hidden relationships, a private life shrouded in mystery."

Jay Scott, leaning against the wall, chimed in. "A hidden family, maybe? It was all speculation, wasn't it?"

"Mostly," George replied, his gaze distant. "But in cases like this, even rumours can have a kernel of truth. We can't ignore the possibility of unknown connections."

The room fell silent, each member contemplating the implications. The idea that the Ripper might have had a secret family, relationships that had escaped decades of scrutiny, added a new dimension to the case.

"We need to dig deeper," George continued, his voice unwavering. "Review old interviews and talk to anyone who knew him personally. Anything that sheds light on his private life."

The team nodded, energised by the new lead. As they dispersed to their tasks, George remained at the table; the files spread out before him. The notion of a hidden aspect of Sutcliffe's life niggled at him, a puzzle piece that might be crucial to understanding the current case.

Chapter Five

At the front of the Incident Room, Detective Inspector George Beaumont prepared to address his team, his presence commanding attention. "Any updates?"

Police Constable Andrew Finch stepped forward, a file in hand. "I've compiled the overnight reports," he announced, his voice steady and clear. The room quieted, all eyes turning to him.

As Andrew detailed the latest developments, George noted the precision of his delivery. Every fact was meticulously presented, each observation sharp and focused. Andrew's knowledge of the case details was extensive, more than what his role would typically entail.

"There's a pattern in the timings of the attacks," Andrew pointed out, highlighting specific lines in his report. "And if we consider the historical context of the original Ripper's methods..."

George raised an eyebrow, intrigued. Andrew's analysis delved deep, showing engagement beyond routine duty. It was as if Andrew had immersed himself in the case, living and breathing the details.

The briefing continued, but George's mind lingered on Andrew's presentation. The constable's keen interest and detailed knowledge of the case were unusual for his rank. It was a level of dedication that bordered on obsession.

* * *

"To understand criminality, we must confront humanity's darkest corners." Professor Mark Finch's Scottish brogue echoed off the crowded lecture hall walls. He clicked the projector remote, the screen filling with a chilling image—a collage of pictures of Dennis Nilsen, Harold Shipman, Beverley Allitt, Fred and Rose West, and Ian Brady.

"What drives seemingly ordinary people to commit extraordinary evil? Today, we examine one such enigma—the serial murderer."

Finch began pacing the stage slowly. "Of course, our morbid fascination with these real-life monsters often overshadows the true cost of their crimes. The torn families and destroyed communities left in their wake."

He paused, letting the room absorb his words before continuing. "Perhaps none exemplifies this killer celebrity phenomenon more than the Yorkshire Ripper. For years, this shadowy figure held Northern England hostage through a brutal murder spree targeting women."

Sutcliffe's face appeared on the screen.

With another click, the projector showed photos of the Ripper's gruesome handiwork—bodies obscenely posed and eviscerated. Students gasped and shifted uneasily as Finch studied the horrific images.

"Thirteen confirmed victims attributed to the Ripper before Peter Sutcliffe's 1981 conviction ended the nightmare." Finch's voice hardened. "Though for the families involved, the nightmare never truly ends."

He began pacing again. "Now then, what fascinates criminologists is how one twisted man could wield such fear over an entire society. Reduce once-vibrant communities to ghost towns after dark. Make citizens view their own neighbours with suspicion and dread."

Finch paused next to a student in the front row. "Imagine not feeling safe walking home from this very lecture hall at night. Worrying that any passing stranger could be the Ripper himself, waiting to strike. An entire region gripped by paranoia over one killer."

Returning to the podium, Finch folded his arms grimly. "The Yorkshire Ripper became more than a man. He embodied primal terror, the depths of depravity lurking within. A faceless evil that stripped away the illusion of order and reason. Turned bustling modern neighbourhoods into hunting grounds."

He lowered his voice. "In many ways, the legend and fear surrounding this spectre mattered more than the broken mortal behind it all. Society endowed him with mythical power to stalk the night. He became the new bogeyman."

Finch glanced up at the horrific images still projected. "But in focusing on the Ripper's twisted celebrity, we risk forgetting the true cost. Thirteen innocent lives were cut short. Families destroyed. Communities shaken to their core."

His dark eyes scanned the silent room. "So, I ask you this— how does a supposedly civilised society allow such evil to take root in its midst? And when it takes that dreadful form, how should we... no, how must we confront it?"

Letting the provocative question hang in the air, Finch clicked to a new slide. "Next week, we will explore profiling techniques police investigators use to get inside these deviant minds. But consider my challenge until then: how can society face darkness without losing our own humanity in the process? The Ripper lost his. We must guard ours more closely."

As students slowly gathered their belongings to leave, Finch noticed his friend George Beaumont waiting by the exit. The professor's chest tightened, realising why the Inspector likely needed to see him so urgently.

The Ripper's twisted legacy was haunting Yorkshire again.

Steeling himself, Finch approached George, knowing his friend would do everything possible to hunt this new evil down.

* * *

George slid into the worn wooden booth in the back corner, away from the other Drysalter patrons. He checked his watch. 7.58 pm. Finch would arrive any minute.

Sure enough, right on time, the front door swung open, ushering in a bitterly cold draft along with a tall figure in a wool coat. George raised a hand in greeting as his old friend Mark Finch approached the table.

"Now then, George. I must say I was surprised to see you in my lecture," Finch said, unwinding his scarf before sitting down. His Scottish accent was still prominent even after years of living in Leeds.

George gave a grim nod. "Sorry to drag you out on short notice, but I really need your help, mate." He paused. "I was surprised you left the case when you did. And that you didn't contact me once you found out about Abigail Trent."

The DI was referring to the fact that Finch left the case once George had apprehended Freddie Harman, assuming he was both the Ripper copycat and the Leeds Ritual Killer.

Finch's expression turned sombre, and he ran a hand through his hair. "I'm as surprised as you are that Harman isn't this copycat," said Finch. "When I heard the news and realised it wasn't just sensationalised media shite, I knew I should have rung you, George." He paused. "But I was embarrassed." He sighed. "I'm sorry, George."

Finch stood up and went to the bar. Two minutes later, he was back with two pints of bitter. Finch took a big sip of his and then said, "So, how can I help?"

Cautiously, George said, "This killer...he's now mimicking the Ripper's methods very closely."

Mark frowned. "Explain."

"He's now emulating Sutcliffe fully," said George. "It's the precision of the wounds, the posing of bodies. It's deliberate replication now."

"And before, it was just killing prostitutes?" Finch said.

George nodded and slid a folder across the table. Finch opened it slowly, his face paling at the horrific contents. Crime scene reports and photos of the recent victims, brutally gutted and displayed like macabre art.

"Jesus fucking Christ," Finch said as he closed the folder, clearly shaken. "You're right. It's like Sutcliffe himself has risen from the grave. What cancerous purpose drives a man to re-enact such violence?"

"That's what I'm hoping you can help me with, mate," George replied. "I need to get inside this bastard's mind. Figure out his obsession with the original Ripper before he kills again."

Finch took another long draft of his bitter, gathering his thoughts before speaking. "Well, I imagine celebrity plays a large role. The Yorkshire Ripper became a legend, the modern bogeyman. This copycat is clearly infatuated with that narrative and seeks to carry it on."

Mark tapped the folder. "Yet it may be more personal than mere legend. The intimate precision of the rituals implies a deep connection to the original crimes. Perhaps even a personal motive like revenge."

George considered this unnerving theory as he sipped his beer. A killer avenging past Ripper victims through fresh blood? It was plausible, yet raised more questions about the impersonator's intent.

Finch continued sombrely. "Of course, by recreating these infamous slayings, the perpetrator knows he will sow fear and paranoia in Leeds anew. Devious, really, how the Ripper's legacy gifts him that power so easily."

He locked eyes with George. "Make no mistake, you face a cunning and dangerous adversary. This is more than a man, George; it's an ideal, risen again to prey upon Leeds. Catching him will be no small feat."

George absorbed the grave warning silently. In truth, part of him relished the chance to prove himself, to force the Ripper's spectre into flesh-and-blood form and defeat it. This time for good.

Finch seemed to read George's thoughts. "I know Harman not being the Ripper makes this case especially meaningful to you, but do not let that cloud your mind or judgement, matey." His tone softened.

"What are you suggesting?" asked George.

"Nothing, mate. I just want you to be careful, that's all."

George nodded slowly, seeing the wisdom in Finch's counsel. They finished their pints in contemplative silence before stepping back out into the cold night air.

George extended his hand. "Invaluable as always, mate. Cheers."

Finch shook firmly. "Let me know if you need me, OK?" His eyes turned skyward pensively. "Leeds has overcome darker days before. It'll do so again, mate."

With a final farewell, the two men parted ways into the night.

Chapter Six

The scent of home cooking filled the kitchen as Isabella checked on the roast in the oven. At the table, George Beaumont bounced his baby daughter Olivia on his knee, eliciting delighted giggles. For a moment, the chaos of the case faded into domestic tranquillity.

Until his mobile rang.

With an apologetic look, George handed Olivia to Isabella before stepping into the other room. "DI Beaumont here. What's up?"

DS Mason's voice came through, urgent. "George, we just got a call on the tip line from an estate agent. Someone spotted a man behaving oddly around a vacant Chapeltown warehouse earlier tonight. The caller ID'd the prowler as a local store owner."

"Maybe he wanted to rent the warehouse out?" said George.

"I thought that too, George, but he has dark hair and a dark beard," Mason said.

George's pulse quickened. He didn't want to get too caught up on the e-fit they had from the Bradford murders, especially as a man could easily shave and cut their hair, but it was something. It could also be everything. This could be the break they needed. "Good work, Luke. Get Uniform there straight away and call me with whatever they find. I'm on my way."

Returning to the kitchen, George met Isabella's weary gaze and knew she understood. "I'm sorry, gorgeous."

"I get it." Isabella forced a brave smile, though disappointment was evident in her dark eyes. "Just please be safe out there." She lifted his coat from the hook herself and helped him into it. Ever the dutiful partner. "And don't do too much; I know you've been struggling with your injuries, even if you try to pretend you aren't."

George pulled her and Olivia into a hug, wishing he didn't have to leave his little family. But the Ripper's shadow still loomed over Leeds, and it was his sworn duty to dispel it.

Kissing them both goodbye, George hurried out into the night. Twenty minutes later, he was at the warehouse, watching the search team comb the filthy interior. "Anything so far?" he asked Mason.

"Take a look for yourself, son." Mason waved him over to a grimy workbench. Two items lay there in evidence bags—a ball pein hammer coated in dried blood and a Phillips-head screwdriver.

"Fucking hell," said George.

"Bastard must've stashed them here to taunt us," Mason spat. "CSI's on the way to process for prints or DNA, but I doubt we'll be that lucky."

George's jaw clenched at the brazen mockery. The Ripper was playing games, and they were always one step behind. How long until this phantom tired of eluding capture and got careless? Made a mistake? Soon, George hoped.

After an hour, SOC Manager Lindsey Yardley approached, looking defeated. "No usable prints or biological traces that we can see initially. Whoever left them on display was careful."

George cursed under his breath. It was just another dead end.

"But I'm sure we can match the blood to one of the victims," Lindsey said.

* * *

George concluded briefing his team on the latest dead end at the warehouse. He could see the growing frustration on their faces mirroring his own. This phantom was adept at keeping them staggering in the dark.

"There must be something we're missing," George insisted, trying to spark new theories. "Our suspect clearly has an intimate obsession with the Ripper's methods." He checked his watch. It was late, but they'd worked later before. Much later. "Let's revisit victimology—were there any connections between the original spree and our recent victims?" He paused, then added, "And I need somebody to visit the shop owner in Chapeltown first thing in the morning."

"I'll get on it ASAP," DC Candy Nichols said.

Jay grinned. "I'll go with DC Nichols, boss, if that's OK?"

George nodded. They'd no doubt be waking up together, so it made sense for them to leave together.

As his team reluctantly delved back into the ancient case files, George's mind churned, too. What crucial piece of this puzzle continued eluding them?

His contemplation was interrupted by DCI Atkinson barging into the room, face like a thundercloud. "A word, George. In private." George's jaw clenched, but he followed Atkinson into the open office and then to his private office.

Once the door closed, Atkinson wheeled on him. "Explain

to me how, after all the time and resources invested, you're no closer to identifying this killer? Three victims already, and what progress, exactly?"

George bristled at the accusatory tone. "With respect, sir, this is a difficult case, as you very well know." The case had been passed from a DI in Bradford to DSU Smith and DCI Atkinson before being passed to George. "We're pursuing every—"

Atkinson cut him off. "I'm aware it's a tough nut to crack but don't pretend this is your first challenging case. The fact is you got lucky with Harman. Without him leaving his saliva behind, you'd never have caught him." He paused and ran a hand through his dark beard. "And I've seen you limping recently." Atkinson cleared his throat. "We have a dangerous maniac roaming free in our city, and I'm not sure you're fit enough to be chasing him!"

George's eyes narrowed. "I am, sir."

"Bullshit," Atkinson spat. "I'm starting to doubt whether you're up for the task of stopping him."

George's fists balled in anger. How dare Atkinson impugn his competence when he had botched the Ripper investigation in Bradford and gotten nowhere? "DSU Smith clearly thinks I'm capable."

"He may do, but I don't. And I'm your boss, remember that!"

George wanted to argue with the DCI but held his tongue. Losing his temper would only prove Atkinson's point about instability under pressure. He took a slow breath before replying evenly. "You know I'll do whatever it takes to catch this killer. My commitment isn't in question."

Atkinson seemed unconvinced. "If that's the case, then see

that the next progress report contains more progress. The public is desperate for this man off the streets." The DCI narrowed his eyes. "I'd hate for you to fail and further erode the public's fragile trust in the police." He shrugged. "That wouldn't do much for any promotions, would it?"

The backhanded warning made George grit his teeth to the point of pain. He wanted to ask the DCI what his problem was, but he simply nodded curtly before returning to the Incident Room, Atkinson's harsh words ringing in his ears.

His team picked up on the scowl clouding his face and prudently avoided comment. George stared up at the Big Board, the photo of bright young Abigail Trent staring back at him. She deserved justice. They all did. And he was failing them so far.

Atkinson's harsh assessment gnawed at him. Was he genuinely losing his edge? Allowing pressure to cloud his deductive skills? Self-doubt permeated his mind like corroding acid.

No. He refused to accept defeat so easily.

This killer was cunning, but George had bested cunning foes before.

Chapter Seven

The shrill ring of George's mobile pierced the tranquillity of the living room. He glanced at the caller ID and sighed before answering.

"Hi, Mia."

"Are you still picking up Jack today?" His ex-fiancée's voice held a sharp edge.

George mentally kicked himself. Amidst the chaos of the case, he'd forgotten about picking Jack up that morning.

"Yep, I'm on my way now," he lied, grabbing his keys.

The drive to East Ardsley took twenty tense minutes. Two-year-old Jack greeted him with youthful excitement when he arrived, oblivious to his father's lapse. Scooping the giggling toddler into his arms, George felt a pang of guilt. He hated letting Jack down.

"Bye then," Mia said crisply from the doorway, pretty features hardened by lingering resentment. "I'm going out and won't be back until later." She paused. "Oh, and try not to forget about him next week."

George bit back a retort and simply nodded before buckling Jack into his car seat. At least he had a few hours before his late shift to make up for his mistake.

Back home, Jack was contentedly scribbling with crayons

on the carpet while George brewed coffee in the kitchen. For a blissful interval, the weight of the case lifted, and domestic calm reigned.

George settled onto the sofa, smiling as Jack crawled into his lap, clutching a crude drawing. "This is you, Daddy!"

"That's brilliant, son." George ruffled his son's blond hair, cherishing the simple joy radiating from him. If only such innocence could persist.

But the moment was shattered by the harsh ringtone cutting through the air. Not now, George thought bitterly, even as protocol compelled him to answer.

"DI Beaumont."

DS Mason's urgent voice greeted him. "George, we've got a significant lead on the Ripper. A DIY shop on Kirkstall Road says he sold a bulk of ball pein hammer and Phillips-head screwdrivers to a man three nights back. Same type the killer used on the last victim."

George closed his eyes, pulse quickening even as disappointment twisted his gut. This was the first concrete break in the case, yet it meant abandoning his son. Again.

"I'll be right there, Luke. Have CCTV footage from the shop sent to the Incident Room."

Ending the call, George turned to Jack, whose smile had faded into a fretful pout. "I'm so sorry, son, but Daddy has important police work." The words felt hollow, guilt rising in his throat.

He called Mia, bracing for her annoyance. She answered on the second ring.

"What?" Her tone dripped accusation.

"A solid lead just came in on a case I'm working on."

"Unbelievable. I should've known your damn job would

interfere again."

George flinched but stayed silent. Arguing wouldn't help.

After a terse goodbye, George gathered up a protesting Jack and secured him in the car seat. The toddler began crying inconsolably.

"I know you're upset with me, son. I'm upset, too. But we'll spend the whole day together next week, OK?"

Jack simply wailed louder as George pulled away, his tiny face screwed up in distress. The sight was like a knife twisting in George's heart. But duty propelled him forward.

* * *

The CCTV footage from the DIY shop proved worthless–just another dead end. The suspect made his purchase wearing a hoodie and cap, obscuring his face from the cameras. George cursed and slammed his fist against the steering wheel, the sharp pain barely registering.

With no other leads to pursue, he headed to Mark Finch's house, which was nearby.

"The Ripper's pattern is deliberate, calculated," George began, his eyes scanning the crime scene photos. "It's like he's recreating the past, not just imitating it."

Finch nodded, his gaze fixed on a black-and-white photo. "Yes, there's a precision to it. It's as if he's claiming a legacy... almost a form of... familial redemption." His voice trailed off, a distant look in his eyes.

George looked up, catching the odd tone in Finch's voice. "Familial redemption? That's an interesting take."

Finch quickly refocused, the momentary lapse gone as fast as it appeared. "Well, the original Ripper was abandoned, misunderstood. Maybe our guy feels a kinship, a need to complete what was started."

There was a depth to Finch's analysis that went beyond professional insight. It bordered on empathetic, a little too personal. George felt a twinge of curiosity but shelved it for later.

"Kinship?" George echoed, his brow furrowing slightly.

Finch leaned back, his expression reverting to its usual analytical demeanour. "Figuratively speaking. He could be seeing himself in the Ripper's story, filling the void left by his idol."

George nodded, mulling over Finch's words. "We need to get into his head and understand his motives." He started gathering the files, his mind already racing with theories. He stood up, ready to leave.

"Be careful, George. This type of killer he's not just playing a game. He's rewriting history in his mind."

* * *

Morose resignation compelled him back to Mia's house, hoping she might allow him to apologise and see Jack again. But the darkened windows and empty driveway indicated she was gone.

Typical.

George pulled out his mobile and dialled her number, tension coiling in his gut. It rang five times before her voicemail answered coldly. He hung up without leaving a message.

Leaning back in the seat, George closed his eyes and let despair wash over him. He'd abandoned his son for nothing, just as he always did. The job consumed him; its tendrils crept into every aspect of his life, choking out the relationships that mattered most.

And still, the Ripper evaded capture, laughing from the shadows. Another family torn apart by grief and loss. Only this time, it was George's own.

He glanced at the empty car seat in the rear-view mirror, imagining Jack's sweet face twisted in distress. The shrill echoes of his crying as George drove away on a fruitless pursuit. His son's innocent heart broken by the father who kept failing him.

The pain cut deeper than any knife. George pressed his forehead against the icy glass and let muted sobs wrack his body. He lingered there, wallowing in self-loathing as dusk descended and etched the windows in frost.

Nearly half an hour passed before George finally sat up and scrubbed the tears from his face. His breath puffed visibly in the chilled car as he stared out at the dark, silent house. He couldn't change the past. But the future remained unwritten.

George started the engine; jaw clenched with resolve. He would make this right somehow. Mend the trust he'd broken today. He had to, for Jack's sake. His son deserved a father who put family before this endless, thankless crusade. Who didn't live solely for the next crime scene, lead, or faceless killer.

Chapter Eight

Detective Inspector George Beaumont and Detective Constable Candy Nichols navigated the narrow, winding streets to the house where Abigail was last seen. The sky, a palette of greys, mirrored the grim mood inside their vehicle.

The modest two-story house with peeling paint stood silently in the sleepy neighbourhood. It starkly contrasted the vibrant life it must have hosted the night of the party. As they approached, Candy's phone buzzed with a message: "Abigail's phone pinged last near here at 1.43 am."

George nodded, his eyes scanning the surroundings—a seemingly ordinary setting he knew held darker undertones.

A young man greeted them at the door, his eyes bloodshot, hair dishevelled—a remnant of the previous night's revelry. "I'm Tom, Abigail's friend," he mumbled, ushering them into the living room. The room was a chaos of overturned furniture and empty bottles, the party's aftermath.

With her keen observer's eye, Candy noticed a picture on the mantelpiece—Abigail, beaming, arm in arm with Tom. "Can you tell us about last night?" she asked, her voice firm yet empathetic.

Tom slumped into a chair, his face a mask of worry. "It was just a regular party. Abi was here, having fun. She left around half one and said she was getting a lift home."

George, leaning against the wall, interjected, "Did she say who she was leaving with?" His voice was sharp, cutting through the haze of Tom's memory.

"No, she didn't. I just saw her head out," Tom replied, his gaze drifting to the floor.

Candy and George exchanged a look, an unspoken agreement passing between them. "Did anything unusual happen at the party? Anyone unknown or out of place?" Candy pressed further, her mind racing with possibilities.

Tom hesitated, then shook his head. "Nothing I can think of. It was just the usual crowd."

As they prepared to leave, George paused by the doorway, turning back to Tom. "If you remember anything, anything at all, give us a call." His tone left no room for argument, a subtle undercurrent of urgency in his words as he handed over a business card.

The steady rhythm of the rain against the car windscreen set a sombre tone as George Beaumont and Candy Nichols left the house behind. The image of Abigail's last known moments, captured in a fleeting frame of laughter and light, contrasted sharply with the grim reality of her disappearance.

"Let's focus on her lift," George suggested, his mind racing through the possibilities. "If she didn't take a taxi, and no one at the party saw her leave with someone, we need to find out who offered her that lift."

Candy nodded, tapping her tablet to access the city's transportation network records. "I'll check for any registered taxis or ride shares in the area around the time she left the party."

The car hummed through the streets, the city still cloaked in the winter gloom. George's eyes were alert, scanning every corner, every shadow. In his line of work, the quiet of dawn often concealed secrets waiting to be unearthed.

Candy's voice broke the silence. "There's no record of any registered taxi or ride share pickups at that time near the party location." Her brow furrowed in concern. "Either she got into a private car, or..."

"Or she never left the vicinity," George finished her thought, the implications hanging heavily in the air.

They reached Tom's house again. The rain had stopped, leaving the world washed anew, but the mystery of Abigail's disappearance remained as murky as ever.

Splitting up to cover more ground, they canvassed the neighbourhood. George's approach was methodical, with each query carefully extracting information. With her natural charm, Candy gently prodded the residents, her questions soft but insistent.

An elderly woman, Mrs Harrow, living two doors down, offered a glimmer of hope. "I saw a car late that night. An old model, dark-coloured. It was parked just down there," she pointed towards the end of the street. "Stayed there for a good while, then drove off. Odd, it was."

George jotted down her statement, his mind piecing together the scant evidence—an unknown car, a murdered girl, and a timeline that was slowly narrowing down.

Back in their car, George and Candy shared their findings. The puzzle was starting to take shape, but the picture it was forming was unsettling.

"We need to find that car," George stated, his voice a determined echo in the cramped space of the vehicle. "It's our best lead yet."

Candy nodded, already sending out an APB based on Mrs

Harrow's description. The police network would now be on the lookout, every patrol car, every traffic camera an extension of their search.

* * *

The lead on the car, which had momentarily promised a breakthrough, fizzled out into the mundane reality of everyday life. Detective Constable Jay Scott and Detective Sergeant Tashan Blackburn returned with the news, their expressions a mix of frustration and determination. The car, an old model spotted by Mrs Harrow, belonged to a woman whose boyfriend used it for early morning shifts. Both their alibis were solid, confirmed independently by Jay and Tashan.

In the squad room, the atmosphere was tense, a palpable mix of urgency and disappointment. George Beaumont leaned back in his chair, his gaze distant, processing the news. Sitting across from him, Candy Nichols rifled through the case file, looking for any missed detail or overlooked clue.

"We're back to square one, boss," Jay said, leaning against the desk. His voice held a tinge of weariness, a sentiment echoed in Tashan's solemn nod.

"Not necessarily," George countered, his voice cutting through the defeatism. "Every cleared lead narrows the field. We're looking for a needle in a haystack, but at least we're eliminating some hay."

Candy looked up, her eyes meeting George's. "What about checking CCTV footage around Tom's house, sir? Maybe we can spot Abigail after she leaves the party and see if she meets someone."

George said, "We've already checked council and private

footage, Candy."

"What about dashcam footage or footage saved on doorbell cameras?" asked Tashan.

"Good idea. Tashan, take the lead on this, take Jay with you and canvass the area. Then, comb through any footage from that night. Look for anything out of the ordinary."

The team sprang into action, a renewed sense of purpose invigorating their steps. As Jay and Tashan set off, Candy turned to George. "What if she never got into a car? What if she walked away from the party?"

George pondered the possibility, his mind racing through scenarios. "Get in touch with Sergeant Greenwood and ask him to start a search around the neighbourhood. She might have taken a detour, something unplanned."

As the day wore on, the team sifted through hours of footage, their eyes straining for any sign of Abigail. The neighbourhood search commenced door-to-door inquiries, painting a picture of the night. Yet, as the sun descended below the horizon, they were no closer to finding Abigail.

* * *

George Beaumont sat across from an elderly man, Harold Jenkins, who had known Peter Sutcliffe in the years before his infamy. The man's hands were clasped tightly on the table, his eyes reflecting the memories of a past long gone.

George leaned forward, his voice calm yet insistent. "Mr Jenkins, you knew Sutcliffe personally. Can you tell me about him? About his life outside of what the public saw?"

Jenkins shifted uncomfortably in his chair, a frown creasing his wrinkled forehead. "Peter was a private man, kept to himself mostly," he began, his voice wavering. "But there were always whispers..."

"Whispers?" George prompted, sensing the hesitation, the undercurrent of something more.

Jenkins looked up, his gaze meeting George's. "About his life, things he never talked about. People said he had secrets, parts of his life he kept hidden, even from those closest to him."

George frowned. No shit, Sherlock. The man kept his secret of being the Ripper for years. Still, his attention sharpened, his mind processing each word. "Did you ever hear anything specific? Any details about these secrets?"

Jenkins shook his head, a shadow passing over his face. "No, nothing concrete. Just rumours, you understand. But in a town like this, rumours sometimes have a bit of truth to them."

George made a mental note of Jenkins's words, the unspoken implications hanging in the air. The interview continued, delving into Sutcliffe's known history, but George's thoughts lingered on the hinted secrets, the whispered aspects of a life shrouded in darkness.

As the interview concluded, George thanked Jenkins and stepped out into the corridor, his mind racing. The idea that Sutcliffe had hidden parts of his life, secrets that had never surfaced, added a new layer to the current investigation. What were these secrets, and how did they tie into the Ripper's legacy?

Back in his office, George sat in contemplation, the interview playing over in his mind. Jenkins's words, the hints at an unseen side of Sutcliffe, were a subtle thread in a larger tapestry. George knew that to catch the current killer, he needed to understand the past, no matter how deep he had to dig into the shadows of history.

At this late hour, he was alone but for the victims' sightless stares, gazing back from the glossy prints. The other detectives had returned to their families hours ago, leaving George to his tireless and futile vigil.

As though a ghost, Abigail Trent had just disappeared.

The door creaked open, and DS Mason entered cautiously, two steaming mugs in hand. George didn't look up from the pages spread before him.

"No breaks tonight, eh lad?" Mason said gently as he placed a tea beside the DI. "You look proper knackered."

George just grunted, not wanting platitudes. The answers were here somewhere amidst the bloodstained evidence and sterile reports. He just had to dig deeper.

Mason pulled up a chair beside him with a weary sigh. They sat in resigned silence under the oppressive white lights, sipping their tea for a while. The station walls muffled the sounds of life outside—lovers laughing, friends embracing, families drawn together.

"What's got you tormenting yourself here alone, George?" Mason finally asked. "Isabella must be missing you tonight. And little Olivia."

George's gaze drifted to the baby photos framed on his desk at the mention of his daughter's name. Toothless smiles and tiny waving hands, snapshots of innocence he hardly saw any more. Needle-sharp regret pierced his heart. He looked at his picture of Jack and had to fight away the tears.

"I don't know how to be there for them, Luke," he admitted softly. "Not with this bastard still out there. The job consumes me. Has done for years now." George's fingers tightened around the mug. "But I've never been this bloody powerless to stop it before. Can't focus on anything but the next lead, the next body."

Mason nodded sympathetically. "I understand, son, believe me. But don't let this Ripper rob you of what matters most. Your family." He gestured at the photos. "They need you, not just in body, but in spirit."

George turned back to the files in front of him, the broken lives cruelly extinguished. "These victims need me, too. Their families. Someone has to find justice for them."

"And you will, but not by burning yourself out," Mason said firmly. "Go home. Be with your wife and daughter. You'll return with a better frame of mind, trust me." He squeezed George's shoulder as he stood to leave.

Alone again, George contemplated Mason's words. He was right—this obsessive spiral only bred failure. Finally closing the folder, George gathered his things and headed out into the cold night air, breath pluming before him.

The hunt could wait one night. Right now, his family needed him more.

* * *

The scrape of a chair being dragged across the floor grated on George's frazzled nerves as DCI Atkinson sat across from him. George had been ordered to Atkinson's office immediately. The detective inspector braced himself for another confrontation.

"You look like shit, Beaumont," Atkinson remarked, eyes narrowing at the DI's haggard appearance. "When's the last time you slept?" He shook his head in exaggerated disappointment.

George remained silent, refusing to be baited.

"I mean, Christ, your face alone is likely frightening the public," Atkinson continued. "Hard to inspire confidence like that, isn't it?"

"I'm fine, sir," George said tightly.

Atkinson leaned forward, his smile not reaching his eyes. "Are you sure? I've noticed that nasty limp is coming back. Not fully recovered, eh?"

George's jaw clenched. "The injury is irrelevant. Now, unless you actually have something productive to discuss—"

"Oh, I do," Atkinson interjected. "I'm ordering you to take leave. Effective immediately."

"What?" George sputtered. "Sir, you can't! We're making progress on—"

"It wasn't a request, Detective Inspector." Atkinson's voice turned icy. "You're unfit for duty in your current state. Obsession is no substitute for diligent police work, which you apparently can't provide currently."

George's frayed temper finally snapped. He surged to his feet and planted his hands on Atkinson's desk, looming over the seated man.

"Don't you dare question my dedication," he growled. "No one wants this bastard caught more than me. I won't sleep until he's stopped!"

Atkinson seemed unfazed by the outburst. "And that right there is the problem. Your judgement is compromised, Beaumont. You've lost all objectivity because it's become a personal vendetta for you." His eyes glinted with perverse satisfaction. "I'm suspending you for your own good. And the good of this investigation."

"You arrogant bastard," George spat. "Both you and Smith

failed!" He paused, and his tone turned to venom. "I'm the best chance at catching the Ripper!"

Atkinson stood abruptly, meeting George's glare. "You're off this case, effective immediately. Now get out of my sight."

George trembled with impotent fury, hands curled into fists. Every instinct screamed at him to fight back, to defy this pompous arsehole's attempt to derail him.

But Atkinson was still his superior. With monumental effort, George mastered his rage. He could do more good on the outside than rotting away powerless on suspension.

Without another word, he turned on his heel and stalked out, Atkinson's taunting laughter echoing down the hall. This was only a temporary setback, George vowed. Atkinson couldn't keep him from the hunt forever. No one could.

* * *

The frigid night air did little to rouse George from his stupor as he left the pub, where he'd attempted to drink his stress away. Physical and emotional exhaustion borne of endless dead ends and strain had finally caught up, turning his limbs to lead. The short walk to his car stretched on forever.

Fumbling with numb, clumsy fingers, George unlocked the vehicle and collapsed into the driver's seat. He knew driving in this condition was foolish, but the thought of waiting even a minute longer to get home was unbearable.

As the engine sputtered to life, the vibrating seat jarred his aching body. George's bleary gaze struggled to focus on the headlights slicing through the darkness ahead. He just needed rest. To close his eyes for a moment...

A sharp rap against the fogged window glass startled George

from the precipice of sleep. Squinting through the mist, he made out the distinctive silhouette of a police hat and high-visibility jacket.

"Evening, sir. Everything alright?" the officer inquired, shining a torch into the car.

George fumbled for his badge and ID. "Detective Inspector Beaumont, West Yorkshire Police," he managed. "I'm fine, just... I just need to get home."

The beam moved to illuminate George's dishevelled appearance and bloodshot eyes. The officer frowned, mouth set in a firm line.

"With respect, Detective Inspector, you look absolutely shattered." His tone allowed no argument. "Time to hand over the keys and phone a taxi. I'll give you a lift to the station if walking's beyond you now."

Chagrin pierced George's stupor. He was in no state to argue either, much as it galled him to be handled like some reckless drunk.

As he moved slowly to comply, the officer's stern expression softened. "Apologies for the hard-line, sir, but I know the dangers of driving exhausted all too well. Lost my own brother that way." He paused. "Can't have you becoming another grim statistic. Not on my watch."

George nodded wearily as he hauled himself from the car. "You're right, of course. Reckless of me to consider driving just now." He sighed, breath pluming in the icy air. "I'll call that taxi. Get home safe to the family." He paused. "Thank you. Really."

The officer clasped his shoulder. "You're working the Ripper case, aren't you?"

George nodded.

"I'm Andrew Finch," the PC said, offering his hand.

"Finch?"

The Yorkshireman nodded. "That's right, PC Finch if you want to put in a good word," he said with a wink. "I was at the briefing earlier."

"I remember." Despite his fatigue, George managed a wan smile. "And I'll do just that, thanks again."

Bidding the officer goodnight, George watched the patrol car pull away before dialling for a taxi.

* * *

The silence in George's cramped home office felt oppressive as he sat brooding behind his desk. Isabella was already in bed when he returned home.

A half-drunk cup of coffee had long gone cold, matching the darkness pervading his mood. With no active leads to pursue, and his suspension from the case, frustration and bitter helplessness festered within.

His gaze fell on the framed photo positioned beside his monitor—a candid shot of Olivia's christening. George remembered the radiant joy on Isabella's face as she held their swaddled newborn, the pure love shining in her eyes. He touched the image tenderly, heart aching.

When had he last seen Isabella smile like that? Their fractured bond was yet another casualty in his relentless crusade against the Ripper. She tried to hide the pain his detachment caused, but George saw it in the sorrowful glances when he worked late again. In her slowly fading hopes that he might regain the balance he'd lost. That her partner, not just the obsessed DI, would return to her.

Before he could think better of it, George grabbed his mobile and selected Isabella's number. She answered on the third ring, voice hoarse with sleep.

"George? Is everything alright?"

He winced, realising the late hour. She may not have been asleep before, but she certainly had been when he called. "I'm sorry; I didn't mean to wake you." He hesitated. "I've just... missed you lately. And I wanted to apologise again for missing tea. The case demanded my focus, but that's no excuse—"

"Shhh, it's okay," Isabella soothed, a tinge of sadness in her tone. "I just want you to take care of yourself too. You've hardly been eating or sleeping lately. It worries me."

George's thumb brushed over the fading photo, heart squeezing with remorse. "I know, and I'm sorry. But this Ripper case... it's slowly consuming me, Iz. I can't switch off, can't stop chasing leads. Not while he's still out there."

Silence hung on the line before she responded gently. "Just promise you won't shut me out? We're in this together, even when the job pulls you away." A pause. "Olivia asks for her Dada every day, you know."

A lump formed in George's throat at this. He had to be better—for all their sakes. "I'm here, Iz. I'll try harder to be present again, I swear it. We'll get through this darkness together."

"I know we will." Her voice trembled with restrained emotion. "Olivia and I both need you. And Jack does, too. Please take care of yourself, too, not just during this case. We'll still be here when it's over."

"I don't deserve you," George whispered.

"No, you deserve so much more," Isabella replied fiercely. "Now come to bed and sleep, you dickhead. And have breakfast tomorrow with us before work?"

George smiled wearily as some tension uncoiled in his chest. "Absolutely. I'll cook up those pancakes Olivia loves."

"I expect you in here naked in ten minutes," Isabella replied.

George grinned and shut down his computer.

Chapter Nine

George stood paralysed, screams trapped in his throat as the Ripper plunged the knife again and again into Isabella's convulsing body. Crimson blossomed across the flower print of her nightdress; the one George gave her last Christmas.

Somewhere, a baby wailed, cries rising in animalistic terror as the killer's shadow fell across the cot. George struggled against invisible bonds, mouth frozen in a rictus of anguish. Olivia's screams reached a crescendo accompanied by a sickening crunch of bone.

The Ripper turned, face obscured by swirling darkness. Only the flash of the blade arcing high remained clear, poised to obliterate the last flicker of family George clung to.

He thrashed violently, trying to force frozen limbs to obey his screaming mind. But like all the nights before, paralysis kept him pinned—a spectator to the massacre of everything that gave his hollow existence meaning.

With a strangled gasp, George jerked upright in bed, sheets tangled around his sweat-soaked body. Next to him, Isabella stirred, mumbling something soothing before slipping back into undisturbed sleep.

Pulse still racing, George slipped from under the stifling covers and stumbled to the bathroom on shaky legs. He groped for the light switch, squinting against the sudden fluorescence assaulting his dilated pupils.

The face staring back at him from the mirror seemed a stranger's—bloodless lips stretched over gritted teeth, veins bulging at the temples, eyes full of primal dread. George sagged against the sink, sucking deep lungfuls of air to slow his wild heartbeat.

Just a nightmare, he told himself. His family was safe, the darkness held at bay for now. But visceral remnants of the vision still clouded his mind, refusing to fade back into the subconscious depths they crawled from.

Because it was more prophecy than Fantasy—a grim warning of the devastation awaiting if he failed, George had stood helpless in dreams before, seeing his loved ones' blood spill— first, the vampire and Isabella at Halloween, and now Olivia too.

George gripped the sink tighter, knuckles blanching. Never again. He swore the visions would not become reality. Not when he still drew breath.

Staring himself down in the mirror, George recalled his oath to Isabella only hours ago—no more empty promises that they came first.

He splashed cold water on his face and took a deep, steeling breath. He'd speak with Smith in the morning and ask to be SIO again.

Emerging from the bathroom, George slid back into bed and pulled Isabella's sleeping form close. Her warmth and the sound of gentle breaths worked their magic, easing the lingering tension from his body.

Chapter Ten

The conversation in the Incident Room quietened as Detective Inspector George Beaumont stepped up to address his team, newly dubbed the Ripper Task Force. DS Luke Mason, DC Jay Scott, DC Tashan Blackburn, and DC Candy Nichols all gave him their full attention, faces etched with solemn purpose.

"I want to be honest with you all this morning," George said. "Last night, I was removed from the case because I couldn't give my all." He paused. "However, due to increasing OCG activity, this morning DSU Smith has allowed me to continue as SIO, under the condition that I delegate more."

George saw smiles beaming back at him, giving his confidence a boost. "Thank you, each and every one of you," George began. "But I need you all to know that the Ripper has haunted this city long enough. It's our sworn duty to protect Leeds and bring this pretender to justice."

Mason spoke up first, conviction resonating in his gruff voice. "Too right, son. We won't fail the public again, not like last time." The older man's eyes took on a distant sheen as he recalled the terror of the original 1970s murders.

George clasped Mason's shoulder firmly. "Not on my watch, Luke. Together, we'll uncover whatever depraved motive drives this impersonator to further defile the Ripper's bloody legacy."

"We're with you, boss," Jay said. "This sick bastard will slip up eventually, and we'll be there to grab him." Candy and Tashan nodded their agreement.

"So where do we start, sir?" Tashan asked. "Re-examining old evidence? Victim profiles? Witness statements?" His notebook was poised to jot down notes.

George smiled approvingly. "Eager and astute as always, Tashan. I want you and Candy to revisit the crime scenes. Every minute detail may prove crucial."

The two detective constables headed out briskly, their focus honed like bloodhounds on a fresh scent. George then turned to Jay and Mason. "Meanwhile, you two will join me in checking out a new lead. The owner of a gym in Holbeck mentioned a man harassing female customers the past few weeks. Hates prostitutes, apparently. He could be our guy."

Jay cracked his knuckles. "Happy to knock some heads if needed, boss."

Mason shot him a look. "Easy there, lad. You can't go kicking down doors on a casual tip. But we'll gather intel discreetly." He checked his watch. "Lead the way, George. Ripper's days are numbered."

Departing the station, the three men drove in tense silence, mentally prepping for the possibility, however slim, that their query could produce the break in the case they desperately needed.

* * *

George and Mason approached the secured storage locker containing artefacts from the original Ripper investigation.

Unfortunately, the tip from the gym had been a dead-end.

George hesitated, hand hovering over the lock. "Are you sure you're ready for this, Luke?"

Mason's jaw was clenched, his eyes distant and haunted. As if in a trance, he nodded for George to proceed. With an ominous metallic clang, the locker opened to reveal its ghastly contents—a bloodstained timber mallet, twisted lengths of rope, and other implements recovered from crime scenes decades ago, now preserved behind glass.

George heard Mason's sharp intake of breath as he reluctantly met the older man's gaze. "Christ, every foul memory comes flooding back just looking at those damn things," Mason muttered through gritted teeth, an involuntary shudder wracking his body.

Seeing his mentor so shaken pierced George's heart. He grasped Mason's shoulder firmly. "I understand this is difficult. But it's necessary, Luke." At Mason's hesitant look, George added gently, "We can leave if it gets to be too much."

Taking a deep breath, Mason quickly wiped a stray tear from his cheek and straightened up. "Aye, let's just get this over with."

They began meticulously cataloguing each piece of evidence, comparing details to the original case files. With clinical detachment, George noted traces of blood and hair still adhering to the hammer's head, likely from the vicious bludgeoning of young Barbara Leach in Bradford.

Mason kept his emotions in tenuous check until they reached the screwdrivers. "He used to sharpen these and use them to—" Mason rasped, unable to tear his eyes away. "Sutcliffe was a sick bastard..." He trailed off as revulsion twisted his features.

George quickly guided the shaking man to a chair before he

collapsed. Kneeling before him, George spoke firmly but with compassion. "Stay with me, Luke. I know this dredges up pain. But use it; let your hatred for these horrors strengthen your resolve now." He gripped Mason's hands tightly. "Make this second chance count."

Gradually, Mason's rapid breaths slowed again as he clung to George's steadying words like a lifeline. When he finally looked up, steely purpose had returned to the depths of his haunted eyes.

"You're right, son," he acknowledged with a weary nod. "Reliving the past won't undo it." Mason rose, squaring his shoulders. "But we can damn well make sure this city never suffers this evil again."

George smiled proudly at his mentor's resilience. Together, they resumed cataloguing the evidence, though Mason occasionally had to steel himself when confronted with an especially gruesome artefact.

* * *

The lurid contents of the case files seemed to leer up at George from the spread pages as he hunched over his desk, scrutinising every chilling detail. Meticulously compiled dossiers on each original Ripper victim lay before him in gruesome testimony—crime scene photos, autopsy reports, psychological profiles. He knew he needed to reassemble all pieces of the grotesque puzzle if he hoped to thwart this impersonator.

George forced himself to study each eviscerated body dispassionately, searching for insights into motive and methodology. But within the macabre patterns, half-glimpsed human details occasionally pierced his detachment...a blood-matted lock of blonde hair, lips frozen open mid-scream, a once-treasured bracelet clinging to a mutilated wrist.

Shaking off the discomfort, George pulled out the most recent crime scene images to compare. Though separated by decades, the impersonator's savage handiwork clearly echoed that of his idolised predecessor.

The shrill ring of his mobile pierced the brooding silence of George's office. He frowned at the caller ID before answering briskly. "DI Beaumont.

"George, it's Lindsey." The CSI manager's voice held an odd tension.

"Everything OK?"

"My team's still processing the alley where the latest victim was found. But we discovered something unsettling... a note left at the scene addressed to you."

George sat bolt upright, pulse quickening. "Go on."

"It's taunting, sir. Deliberately left for us to find. No prints or DNA present, unfortunately." Lindsey hesitated before continuing. "It says, 'Catch me if you can, DI Puppet'."

George's fist involuntarily clenched at the audacious challenge. So their suspect was done lurking in the shadows; he wanted direct engagement now. "Bag it for evidence and keep the note confidential for now. He craves a spotlight, so we deny it."

"Yes, George. I don't mind telling you, this bastard's getting cocky," Lindsey said soberly.

After ending the call, George leaned back, stroking his chin thoughtfully as he deliberated how best to respond to this dramatic escalation. Clearly, their publicity-hungry murderer felt emboldened, desperate to propel the deadly game to a new level.

Such brazen taunting confirmed the profile George constructed—their suspect was an organised killer driven by ego, the desire for infamy and control. By flaunting his escape from justice so far, the perpetrator risked making critical mistakes if his mania continued unchecked.

"Let the arrogant prick crow while he still can," George muttered to himself. "His thirst will force the errors we need."

Still, this 'puppet' reference unsettled George, implying that the killer had intimate knowledge of the investigation's frustrations. A leak from within the department? The thought made George's blood run cold. But he could not rule out any possibilities yet.

For now, discretion was imperative. George picked up his office phone and dialled Candy's extension. "DC Nichols, please quietly retrieve the evidence bag with the note left by our suspect. Bring it directly and discreetly to my office."

He sat back and steepled his fingers contemplatively until a soft rap at the door heralded the officer's arrival. Candy handed over the sealed bag, her bright eyes brimming with questions. George forestalled them with a raised hand.

"Candy, can we keep this note between us, please?"

Candy nodded her understanding before departing.

Alone again, George carefully examined the note, gleaning what he could from the sloping, eccentric handwriting. Though the words themselves seemed troubling, they marked a pivotal moment—his nemesis could no longer resist direct engagement. And eventually, through patience and cunning, that compulsion would spell the bastard's demise.

* * *

George concluded updating the Ripper Task Force on the latest developments, including the unsettling taunting note left at the crime scene. He could see frustration and self-doubt creeping into the downcast eyes of his team. Despite their tireless efforts, the impersonator remained as elusive as ever.

Detective Chief Inspector Atkinson broke the gloomy silence, making little effort to conceal his scorn. "So after all this time twiddling about, you've got nothing to show except more meaningless psychobabble about his motivations. Is that correct, Detective Inspector?"

George bristled, biting back an acidic retort. "With respect, sir, criminal psychology has proven key to constructing an offender profile. We must understand his twisted drives to—"

"Must we?" Atkinson interrupted derisively. "Seems to me the only useful approach is proper investigative legwork to find real, actionable evidence. Not academic navel-gazing." His glare lingered on George. "So far, you've delivered inadequate results on both fronts."

George shot up from his seat, nostrils flaring. "My team has worked themselves to the bone chasing every potential lead! But this cunning bastard leaves practically nothing behind to work with."

Atkinson rose slowly to meet his gaze, a smug half-grin forming. "The old 'he's too clever for us' excuse, eh? Spare me the drama, Beaumont. Your job is to outwit such deviants through diligent police work." He shook his head in mock disappointment. "Seems you lack the capability required."

"How dare you!" George slammed his fists on the table, sending case files scattering. "If you believe you can do better capturing this fiend, be my guest! Otherwise, back the hell off and let us work!"

Absolute silence descended after the enraged outburst. George trembled with adrenaline, even as regret trickled in for losing composure. But Atkinson's goading had pushed him past endurance.

The DCI leaned over the table, eyes glinting. "I'd mind that temper if I were you, Detective Inspector. Makes you seem unbalanced, irrational." He flashed a frigid smile. "Hardly the image needed from the investigation's leader, wouldn't you say?" He paused. "I wonder how DSU Smith would react if you spoke to him like you've just spoken to me."

Before George did something rash, he turned sharply on his heel and stormed from the room without looking back.

Chapter Eleven

The scent of fresh coffee temporarily lifted George's spirits as he handed Mason a steaming mug across the organised chaos of his office desk. Case files and crime scene photos competed for space with empty takeaway containers and crumpled energy drink cans—the residue of endless hours puzzling over sparse leads.

George sank into his chair with a weary sigh, massaging his throbbing temples. "This bastard really knows how to cover his tracks. Barely left us crumbs so far."

Mason sipped his coffee thoughtfully before replying. "Aye, he's a cunning one, alright. Got us chasing phantoms while he watches from the shadows, smug as can be." The older man shook his head ruefully. "Can't decide if we're out of our depth or just unlucky."

"A bit of both, maybe." George managed a wan smile. "It doesn't help that Atkinson seizes every chance to undermine me. The constant scrutiny only slows progress."

Mason waved his hand dismissively. "Ah, don't mind that pompous twat. He's just threatened by someone clearly more capable. Your talents intimidate him."

When George didn't appear convinced, Mason leaned forward resolutely. "Now you listen here, son. We've overcome far worse in our day, you and I. This Ripper impersonator he's just another piece of scum we'll outfox soon enough. Have faith."

George absorbed the impassioned words, feeling his stagnant spirits begin to stir again. Mason had a knack for fortifying resolve even in the darkest moments. It was a gift George desperately needed now.

"Too right, Luke," he acknowledged finally. "We'll smoke this rat out of hiding eventually. He's gotten the better of us so far, but the tables will turn." George clenched his fist. "And when they do, I'll be ready to strike without mercy. The Ripper's reign ends here."

Mason grinned and raised his mug in salute. "That's the tenacious spirit I know! Reminds me of your early days, son. You were born to hunt monsters, George. And your cunning has only sharpened with experience."

George returned the toast, some balance restored. There would be twists and turns ahead in this deadly chess match. But if anyone could anticipate the Ripper's next movements and trap him, it was the skills Mason helped nurture all those years ago.

The brief moment of camaraderie had steadied George's nerves, rekindling momentum and clarity of purpose. Mason was right; self-doubt served no one. He had been sworn to this gruelling calling for a reason. Now was the time to prove himself worthy of the charge.

Draining his mug, George felt replenished for the difficult work ahead. "We'll review the case notes again. Something we've overlooked will reveal itself."

Mason nodded approvingly and squeezed George's shoulder on his way out.

Alone again, George squared his shoulders and turned his focus to the puzzle laid out before him.

* * *

The archives were a maze of dusty files and forgotten histories. George Beaumont and Mark Finch sat at a table cluttered with folders, the air around them heavy with the scent of ageing paper. They were sifting through the old case files of the Ripper, each page a reminder of the horrors from the past.

George picked up a file, his eyes scanning the contents. Suddenly, he paused, his brow furrowing. "Look at this," he said, holding out a document to Finch. The file was heavily redacted, swathes of black obscuring the text.

Finch leaned in, his eyes narrowing as he examined the document. "What are they hiding here?" he muttered, a hint of frustration in his voice.

"It's a gap in Sutcliffe's profile," George observed, a sense of unease settling over him. "Why would they redact this information?"

Finch shrugged, his expression unreadable. "Could be a variety of reasons. Protection of an informant, sensitive details."

George wasn't convinced. He tapped the file thoughtfully. "It feels like more than that. Like there's a piece of his life, they wanted to keep hidden."

They continued their review, but the redacted file stayed in George's mind, a puzzle piece that didn't fit. He made a mental note to dig deeper, to uncover the truth behind the black lines.

The clock ticked on, marking the passage of time as they

delved further into the archives. The room around them felt like a vault of secrets, each file a keeper of untold stories.

Later, after Mark had left, George's thoughts lingered on the gaps in Sutcliffe's profile. What were they missing? What secrets had been buried in these archives, hidden from the world?

The shrill ringing of his office phone jarred George from his brooding contemplation. Rubbing his eyes, he cleared his throat before answering briskly. "DI Beaumont."

Instead of a voice, only the faint static hiss of an open line greeted him. George frowned, about to hang up, when he detected the unmistakable sound of rhythmic breathing drifting through the receiver.

His pulse quickened. "Who is this?" he demanded sharply.

The breathing grew louder and more laboured, almost a sinister panting. The hairs on George's neck stood up as he gripped the phone tighter. "I'm going to hang up if you don't speak!"

After a tense pause, a chilling, raspy voice finally issued from the speaker, so soft George had to strain to hear.

"The Ripper... he will rip you... too..."

George shot to his feet, nearly upending his chair. "Who the hell is this?" he shouted, but the line was already dead, the dial tone buzzing mockingly in his ear. Slamming the phone down, George began furiously punching buttons to find the number to trace the call, heart hammering against his ribs.

But as expected, the number was withheld. Cursing bitterly, George swept stacks of files off his desk in a sudden, violent outburst. He stood shaking with impotent fury over the mess.

The bold, threatening call confirmed that the Ripper was tracking the investigation closely enough to obtain George's direct office line, which was kept confidential for security. Was it the taunting words of the monster himself or some cruel prankster? Regardless, George realised with chilling certainty that he was now a target in this twisted game.

He paced like a caged animal, thoughts racing wildly. Clearly, their adversary was done being a faceless ghost. Even the investigation's leader was no longer untouchable. George's jaw tightened. If this was psychological warfare, then so be it. He would not bend or break so easily.

A knock at the door interrupted his seething introspection. DS Mason poked his head in, surveying the debris and George's dishevelled, manic appearance with concern.

"Everything alright, son? Heard a commotion..."

George took a deep breath, regaining composure before meeting Mason's eyes. "Just a disturbing prank call, nothing to worry about. I'm sorry for the disruption."

Though Mason seemed unconvinced, he simply nodded. "Well, try not to let it rattle you too badly. We need that sharp mind of yours focused." He gestured at the mess. "I'll send someone to tidy this up. And do heed an old man's advice—get some rest soon, eh?" He winked. "You look like shit."

After Mason departed, George sank down heavily in his chair again. Rest seemed unlikely, with the Ripper's threat still echoing in his mind. But he refused to let this killer believe he could be unnerved so easily.

Jaw set with defiance, George began reassembling the scattered paperwork. There was too much at stake now to indulge fear or hysteria. If this was the opening salvo in a new phase of their deadly game, so be it.

* * *

Professor David Yates' cramped university office threatened George's nostrils as he paced before the cluttered desk, urgency lending passion to his appeal.

"Professor, you're one of the foremost experts on the Ripper's criminal psychology. I need your insight into his twisted motivations if I'm to stop this copycat from prolonging his bloody legacy."

Yates removed his spectacles, regarding the agitated inspector thoughtfully. "Violent impulses leave complex fingerprints, Detective. Especially ones echoing through history as this entity has."

He steepled his fingers contemplatively before continuing. "Consider the intimate mimetic quality of the murders. This indicates a deep, personal fascination with the original killings. Perhaps even an act of homage by a relative of Ripper victims seeking long-delayed catharsis through blood."

George's eyes widened slightly as he processed the chilling theory. "A vengeance spree? You really think that's plausible?"

"More than mere spectacle seekers, at least. Trauma endures, Inspector. The vulnerable never forget being prey." Yates held George's gaze intently as if glimpsing the darker truths coiled in the depths of men's hearts.

George carded a hand through his hair, thoughts racing ahead to the investigation. "If you're right, we've been pursuing this all wrong. The victims hold the key, not the locations." He stood abruptly and grabbed his coat. "I need to speak to my team immediately."

Yates rose and extended his hand. "My door is open if you require more insight, Inspector. Into this disturbed mind, or your own."

George felt the weight of the professor's stare as they shook hands. What exactly did he know about the creeping obsession emanating from the abyss within? With a muttered thanks, George hastened away, determined not to let introspection deter him now. Too much depended on swift action.

Back at the station, George assembled his subordinates, seeing his own haggard features reflected in their exhausted faces.

"We have hard new lines of inquiry to pursue," he announced without preamble. "To understand this killer, we look to the past. Surviving relatives of Ripper victims may hold vital clues."

He could see the understanding and dread creeping into their eyes. But it had to be done—no more dead ends.

After assigning the detectives each a list of families to delicately interview, George grabbed Mason and headed for the car, the older man hurrying to match his brisk stride.

"Where we off to in such a rush, son?" Mason inquired as he slid into the passenger seat.

"Chapeltown. His Leeds killings all occurred there so far." George's knuckles whitened on the wheel. "If Yates is right, our boy will strike close to home again soon. We'll be ready this time."

* * *

The distant roll of thunder echoed George's brooding as he sat hunched at the kitchen table, bleary eyes staring past the untouched meal Isabella had saved for him. She rested a hand lightly on his shoulder, her voice gentle.

"You look absolutely knackered, gorgeous. How did tonight

go?"

George simply shook his head, her question reviving the bitter taste of failure. "Just shadows. Always slipping through my grasp." He exhaled sharply. "I'm no closer to stopping him than the night this nightmare started."

Isabella wrapped her arms around him from behind, offering wordless comfort as she felt the tension radiating from his rigid frame. She hated seeing George torment himself like this as the investigation stalled.

"You'll find the piece that breaks the case wide open," she assured softly. "But run yourself into the ground, and you're no good to anyone. Trust me."

"Thank you."

"Come to bed, George." She took his hand, coaxing him up from the table and into her soothing embrace.

Reluctantly, George allowed himself to be led away, the siren call of oblivion in slumber growing more seductive by the moment. But surrendering fully to that refuge remained difficult, knowing the Ripper still roamed free out there somewhere, taunting them all.

In a cramped basement flat by the River Aire, the blooded glow of a darkroom lamp revealed glossy photos strung up to dry—the Ripper's gruesome homage immortalised in vivid detail. A gloved hand caressed the images almost sensually, admiring their macabre artistry. This tribute deserved an audience, and he knew just who to bestow that honour upon.

The killer lovingly clipped newspaper reports of the spree, savouring each line that amplified fear and chaos. Though pseudonymous reportage, the message below was clear—your legacy endures. I remain your faithful servant. Father.

The Ripper could not resist responding to such florid devotion. After all, immortality came through spilling both blood and ink. What better venue for their fatal waltz to continue than the city that birthed them both? Not physically, of course, but metaphorically.

Soon, there would be no more need for restraint or patience. The grand finale approached, scripted by destiny's guiding hand. And George Beaumont was destined for the starring role: worthy adversary turned sacrificial lamb. The cycle neared completion.

Until then, the Ripper sharpened his blade and prepared the altar, humming with anticipation. Like his father, God had spared him so far from the police's hapless pursuit, precisely as the whispered voices promised. The beasts in human form could not perceive what their feeble minds refused to comprehend.

But George was different—a worthy foe at last. The Ripper sensed they shared the same primal current flowing through their veins, driving them toward the inevitable collision ahead. Noble hunter and cunning beast, predator and prey... their tragedian roles interim only.

The Ripper smiled beneath his mask, likening him to Sutcliffe, breath quickening. Soon, the final act would unfold on destiny's stage, written in spurting arteries and frantic screams. Then Leeds would behold divinity's exquisite terror once more and tremble before death's grinning rictus.

The photos were ready now—a worthy gift for George, who deserved the highest honours. The Ripper gathered his trophies carefully and stepped out into the cold night fog. The hunt would resume tomorrow.

Chapter Twelve

The early morning sun cast a grim light over the desolate waste ground, doing little to dispel the chilling air that hung heavily around the new crime scene. Detective Inspector George Beaumont, his expression a hardened mask of resolve, stood over the body of Emily White. Her lifeless form, sprawled and mutilated, echoed a haunting familiarity that clawed at the edges of Beaumont's mind.

Barbara Leach—the thought flickered through Beaumont's seasoned consciousness. The resemblance was uncanny, deliberate. Each vicious stab wound that marred Emily's body mirrored the brutality inflicted upon Leach, a sinister echo of the Yorkshire Ripper.

Beaumont crouched, his eyes tracing the ruthless precision of the killer's work. The disposal of Emily's body in such a barren place was a bold message - a morbid signature left by a murderer whose intention was not just to kill but to recreate the Ripper's most infamous act of violence.

Dr Ross, the pathologist, approached, his face set in a grim line as he donned his gloves. He exchanged a brief, knowing glance with Beaumont. Their years of working together formed an unspoken language of mutual respect and shared burdens.

"Same MO as Abigail Trent," Dr Ross confirmed, his voice steady despite the gruesome scene before him. He knelt beside the body, his hands moving methodically as he began his examination. "The killer's not just mimicking the Ripper. He's perfecting the method."

Beaumont's jaw tightened. The killer was evolving, learning from each murder, each act a step closer to some twisted ideal. It was a dangerous game of cat and mouse, and Beaumont felt the weight of the challenge pressing down on him.

PC Andrew Finch approached tentatively. "Sir, we've cordoned off the area, but a lot of media pressure is building up."

George nodded, his gaze never leaving the body. "Keep them back. This scene is our only voice from Emily now. We can't afford contamination."

As the team set to work, George observed Andrew. The constable's involvement was deeper than usual, his observations sharp, his queries pointed. He moved through the scene with a keen eye, occasionally jotting down notes that seemed more thorough than standard procedure.

"Found something over here, sir," Andrew called out, gesturing to George to a secluded area. He pointed to a set of barely discernible footprints, partly hidden. "Looks like our suspect might have been watching from here."

George knelt beside Andrew, examining the find. "Good catch, PC Finch," he commended, though a part of his mind noted the constable's heightened alertness. It was as if Andrew was piecing together a puzzle only he could see.

Turning back to Dr Ross, Beaumont asked, "Time of death?"

"Rough estimate, between midnight and 2 AM," he replied. "I'll know more after the postmortem."

George stood up, his eyes scanning the desolation around

them, finding PC Andrew Finch. Throughout the morning, Andrew's presence at the crime scene was like a taut string, his engagement bordering on personal investment. He offered insights that went beyond the observations of a regular beat officer, his comments occasionally hinting at a deeper understanding of the criminal mind.

George found himself mulling over Andrew's behaviour. It was meticulous and involved, almost as if he were connected to the case in a way that went beyond his duty.

He stored it in the back of his mind and looked around. The waste ground was a stark canvas, empty, but for the tragedy, it cradled. He pondered the killer's choice of location - was it a message, a symbol, or merely a matter of convenience?

"George," Dr Ross' voice broke through his thoughts. "There's something else. The killer left a mark, not on the body, but nearby. It might be significant."

Beaumont followed his pointing finger to a nearby wall, where a symbol was crudely painted - an eerie replication of a symbol found in the Ripper's case files. His heart sank as the realisation hit him: this killer was not just reliving the past; they were taunting the present.

"Get Forensics to take a look at that. Every detail matters," George instructed his mind already racing with theories and possibilities.

* * *

Detective Inspector George Beaumont stood at the head of the briefing room, his team assembled before him, their faces a mix of determination and unease. The image of Emily White's body, so hauntingly reminiscent of Barbara Leach's, loomed large in their minds.

Beaumont cleared his throat, his voice steady despite the turmoil that churned within. "We're facing a calculated killer," he began, his eyes scanning the room. "This latest murder is not just a copycat of the Ripper's work; it's a deliberate echo of one of his most infamous kills - Barbara Leach."

Detective Sergeant Luke Mason shifted uncomfortably in his seat, the memory of the Leach case still vivid in his mind. "I remember the panic that swept through Leeds after Leach's murder," he said, his voice barely above a whisper. "The fear, the anger... It's happening all over again."

Beaumont nodded solemnly. "That fear is exactly what this killer is banking on. They're not just taking lives; they're trying to resurrect the Ripper's reign of terror."

The room fell silent, the weight of Beaumont's words hanging heavily in the air. Each officer knew the stakes had been raised; this was no longer just a hunt for a murderer but a race to prevent a city from being consumed by fear.

"Forensics found something at the scene," Beaumont continued, bringing up a photo of the crude symbol discovered near Emily's body. "This was painted on a wall nearby. It's identical to a symbol from the Ripper's case files."

A murmur ran through the team. The symbol, so stark and foreboding, was a chilling reminder of the past they were now grappling with.

"We need to dive into the Ripper's files again," Beaumont said decisively. "Anything that can give us an edge, any pattern or detail we might have missed."

Detective Constable Candy Nichols raised her hand. "Sir, should we consider the possibility that the killer might be someone with inside knowledge of the original case? Someone who had access to the files?"

Beaumont paused, considering. "It's a possibility we can't ignore," he admitted. "We need to keep an open mind on all fronts."

The team sprang into action, files and photos spread across tables, the buzz of conversation filling the room. Beaumont watched them, a sense of pride mixed with apprehension. They were a skilled team, but they were venturing into uncharted waters, chasing a shadow that danced just out of reach.

* * *

Isabella Wood sat motionless, her eyes fixed on the television screen. The flickering images painted a grim picture - a crime scene swarming with police, the fluttering of crime scene tape in the cold breeze, and at the centre of it all, Paige McGuiness, reporting live.

McGuiness stood with an air of confidence that seemed almost out of place amidst the chaos. Dressed in a tailored business suit that spoke of professionalism and heels that clicked authority with each step, she commanded attention. Her raven-black hair, cut in a severe bob, framed her face, emphasising her sharp features and determined expression.

"As the city wakes up to yet another gruesome murder, fears grow that the Yorkshire Ripper has returned," McGuiness began, her voice steady and clear. "Emily White, a young woman with her whole life ahead of her, was found brutally murdered and mutilated, in a manner eerily reminiscent of the Ripper's infamous spree."

Isabella's hands tightened around the remote. The words'

Yorkshire Ripper' echoed in her mind, a chilling reminder of a past that the city had struggled to move beyond. The memories of those dark days, the paranoia and horror that had gripped Leeds, were resurfacing with a vengeance.

McGuiness continued, her report painting a vivid picture of the fear that was once again taking hold of the city. "Residents are advised to be vigilant and report any suspicious activity. The police are doing everything in their power to track down the killer and bring an end to this reign of terror."

The camera panned over the crime scene, lingering on the huddled figures of the forensic team, then cut back to McGuiness. Her expression softened slightly, a hint of empathy breaking through her professional demeanour. "Our thoughts go out to Emily's family during this difficult time," she said, her voice tinged with a sombre note.

Isabella felt a shiver run down her spine. The horror of what was unfolding was all too real, and McGuiness' words only served to amplify the growing sense of unease. She found herself gripping the remote tighter as if trying to hold onto something solid in a world that was spiralling into chaos.

Suddenly, the screen split, showing a panel of experts, each ready to weigh in on the situation. There were criminologists, former detectives, and even a psychologist, all speculating on the killer's motives, the pattern of the murders, and what it meant for the city.

Isabella listened, but their words seemed to blend into a cacophony of theories and conjectures. The only truth she knew was the fear that was spreading like a shadow over Leeds, a fear that was becoming all too tangible.

As McGuiness wrapped up her report, Isabella switched off the television, the room falling into silence. The weight of what she had just seen and heard hung heavily in the air.

Chapter Thirteen

George sat hunched over his desk, the phone pressed tightly to his ear. The din of the station continued faintly in the background, a distant reminder of the urgency that enveloped them. He waited, listening to the ringtone until a familiar voice answered.

"Mark Finch," came the crisp, analytical tone.

"Finchy, it's George. I need your perspective on the Emily White case," George said, cutting straight to the chase.

There was a brief pause, then Finch's voice, continuously measured, replied, "I've been following the news. It's unsettling, to say the least."

George leaned back in his chair, his eyes fixed on the file splayed open before him. "It's more than unsettling. This killer isn't just mimicking the Ripper; they're recreating specific murders. I need to understand why. Why this murder? Why Barbara Leach's case?"

Finch's sigh was almost inaudible, but George knew him well enough to catch the subtle shift in his tone. "The original Ripper case, especially the Leach murder, was a turning point. It wasn't just the brutality of the killings; it was the fear they instilled, the hysteria they provoked. This copycat might be trying to evoke that same level of terror."

George drummed his fingers on the desk, considering Finch's words. "So, you're saying it's about more than the killings. It's about recreating the fear, the chaos?"

"Exactly," Finch affirmed. "This killer is not only obsessed with the Ripper but also with the impact he had on the nation. By mirroring one of the most shocking cases, they're trying to reignite the same horror."

The pieces were beginning to fit together in George's mind, forming a chilling picture. "They want to be remembered, to leave a mark on history."

"There's likely an element of ego, yes," Finch said. "But don't overlook the psychological aspect. This could be their way of asserting control and demonstrating power over their victims and the public consciousness."

George's gaze drifted to the window, the night skyline of Leeds stretching out before him. Once a place of vibrant life, the city now felt like a stage for a dreadful play.

"Mark, what's the next move if this is about evoking fear? How do we figure out where this leads?" George asked, a sense of urgency threading his voice.

Finch was silent momentarily, then replied, "Look for patterns, not just in the murders, but in the timing, the locations. And George, be prepared for escalation. If this killer is chasing the Ripper's shadow, they'll want to outdo him."

The call ended with a promise of further analysis, leaving George alone with his thoughts. The idea of escalation sent a shiver down his spine. If Finch was right, and this was about surpassing the original Ripper, then the city was on the brink of a descent into terror, unlike anything they had seen before.

* * *

Outside the imposing facade of Leeds Police Headquarters, a sea of protesters swelled under the grey sky, their anger as palpable as the chill in the air. Placards bobbed above the crowd, each emblazoned with bold, accusatory words: 'Not Again!', 'Justice for the Victims!', 'Stop the Ripper!'. The clamour of their voices, raised in a cacophony of frustration and fear, reverberated against the stone walls of the building.

George stood by the window of his office on the second floor, observing the scene unfold below. He understood their fear, their anger. It was a physical manifestation of the city's pulse, racing with anxiety. The protesters weren't just demanding justice; they were voicing the terror gripping Leeds' heart.

A chant began, a rhythmic, haunting refrain that echoed the sentiment on the signs: "Not again! Not again!" The words were a stark reminder of the city's dark history, a past everyone hoped was buried deep.

Detective Sergeant Luke Mason joined George at the window, his expression a mixture of concern and determination. "They're scared, George," he said his voice low. "And angry. They think we're not doing enough."

George turned from the window, his gaze firm. "Their fear is justified, Luke. But they need to understand we're doing everything we can. This isn't just a case for us; it's personal."

Luke nodded, the weight of responsibility evident in his eyes. "I know, but the longer this goes on, the more restless they'll get."

The sound of a megaphone broke through the chants, a protester's voice amplifying the crowd's sentiment. "We won't be victims again! The police must act now!"

George's jaw tightened. The situation was a tinderbox, and every passing moment, every unsolved clue was a spark that threatened to set it off. He knew they needed a breakthrough, and soon.

Back in the bullpen, the team was a whirlwind of activity. Phones rang incessantly, and detectives hunched over computers, analysing every scrap of data they had. The tension in the room was almost tangible, each officer acutely aware of the eyes of the city upon them.

Detective Constable Candy Nichols approached George, a file in her hands. "Sir, we've got something. CCTV footage from near the crime scene. It's not clear, but it could be our suspect."

George took the file, a glimmer of hope igniting amidst the uncertainty. "Good work, Candy. Let's get this analysed immediately. Any lead, no matter how small, could be the key."

As the team rallied around the new lead, George's thoughts returned to the protesters outside. They were a stark reminder of the stakes at hand. This was more than a case; it was a battle for the soul of Leeds. The city looked to them for protection and answers, and he would not let them down.

Leaving the buzz of the bullpen behind, George stepped into his office, closing the door on the chaos. He needed a moment, just a brief respite, to gather his thoughts. The weight of expectation, the burden of fear, the relentless pressure of the case - it all converged, threatening to overwhelm him.

* * *

Late afternoon light filtered through the blinds of George Beaumont's office, casting long shadows across the floor. He sat at his desk, surrounded by personnel files of the officers involved in the case. Methodically, he reviewed each one, seeking insights into his team's dynamics.

When he reached Constable Andrew Finch's file, George paused. The pages detailed Andrew's career: commendations and an exemplary service record, but something else caught his eye. A marginal note, added by a previous supervisor, mentioned Andrew's intense interest in criminology and historical crimes, with a specific focus on the original Ripper case.

George leaned back in his chair, the file open before him. Andrew's fascination with the Ripper was more than a professional interest bordering on the obsessive. It was an unusual detail, one that painted Andrew in a different light.

The clock on the wall ticked steadily as George contemplated this new information. Andrew's exemplary record was unquestioned, but this intense interest in such a dark chapter of history was intriguing. It suggested a depth to Andrew's character that George hadn't considered before.

George made a mental note to discuss Andrew's historical interests to gauge his perspective. It could be benign, a mere academic curiosity, or a clue hidden in plain sight.

* * *

The clock on the wall of George's office ticked past midnight, its steady rhythm a stark contrast to the tumult of thoughts racing through his mind. The only illumination came from the desk lamp, casting a pool of light over the scattered files and photographs that held the remnants of Barbara Leach's case. George, his eyes red and bleary from hours of scrutiny, leaned closer to an old, grainy photograph, searching for something, anything, that the original investigators might have overlooked.

The silence of the room was broken only by the occasional rustle of paper as George sifted through the evidence, each piece a ghostly echo from a past that refused to stay buried. He had studied these files countless times, memorised every detail, yet now he poured over them with a renewed sense of desperation. The killer was out there, a shadow moving in the night, and George felt the weight of time pressing down on him.

A knock at the door jolted him from his focus. Detective Sergeant Luke Mason peered in, his face etched with concern. "George, you need to take a break. You've been at this for hours."

George waved him off, his gaze not leaving the files. "I can't, Luke. There has to be something we missed, a clue, a connection."

Luke stepped into the room, his eyes scanning the evidence that seemed to consume George. "We've been over these files a dozen times. The killer follows the Ripper's pattern, but they're not the Ripper. We need to think differently."

George's hands paused on a report, his mind a whirlwind of thoughts. "But what if we're not looking at it the right way? What if the answer's been in front of us all along?"

Luke sighed, pulling up a chair. "Then let's look at it together. Fresh eyes might help."

Together, they delved into the labyrinth of evidence, tracing the path of the original Ripper case through the lens of the present. The faded and haunting photographs spoke of a brutality that had once terrorised the city and now seemed to be reawakening.

As they pored over the details, a pattern emerged, subtle and elusive yet undeniable. The locations, the timing, the method - there was a meticulousness to it, a deliberate staging that went beyond mere imitation.

George leaned back, his mind racing. "This isn't just about recreating the murders. It's a message, a narrative. The killer's telling a story, and we're just catching up."

Luke nodded, his expression grim. "And each murder is a chapter in that story. We must figure out the ending before it's too late."

The hours slipped by as they dissected every aspect of the case, the room becoming a microcosm of their relentless pursuit of the truth. Outside, the city of Leeds lay shrouded in darkness, its streets quiet, but a palpable tension simmered beneath the calm.

Finally, as the first light of dawn began to filter through the blinds, George sat back, a deep exhaustion settling over him. The pieces of the puzzle lay scattered before them, a jigsaw that defied completion.

Luke stood up, stretching his weary limbs. "We should get some rest, George. We're no good to anyone burned out."

* * *

A chill in the morning air greeted George as he stepped out of the police station, the rising sun casting long shadows on the streets of Leeds. He pulled his coat tighter around him, the fabric doing little to ward off the cold that seeped into his bones. His phone pinged a sharp sound that cut through the quiet of the morning. An email from Johnathan Duke, the local paper's editor, flashed on the screen.

With a sense of weary resignation, George opened the message. Duke's words were blunt and to the point. He was publishing an article on the Ripper, the email read, no doubt sensationalising the fear that already gripped the city. George could almost hear Duke's larger-than-life voice, booming and theatrical, as if every word he spoke was part of a grand performance.

Shaking his head bitterly, George Googled the morning edition of the paper. The headlines screamed in bold letters: "Yorkshire Ripper Returns" and "Leeds in Fear." It was precisely the kind of sensational journalism Duke revelled in—dramatic, fear-inducing, and bound to sell copies.

George's thoughts drifted to Duke—a six-foot-five American whose presence was as significant as his stature. Duke was a man who seemed to live his life on a stage, every interaction, every performance, every conversation, an act. It was a trait that George found both irritating and fascinating in equal measure.

Duke was nearly as wide as he was tall, a jolly giant of a man who indulged in life's pleasures with an unapologetic zest. George remembered their past meetings, the editor always with a cigarette in one hand and a drink in the other, his laughter booming through the room.

Despite his theatrics, Duke was undeniably the best-connected person in Leeds. His network was vast, his influence far-reaching. George knew that Duke's article, however sensational, would capture the city's attention, stoking the flames of fear and paranoia.

As George walked towards his car, the headlines flashed before his eyes, each passer-by a carrier of the spreading dread. He felt a surge of frustration. The media's portrayal was turning the Ripper into a spectre, a bogeyman that haunted the city's every alley and shadow.

He reached for his phone, contemplating a call to Duke to reason with him, to ask for restraint. But he knew it would be futile. Duke was a force unto himself, a man who believed in the power of the press, for better or worse.

The city of Leeds, already on edge, would now be reading Duke's dramatised account of the Ripper's return. George knew the impact it would have—the heightened fear, the increased pressure on the police, the escalating hysteria.

Chapter Fourteen

DC Jay Scott and DC Tashan Blackburn approached the White family's home in Rodley with a sense of solemnity. They were about to enter a space filled with the rawest form of human grief. The Whites' residence, a modest semi-detached with a well-tended front garden, stood silent, starkly contrasting the turmoil within its walls. The task at hand was never easy, but today, it felt even heavier, knowing the depth of the life that had been cut short.

Mrs White answered the door, her face etched with the unspeakable pain of a mother who had outlived her child. Her eyes, red-rimmed and weary eyes, flicked between the two detectives, searching for answers where there was none to give. Mr White stood a step behind, his posture that of a man hollowed out by loss, his silent nod a greeting devoid of the warmth it might once have held.

The Whites stepped aside, granting entry into their home, a space that now felt too large without Emily's presence. The living room was adorned with pictures of happier times—a smiling Emily in graduation robes, Emily at a family wedding, her laughter forever captured in still life.

Mrs White clutched a cushion tightly, a substitute for the daughter she could no longer hold. Mr White's hands were restless, fiddling with a pen Emily had used—a memento he couldn't part with.

"Tell us more about Emily," said Jay.

"Emily was special," Mrs White began her voice a delicate thread of sound. "She loved her job at the book shop in Leeds... 'Amongst the Stacks' it was called. She would come home with stories about the people she met, the books she read... She believed books could change lives."

Tashan nodded, taking notes. "It sounds like she was very passionate about her work."

"She was," Mr White said, his voice gaining strength as he spoke of his daughter. "It wasn't just a job for her but a calling. She had this way of knowing exactly what book a person needed."

Jay, with his boyish charm and easy smile, tried to offer comfort. "We've heard from her colleagues and friends. They all speak of her kindness and her creativity. She was loved by many."

Mrs White's eyes were bright with unshed tears. "She was our little light. Always helping others, always giving. She organised fundraisers, volunteered... She had this dream of writing a novel one day."

"And she was an artist too," Mr White interjected, pointing to a canvas that was vibrant with colour. "Emily saw beauty in the mundane. She'd paint or write about the people she saw and the lives they led. She had notebooks full of ideas."

Jay looked around, seeing the remnants of Emily's creativity scattered throughout the room—paintings, books, and filled notebooks. It was a testament to a life brimming with potential. "I hate to ask, but can you think of anybody who would want to hurt her? Anybody new in her life?"

"We can't understand... who would do this to our Emily," Mrs White whispered as they all took seats, the detectives careful to maintain a respectful distance. "She was kind; she wouldn't hurt a soul."

Jay leaned forward, his expression sympathetic yet resolute. "We're doing everything we can to find out who is responsible," he assured her. "Emily—she deserves justice."

"We'll do everything we can to find who did this," Tashan assured them, his blue eyes earnest. "Emily's life was meaningful."

The detectives stood to leave, the air in the room heavy with unspoken sorrow. At the door, Mrs White grasped each detective's hand. "Thank you," she said, a gratitude mixed with despair.

* * *

The morning stretched long and restless for Detective Sergeant Luke Mason. Tossing in his bed, the haunting images of the case flashed across his mind's eye—the crime scenes, the fear-stricken faces of Leeds' citizens, the ever-looming shadow of the Ripper. The clock on his bedside table ticked monotonously, marking the passage of sleepless hours. Finally, unable to find solace in the silence of his room, he reached for his phone and dialled George.

The phone rang twice before George's voice, weary yet alert, answered. "Luke? What's wrong?"

"Can't sleep," Mason admitted, sitting up in bed, the phone pressed against his ear. "This whole thing... it's like I'm back in '79, as a rookie, with the city losing its mind over the Ripper."

There was a moment of silence on the other end, a shared remembrance of a time that had shaped them both as officers and as men. "I know," George finally said, his voice tinged with a deep understanding. "It feels like we've come full circle, doesn't it?"

Mason exhaled, a sound more of frustration than relief. "Yeah. And it's not just the murders, George. It's the fear. The paranoia. It's like history is repeating itself, and we're right in the middle of it."

"You're right," George said, and Mason could picture him, likely sitting in his living room, surrounded by case files, the weight of responsibility etched on his face. "But you're not a rookie any more, Luke. We've got experience and knowledge. We'll catch this guy."

Mason nodded to himself, a gesture unseen but understood. "I just hate seeing the city like this. People are scared, George. Scared to leave their homes, scared of their own neighbours."

"It's what the killer wants," George said, his voice hardening with resolve. "Fear is their weapon, as much as the knife they use. But we won't let them win. We'll bring them to justice."

There was a comfort in George's conviction, a reminder of the oath they had taken years ago to protect and serve. Mason felt a renewed sense of purpose, a determination to stand against the tide of fear that threatened to engulf their city.

"I remember when I worked on the Sutcliffe case," Mason said, a distant memory surfacing. "We were so determined to make a difference, to put an end to the nightmare."

"And you did," George replied. "We'll do it again. This killer, this copycat, they've underestimated us. They think they can invoke the Ripper's shadow to cover their tracks, but we'll shine a light so bright, there'll be nowhere for them to hide."

Mason couldn't help but smile despite the grimness of their situation. George's unwavering determination was a beacon in the dark, guiding them through the chaos.

"You should try to get some rest, Luke," George said, his voice softer now. "We've got a long night ahead of us."

Mason agreed, knowing the truth in George's words. "Thanks, George. I needed this talk."

"Anytime, Luke. We're in this together," George replied before ending the call.

Mason set his phone down, feeling a sense of camaraderie that eased the tightness in his chest. He lay back down, the conversation with George providing a semblance of peace amidst the storm that raged outside.

* * *

In the seclusion of his lair, a dimly lit, cramped space lined with clippings and photographs, the yet-unidentified copycat sat hunched over a cluttered table. The only sound was the snip of scissors as he meticulously cut out articles from various newspapers, each headline screaming about the terror that had once again gripped Leeds. His fingers, stained with ink and glue, moved deliberately, almost reverently.

The walls around him were a shrine to his deeds, a chaotic tapestry of news clippings, old photographs of the original Ripper's victims, and freshly added articles about his own escalating crimes. In this hidden sanctuary of madness, he was both a curator and a devotee, basking in the chaos he had unleashed upon the city.

Every article was a trophy, a testament to his skill in evoking the shadow of the Yorkshire Ripper. He placed each clipping carefully, creating a collage that told a story of fear and fascination. The headlines were bold and sensational—'Yorkshire Ripper Strikes Again,' 'City Held Hostage by Fear,' 'Leeds in the Grip of a New Terror.' Each word was a note in the symphony of panic he had composed.

His eyes, gleaming with a feverish intensity, scanned the articles, absorbing the words that spoke of the mass anxiety his actions had provoked. There was a perverse satisfaction in seeing his work recognised, in knowing that he had successfully stirred the memories of a city's darkest days.

As he worked, he hummed a tune, discordant and chilling, a soundtrack to his twisted labour. He revelled in the power he wielded, the ability to conjure fear with a single, calculated act. He was no mere imitator but an artist, elevating the Ripper's legacy to new heights.

The room was a cocoon, isolating him from the world outside, where the consequences of his actions played out. In here, he was untouchable, a mastermind orchestrating a reign of terror from the shadows.

He paused, his gaze falling on a particularly striking headline: 'Leeds in Fear: The Return of the Ripper?' The question mark at the end was almost an insult, a challenge to his identity. He sneered, a sound devoid of humour. They still doubted, still questioned whether he was worthy of the Ripper's mantle.

But he knew better. He was more than a copycat; he was an evolution, the next chapter in a saga of horror and intrigue. He was the one who had brought the Ripper's shadow back to life, who had tapped into the primal fear that lurked in the heart of the city.

He stood up, stepping back to admire his handiwork. The collage was a mirror, reflecting his inner world, a place where violence was an art and terror was a tool. He had created a masterpiece, a living, breathing canvas of fear.

* * *

George Beaumont stood before his Big Board, an expansive canvas where the sprawling complexities of the case were pinned and mapped out, in his home office. Dim light from a desk lamp cast long shadows across the room, accentuating the intensity in George's bloodshot eyes. Sleep had become a rare commodity, sacrificed at the altar of his relentless pursuit of the copycat.

The board was a testament to his methodical nature, a structured chaos of photographs, notes, timelines, and maps. Each piece was meticulously placed, a fragment of the larger, elusive puzzle he was determined to solve. His eyes moved from one clue to another, tracing connections, seeking patterns in the web of evidence that sprawled before him.

In the solitude of the room, surrounded by the ghosts of the case, George's resolve hardened. He would not let this spectre of the past, this shadow that had re-emerged to haunt the streets of Leeds, defeat the city on his watch. The weight of responsibility, the burden of expectation, bore down on him, yet his determination remained unshaken.

He reached out, fingers tracing the outline of a photograph of the latest crime scene. The copycat was meticulous, recreating the Ripper's heinous acts with chilling precision. But in that precision, George knew, lay the key. No criminal was flawless; every act left a trace, a signature that would eventually lead to their downfall.

The room, lined with bookshelves and filled with the relics of his career, felt like a cocoon, isolating him from the outside world. Here, in his sanctuary, George could think and strategise away from the prying eyes and constant demands of the outside world.

His gaze settled on a map of Leeds, pins marking the locations of the copycat's crimes. There was a pattern there, he was sure of it, a geographical puzzle that, once solved, would bring him one step closer to the killer. He leaned closer, his mind racing through theories and possibilities.

The phone on his desk rang, slicing through the silence. George glanced at it, debating whether to let it ring. But duty called, unrelenting and urgent. He picked up the receiver, his voice steady. "DI Beaumont."

The voice on the other end, one of his team members, brought news of a potential lead, a witness who claimed to have seen something on the night of the latest murder. It was a thin thread, but George knew that in cases like this, even the thinnest thread could unravel the entire tapestry of lies and deceit woven by the killer.

"I'll be there in twenty minutes," George said, hanging up the phone. He took one last look at the Big Board, his mind a whirlwind of thoughts and strategies.

Chapter Fifteen

The bell above the book shop door chimed as George and Candy entered the quiet, book-lined sanctuary. Amidst shelves brimming with tales and secrets, they found Emily's boss, Mr Hargreaves, a thin man with spectacles perched precariously on his nose.

"Detective Inspector Beaumont and Detective Constable Nichols," he said, holding up his warrant card, his voice a soft echo in the silence of the store.

"Emily was a gem, truly passionate about books."

George nodded, eyes scanning the store, each book a silent witness to Emily's days. "Can you tell us about her? Her habits, friends, anything unusual before she disappeared?"

Mr Hargreaves adjusted his glasses, a thoughtful frown creasing his forehead. "Emily... she was always here, either working or writing. Quiet, kept to herself mostly." He hesitated a flicker of remembrance in his eyes. "But last week, she seemed... troubled. Distracted."

Candy leaned in, her interest piqued. "Did she mention anything? Anyone bothering her?"

"No, but she received a phone call. She left abruptly that day," Mr Hargreaves recalled, his fingers absent-mindedly straightening a stack of books.

"A call?" George echoed, his mind latching onto the detail. "Did you hear any of it?"

"Just bits and pieces. It was heated, though. She was upset." Mr. Hargreaves's voice trailed off, lost in the memory.

George exchanged a look with Candy, a silent communication of shared thought. "Did she meet anyone here? Someone from outside?"

"Only her writing group. They met here on Thursdays," Mr Hargreaves replied, gesturing to a corner table nestled between towering bookshelves.

"Thank you, Mr Hargreaves. We might be back with more questions," George said whilst handing over his business card, his tone carrying a finality that matched his resolve. "Call me if you think of anything else."

As they left the book shop, the chime of the bell sounding a soft farewell, George turned to Candy. "Let's look into that phone call and the writing group. There's more to this."

* * *

Pursuing the lead from the book shop, George and Candy delved into the dynamics of Emily's writing group. The group, known as the "Leeds Literati," was a diverse assembly of aspiring writers, each with their own story to tell.

Having collected the group members' names, Candy began reaching out, her calls methodical and probing. One by one, they painted a picture of the meetings—passionate discussions and creative disagreements, but nothing that suggested a motive for Emily's disappearance.

Yet, one name kept surfacing—Daniel, a member who seemed particularly close to Emily. "They were often seen together after the meetings," one member noted. "Always deep in conversation."

George's interest was piqued. "Let's bring Daniel in. He might know more about this phone call or if Emily had any problems."

Later, Daniel sat across from George and Candy in an interview room, his fingers nervously tapping on the table. "Emily and I, we were just friends, fellow writers," he began, his voice tinged with anxiety.

"You were seen with her often. Did she ever share anything personal with you? Any concerns or fears?" George asked, his gaze steady and assessing.

Daniel hesitated, then nodded. "She was worried about something. She said she felt like she was being watched, but she wouldn't tell me more. Thought it was just the stress of her writing."

Candy leaned forward, her tone gentle yet insistent. "What about the last time you saw her? Did she mention a phone call?"

"Yeah, she got a call that rattled her. She left in a hurry that day and looked really scared," Daniel admitted, his eyes downcast.

George and Candy exchanged glances, a silent acknowledgement of the new lead. "Did she tell you about the call?" asked George.

Daniel shook his head, the trauma evident on his face and the tears falling from his eyes.

"Thank you, Daniel. We might need to speak to you again," George concluded the interview.

As they stepped out of the room, the pieces of the puzzle were slowly fitting together, but the picture was still incomplete. Emily's fear, the mysterious phone call, her sudden disappearance – they were all connected, but how?

"We need to trace that call, find out who was on the other end," George said, his determination mirrored in Candy's nod.

The pursuit of the mysterious phone call led George Beaumont down a winding path of digital footprints and telecom inquiries. With Josh Fry's technical assistance, they traced the call to its source, a task that consumed hours of meticulous work. Finally, the answer came, but it was not what George had anticipated.

The call originated from a public phone booth in a busy shopping area of central Leeds, a place swarming with people at any given time. George and Candy drove to the site, the booth standing innocuous and unassuming amidst the hustle of city life. It offered no clues, no traces of the caller who had used it to contact Emily.

Determined to exhaust every possibility, they canvassed the area, speaking to shop owners and pedestrians, hoping for a witness who might have seen something. But as the day progressed, it became increasingly clear that this lead was a dead end. The caller had vanished into the anonymity of the city, leaving behind no trail to follow.

Back at the station, George sat at his desk, the frustration evident in his furrowed brow. Candy, equally disheartened, looked over the notes from their inquiries.

George leaned back, his eyes fixed on the map of Leeds on the wall. The red pins and strings seemed to mock their efforts, a tangled web of leads that led nowhere. "Whoever made that call knew how to cover their tracks," he concluded, the realisation bitter in his mouth.

The room was quiet, the weight of the unsolved case hanging

heavily in the air. George's mind, however, was already moving forward, thinking, and planning. "Let's regroup," he said, his voice firm with resolve. "We go back to square one, re-examine every piece of evidence. There has to be something we're missing."

* * *

Evening lamplight filtered weakly through the blinds of the briefing room at the police station, casting long, sombre shadows across the faces of Detective Inspector George Beaumont and his team.

George, his eyes reflecting a night spent in restless contemplation, stood at the head of the table. "Let's hear it," he said, his voice a calm command. "What have we got on the victim's families?"

Detective Constable Jay Scott, a younger officer whose eagerness was often tempered by the grim realities of their work, shifted in his seat. "Sir, I've spoken with every family. Everyone had an alibi for the night of the first Leeds murder. I rechecked them last night, and they're clear for the second murder, too."

A murmur ran through the team, a shared sense of frustration. George's gaze remained fixed on Jay, encouraging him to continue.

Jay hesitated, then plunged forward. "There's something else. Some of the families... they're talking. There's talk that maybe, just maybe, the real Yorkshire Ripper is still out there. That Sutcliffe somehow..."

George's brow furrowed, a silent warning against the conversation's direction. "Jay," he interjected, his tone firm yet measured, "Peter Sutcliffe is dead. That's a fact."

Jay, undeterred, ploughed on. "But what if—"

Detective Sergeant Luke Mason cut in, his scepticism clear. "It's nonsense, Jay. Sutcliffe's gone. This is someone else's doing. Someone who wants the infamy, the notoriety of the Ripper."

Jay's expression was a mix of frustration and intrigue. "But there are theories, conspiracies about COVID, about fake deaths…"

George raised his hand, silencing the room. "Conspiracies, theories—they don't solve cases. Evidence does. This is an elaborate copycat. Someone who's studied the Ripper, who's obsessed with recreating his crimes. We must focus on finding this individual, not chasing ghosts."

The room settled into a tense silence, each officer processing the weight of their task. George's gaze swept across his team, his expression one of unwavering resolve.

"We're dealing with someone cunning, someone who knows how to cover their tracks. But they're human. They'll slip up, and we'll be ready when they do."

The team nodded, a silent affirmation of their commitment. The Ripper, whether a spectre from the past or a shadow in the present, had cast a long, dark pall over Leeds. It was their duty, their burden, to lift that pall.

George's phone buzzed, a terse reminder that the case was ever-evolving. He glanced at the screen, then back at his team. "I've got to take this. Keep digging and keep your focus. This killer is smart, but we're smarter."

As the team dispersed, each returning to their piece of the intricate puzzle, George stepped out of the room, his phone pressed to his ear. The conversation was brief, but his expression upon returning was grave.

"New development," he announced, his voice cutting through the low hum of conversation. "We've received a letter from the killer."

* * *

The task force briefing room was a cauldron of tension, with theories about the suspect's identity flying back and forth, each more speculative than the last. Detective Chief Inspector Atkinson, a man whose stern demeanour was as much a part of him as his warrant card, stood at the head of the table, his patience wearing thin. "Enough theories," he demanded, his voice cutting through the clamour. "I want concrete answers. Who is behind these killings?"

The room fell into an uneasy silence, the air thick with the unspoken acknowledgement of their lack of solid leads. It was then that Mark Finch, here as a favour for George, spoke up. "We should consider the possibility of an accomplice to Sutcliffe," he suggested, his voice calm yet assertive. "Someone who may have been influenced by him in prison and continued the killing tradition after release." He shrugged. "We all wear masks. Some of us just never take them off."

George nodded thoughtfully, considering the implications. "It's a solid lead, Mark. We need to comb through prison records and find anyone who might fit the profile."

Luke Mason stood up, a determined glint in his eye. "I'll start on it right away," he said, leaving for the shared office, his steps purposeful.

As the briefing continued, Detective Constable Nichols, a

young officer with a keen sense of intuition, approached George. "Sir, while canvassing, I stumbled upon something… intriguing. There's local gossip in Chapeltown about an urban legend. They say the real Ripper's spirit still haunts certain areas at night."

George raised an eyebrow, a mix of scepticism and curiosity. "An urban legend, Nichols?"

"Yes, sir," she replied earnestly. "It might sound far-fetched, but in cases like this, folklore can reflect deeper truths in the community's psyche. Maybe there's something there, a clue we're overlooking."

George pondered her words, aware that in the twisted maze of a serial killer's mind, myth and reality often intertwined. "Alright, Nichols. Follow up on it. But discreetly. We don't need more panic."

The briefing came to an end with Atkinson's final words. "Time is not on our side. I want updates every hour. We stop this killer, no matter what it takes."

As the team dispersed, George remained, his gaze lingering on the map of Leeds on the wall, pins marking the haunting trail of the Ripper's shadow. The weight of the case rested heavily on him, a constant reminder of the stakes at play.

He walked to his office, his mind a whirlwind of theories and possibilities. The legend Nichols mentioned nagged at him, a puzzle piece that didn't quite fit yet refused to be ignored. In this dance with the darkness, every step, every misstep, mattered.

Outside, the city of Leeds moved on, unaware of the machinations in the police station, the intricate web being woven to catch a killer. But for George and his team, the clock ticked relentlessly, a steady reminder of the predator lurking in their midst.

In the shared office, Luke poured over prison records, his eyes scanning for any hint of a connection to the Ripper. The task was daunting, but he was resolute. Somewhere in the sea of names and faces lay a key, a link to the monster they hunted.

Back in her corner of the station, Nichols delved into the folklore of Chapeltown, her instincts telling her there was more to the legend than mere ghost stories.

Later, George leaned against a desk, coffee in hand, as the team shared anecdotes from their pasts.

Jay Scott, always the joker, regaled them with tales of his mischievous childhood. Even George cracked a smile, the tension momentarily eased. The conversation turned, as it often does among colleagues, to family backgrounds.

Candy Nichols spoke of her large, boisterous family, her eyes bright with fond memories. The team laughed, drawn into the warmth of her story.

Then, attention subtly shifted to Mark Finch, who had been quietly listening. "What about you, Mark? Any childhood capers to share?" Candy asked, playfully nudging him.

Finch stiffened slightly, his usual composure faltering. "Not much to tell, really," he said, his voice taking on a clipped tone. "Grew up in Scotland, an average childhood. Moved to Leeds as an adult."

George watched Finch closely, noting the slight evasiveness, the way Finch's eyes darted away from the group. The profiler seemed reluctant to delve into his personal history, a stark contrast to the openness of the others.

Before the conversation could probe deeper, Finch deftly redirected. "Speaking of Leeds, did any of you hear about the redevelopment plans for the old market district?" His change of topic was smooth, but George sensed the underlying discomfort.

* * *

When the letter arrived, it was handed to George Beaumont, who was deep in conversation with Detective Chief Inspector Atkinson. The envelope was nondescript, but the weight of it in George's hands felt like a harbinger of something ominous.

As he slit the envelope open with a gloved hand, the buzz of the station seemed to fade into the background. Inside was a sheet of paper, the words typed in an old-fashioned font that immediately evoked images of a bygone era of infamy. George's eyes narrowed as he scanned the contents, recognising the chilling amalgamation of historical terror it represented—a mixture of the Jack the Ripper and Wearside Jack letters.

Atkinson leaned in, his expression turning grim as he read over George's shoulder. "This is a deliberate provocation," he muttered.

The letter was a taunt, a macabre dance of words that echoed the chilling communications of Jack the Ripper and Wearside Jack. It spoke of the murders with a grotesque pride, detailing the acts with an unsettling familiarity. The writer alluded to the police's efforts to catch him as futile, a game he was always one step ahead of.

George's jaw clenched as he read the last line, a direct challenge to him: "Catch me if you can, Oldfield," the West Yorkshire Ripper mocked. "I am the shadow in your streets, the whisper in your fear."

The room fell silent as George folded the letter back up, his mind racing. This was more than a mere copycat; they were dealing with someone who was deeply entrenched in the lore of one of history's most notorious killers. The psychological warfare had begun.

"Get this to forensics," George ordered, handing the letter to a nearby officer. "Check for prints, DNA, anything."

He turned back to Atkinson. "This changes things. He's getting bolder and more confident. It's only a matter of time before he strikes again."

Atkinson nodded, his eyes hard. "You need to step up our game, George. He's taunting you, sure that he's untouchable."

As George walked back to his office, the letter's words echoed in his mind. The killer was not just recreating the Ripper's crimes; he was embodying the very essence of the terror that Jack the Ripper had instilled over a century ago and the crimes of Sutcliffe in the seventies. The historical parallels were not just a pattern to follow but a manifesto to live by.

In his office, George sat down heavily, the letter laid out in front of him. He felt a cold anger settling in his chest. This was a psychological battle as much as it was a physical hunt. The killer was playing a game of cat and mouse, weaving historical infamy into his acts of violence.

He picked up the phone and dialled Mark Finch. "Mark, we've received a letter. It's like he's channelling Jack the Ripper and Wearside Jack. We need a profile update. This guy's not just killing; he's living out a fantasy."

Finch's voice, usually so calm, had an edge to it. "I'll be right over. This is a significant development. It suggests a level of delusion and grandeur that we haven't fully accounted for."

As George ended the call, he leaned back in his chair, his mind a whirlwind of thoughts. The letter was a vital piece of the puzzle, a glimpse into the mind of a killer who was not just mimicking history but trying to rewrite it.

Outside, the city of Leeds went about its day, unaware of the sinister undercurrent that flowed beneath its streets.

* * *

George sat across from a Ripper historian, a man whose life's work was the study of macabre tales from the past. It had been Mark Finch's idea. He'd told George, "History has a way of repeating itself, doesn't it? The past never truly dies."

The historian's eyes, usually so animated when discussing his subject, now darted everywhere but at George, an unease palpable in the air between them.

George leaned forward, his voice steady but insistent. "How could someone replicate these horrific murders so accurately without direct knowledge? It's almost as if they were there."

The historian shifted uncomfortably in his seat, his fingers fiddling with a pen. He avoided George's gaze, focusing instead on a stack of papers on his desk. "Detective, the level of detail in these recreations is... unsettling. It's not just knowledge you can find in books or online. It's intimate, precise."

The implication hung heavily in the room, a sinister possibility that George had already considered. The copycat wasn't just a student of the Ripper's work; he was an aficionado, obsessed with not just the how but the why of those infamous killings.

"But how?" George pressed, his voice a mix of frustration

and desperation. "How does someone get that close to replicating the mindset of a dead killer?"

The historian finally met George's eyes, a haunted look in his own. "I've spent my academic life studying the Yorkshire Ripper, and I can tell you, Detective, there's a fine line between fascination and obsession. Whoever is doing this... they've crossed that line. They're not just replicating the murders; they're reliving them."

George leaned back, the historian's words echoing in his mind. This was more than a case of a killer inspired by history; this was a killer who wanted to be a part of that history, to carve his name alongside the Sutcliffe's in the annals of infamy.

The historian cleared his throat, breaking the tense silence. "There's something else," he said hesitantly. "The Yorkshire Ripper... he had a certain... signature—a way of leaving his unique mark. Your copycat has replicated that, down to the smallest detail. It's as if he's... channelling him."

George felt a chill run down his spine. The word 'channelling' painted a grim picture of the killer's mindset, a mind so warped by its obsession that it could almost bridge the gap between past and present.

"Thank you," George said, standing up. "You've confirmed what I feared. We're dealing with someone who's not just emulating the Ripper. They're trying to become him."

Chapter Sixteen

The evening chill settled deep in his bones as George Beaumont stepped out of the University of Leeds. Journalists immediately swarmed him, their cameras clicking and microphones thrust forward like weapons. The air was thick with anticipation, each journalist vying for a statement, a snippet that could lead tomorrow's headlines.

"Detective Beaumont, is the original Ripper back?" one journalist called out, her voice sharp with urgency.

"Can you confirm if this is the work of an impersonator?" another chimed in, pressing closer.

George moved through the sea of journalists with a stern, unwavering expression. "No comment," he said, his voice a firm rebuke to the barrage of questions. He kept his gaze straight, his steps measured, a man unwilling to fuel the flames of speculation and fear that were already engulfing the city.

Reaching his Mercedes, he slipped inside, the cacophony of voices immediately muffled by the closed door. He let out a deep breath, the brief respite a stark contrast to the chaos he had just waded through. Starting the car, he pulled away from the university, leaving the clamour behind.

Once he was a safe distance away, George picked up his

phone and dialled Luke Mason. The call connected, and he heard Luke's voice, tense yet expectant. "George, any updates?"

George navigated the evening traffic, his mind a whirlwind of thoughts. "It's the same circus out here, Luke. The press is hungry for any scrap of information. They're asking if the original Ripper is back."

There was a pause on the other end, a moment of contemplation. "And what do we tell them?" Luke finally asked.

George's grip tightened on the steering wheel. "Nothing. We keep our focus. This isn't about whether it's the original Ripper or an impersonator. Our job remains the same—to put an end to this brutality."

Luke's response was a mix of resolve and concern. "Understood, son. The team's working round the clock. We're following up on every lead."

As George drove through the streets of Leeds, the city's familiar landscape seemed shadowed by the ongoing terror. The evening lights flickered like distant stars, a stark reminder of the darkness they were battling against.

"We can't let the speculation distract us, Luke," George continued his voice a steady anchor amidst the storm. "This killer, whoever they are, is smart, calculated. We need to be one step ahead."

"I agree, sir," Luke replied. "We're combing through every piece of evidence, every lead. We'll catch this guy."

George nodded to himself, a silent affirmation. "Keep me updated, Luke. Any progress, any breakthrough, I want to know immediately."

The call ended, and George was left alone with his thoughts as he drove on, the Mercedes cutting a solitary figure through the bustling streets. The weight of responsibility, the burden of expectation, rested heavily on his shoulders.

* * *

Back at the station, George gathered his team, his expression grim. "This isn't just about catching a killer," he told them. "It's about stopping someone who's trying to rewrite history in blood. We're not just up against a murderer; we're up against a fanatic."

The team listened intently, the gravity of the situation settling in. The hunt for the Ripper copycat had taken a darker turn, one that delved into the depths of a disturbed mind, a mind that sought not just to kill but to immortalise itself in the darkest possible way.

George's eyes were resolute as he looked at each member of his team. "We need to end this. For the city, for the victims, for justice. We stop this killer, and we stop him now."

As they dispersed to their tasks, a renewed sense of urgency fuelled their actions. The clock was ticking, and with each passing moment, the line between the past and the present, between the Ripper and his disciple, grew ever more blurred.

In the stark confines of his office at Elland Road Police Station, George Beaumont poured over the old case files, the dim light from his desk lamp casting a glow on the weathered papers that held secrets of a dark past. The Ripper's letter, a macabre echo from a bygone era of terror, lay open before him, its words a grim tapestry of taunts and hidden meanings.

Weary yet unyielding, George's eyes scanned each line and word, searching for the subtle nuances that might reveal more than the killer had intended. The letter was not just a communication but a challenge, a puzzle designed by a mind twisted by its dark fantasies.

As he delved deeper, a pattern began to emerge: a rhythm in the phrasing, a careful choice of words that hinted at something more. It was as if the Ripper was playing a game, embedding a coded message within the taunts, a message meant for George's eyes alone.

The air in the office felt heavy, charged with the weight of unspoken revelations. George leaned closer, his mind a whirlwind of theories and conjectures. The letter was a window into the killer's psyche, a glimpse into a mind that thrived on control and manipulation.

"Hidden meanings," George muttered to himself, his voice barely above a whisper. "What are you trying to tell me?"

The words of the letter seemed to dance before his eyes, a macabre waltz of letters and phrases. The Ripper had been meticulous and deliberate in his choice of words. It was a cryptic roadmap, leading to a truth that lay shrouded in shadows.

George's fingers tapped rhythmically on the desk, his mind racing to decode the message. Every word, every punctuation mark, could be a clue, a key to unlocking the Ripper's intent. The killer had thrown down the gauntlet, and George knew he had to rise to the challenge.

He reached for a notepad, scribbling down phrases, rearranging words, looking for patterns. The clock on the wall ticked steadily, marking the passage of time in a room where time seemed to stand still.

As he worked, the pieces of the puzzle began to fit together, forming a picture that was as disturbing as it was enlightening. The letter was more than a taunt; it was a declaration of intent, a roadmap of the killer's plan.

George sat back, a sense of revelation washing over him. The coded message within the letter was a sinister guide, leading him deeper into the labyrinth of the killer's mind. It spoke of a plan, a design beyond merely imitating the Yorkshire Ripper's deeds.

He picked up the phone, dialling Luke Mason. "Luke, get in here. I've found something in the letter. It's a message, a coded roadmap. This killer, he's planning something bigger than we realised."

* * *

Later, the room was silent, every eye fixed on George, awaiting the revelation that might change the course of their investigation.

"There's something in the letter," George began, his voice resolute, cutting through the tension. "The killer references an extra body, one we haven't found yet. It's a deliberate allusion to the mistake Wearside Jack made years ago."

The team absorbed this information, the gravity of the implication settling over them like a shroud. It wasn't just a taunt; it was a calculated move, a clue hidden in plain sight.

Detective Constable Candy Nichols, a young officer who had joined the team recently, shook her head. "The three Rippers, Wearside Jack... they're all just evil," she said, her voice tinged with a mix of anger and disbelief.

Mark Finch, leaning against the wall with his arms folded, looked contemplative. "Evil," he mused, his tone philosophical. "It's a term we use, but what does it truly mean? Some souls seem born possessed by darkness, an inescapable fate that drives them to acts of such cruelty." He paused. "Sometimes, you can understand someone's actions without condoning them. We all have our demons, after all."

The room fell into a reflective silence, each member grappling with the concept. The nature of evil, the darkness that lurked in the human soul, was a mystery they faced every day yet never fully understood.

George's gaze swept across the room, meeting the eyes of each team member. "The ghosts of the victims are all around us," he said, his voice a whisper of determination. "They demand justice, and we will deliver it. This killer, this monster, whatever name we give him, Leeds depends on us to remove this scourge."

The team nodded, a silent vow echoing in the room. They were united in their purpose, bound by a duty that went beyond the call of their badges.

George continued, his words a rallying cry. "We will unravel this message, piece by piece. We will find the hidden body, and we will bring this killer to justice. We owe it to the victims, to the city. We will not rest until this nightmare is over."

As the meeting dispersed, the team moved with a renewed sense of urgency. The coded message in the letter was a puzzle that needed solving, a key that could unlock the mind of a killer who lurked in the shadows of their city.

George remained in the room, the weight of the task ahead settling heavily on his shoulders. He could feel the presence of the victims, their unspoken pleas for justice, their hopes and dreams cut short by a madman's hand.

He looked at the letter again, the words of the killer staring back at him. It was a challenge, a game of wits and wills. But George was undaunted. He had faced darkness before, had stared into the abyss and emerged stronger.

* * *

The clock ticked past midnight; the only sounds were the occasional rustle of papers and the steady tapping of a keyboard. George Beaumont and Mark Finch were the last two left, silhouettes against the glow of George's computer screen.

George, his eyes weary yet focused, analysed a timeline of the crimes. Beside him, Finch was engrossed in profiles of potential suspects.

"It's like we're chasing a ghost," George muttered, more to himself than to Finch.

Finch looked up from his paperwork, his expression contemplative. "Sometimes, I wonder if our paths are really our own choosing," he said, his voice unusually reflective. "Do you think destiny plays a part? Perhaps we're bound to follow in our parents' footsteps, whether we want to or not?"

George paused, turning to look at Finch. The profiler's question hung in the air, oddly out of place. "I believe we make our own paths," George replied after a moment. "Our choices are our own, not dictated by our lineage."

Finch nodded slowly, his gaze drifting back to his screen. "Perhaps. But sometimes, the past has a way of seeping into the present."

The comment lingered in the air, a note of something deeper, something unsaid. George considered it for a moment, a frown creasing his forehead. Finch's musings on destiny and legacy were unusual, but fatigue was setting in, clouding the significance of the words.

George turned back to his work, dismissing the oddity of the conversation. The case was demanding all his focus, leaving little room for philosophical reflections. Yet, as he delved back into the files, part of his mind remained on Finch's words, filed away as a curious anomaly in the profiler's otherwise pragmatic demeanour.

The night wore on; the office bathed in the artificial glow of fluorescent lights.

Outside, Leeds slept, unaware of the two men working tirelessly.

Chapter Seventeen

The evening had draped its cloak over Leeds as George Beaumont stood before his team. "As we tighten the net, we need to be strategic about our next moves," George began, his voice cutting through the room's tension. "I need volunteers for surveillance and additional legwork on the ground."

Constable Andrew Finch was quick to respond, his hand shooting up before George had even finished. "I'll take on extra surveillance shifts, sir," he said, his tone eager, almost urgent.

George glanced at Andrew, noting the intensity in the constable's eyes. It was more than the usual dedication to duty; Andrew seemed personally invested in every detail of the investigation.

"And I can dive deeper into the background checks," Andrew added, leaning forward in his seat, his expression one of focused determination.

George nodded, acknowledging Andrew's offer. "Very well, Andrew. Coordinate with Candy on the background checks. We need to cover all our bases."

As the meeting progressed, Andrew's involvement was notable. He introduced pertinent suggestions, displaying a keen understanding of the case's intricacies. His eagerness to immerse himself in the investigation was evident, a fact that George filed away in his mental notes.

The meeting drew to a close with tasks and roles assigned. The team dispersed, a hive of activity and purpose, but George lingered, his gaze following Andrew as he left the room.

Andrew's heightened eagerness to engage with specific aspects of the investigation was intriguing. It could be a simple case of professional zeal, but George's instincts told him there was more to it. The constable's personal investment in the case was a thread that, if pulled, could unravel unexpected truths.

* * *

George finally managed to return to the sanctuary of his home. The warmth and light of the household stood in stark contrast to the cold shadows of his day's work. He could hear the soft chatter of his family, a soothing balm to his frayed nerves. Yet, as he stepped inside, the weight of the case remained a relentless companion, clinging to him like a second skin.

In the dining room, his family gathered around the table, the aroma of tea and the homely clatter of dishes creating a scene of domestic bliss. George's fiancée, Isabella, looked up as he entered, her smile faltering slightly at the sight of his drawn features. "You're home early," she commented, a note of surprise mingling with concern in her voice.

George managed a nod, forcing his tense muscles to relax as he took a seat. "I needed a break from... well, everything," he admitted, his voice a low rumble.

His young daughter, Olivia, sat in her high chair, her bright eyes and cherubic face a stark reminder of the innocence that existed in stark contrast to the world he was entrenched in. She babbled happily, reaching out her tiny hands towards him.

George looked at her, his heart aching with a love so deep it was almost painful. Yet, even the sight of his baby daughter, usually a sure-fire way to bring a smile to his face, couldn't penetrate the dark cloud that hovered over him. The killer's twisted psyche, the gruesome nature of the crimes, the taunting letter—they all spun a web in his mind, a labyrinth with no clear exit.

Isabella's hand touched his arm, a gentle, grounding presence. "George, you're miles away. Is everything alright?"

He turned to her, the depth of his turmoil reflected in his eyes. "It's this case, Isabella. It's like chasing a ghost. A ghost with a penchant for cruelty and games."

Isabella's expression softened with understanding. She knew the toll his work often took on him, the burdens he carried home. "You can't let it consume you, George. You have to find a way to leave it at the station."

George sighed, his gaze drifting back to Olivia, who was now playing with her spoon, oblivious to the complexities of the world around her. "I wish it were that simple. This killer, he's not just taking lives; he's taunting us, playing a game of his own twisted design."

George's family was a stark reminder of the normalcy that seemed so distant in his line of work. It was a normalcy he fought to protect, a beacon of hope amid darkness.

"I just want to end this, Isabella. To stop him before more lives are lost," George said, his voice barely above a whisper.

Isabella reached out, her hand enveloping his. "And you will. You always do. But don't lose yourself in the process. Remember what you're fighting for."

George nodded, a sense of resolve mingling with the exhaustion. He looked at his family, his haven in a world that too often showed its cruel face. They were his anchor, his reminder of why he did what he did.

For a moment, he allowed himself to bask in the warmth of his family, to let their laughter and chatter wash over him. But the case lingered in the back of his mind, a shadow that refused to be dispelled.

As tea ended and he helped Isabella clear the table, George knew that the night would be long; the killer's riddles and taunts would occupy his thoughts.

* * *

George Beaumont sat alone in the quiet confines of his home office, the only company being the ghostly echoes of a case that refused to let him rest. The room was dimly lit, the light casting long shadows that seemed to dance upon the walls, mirroring the turmoil within George's mind. On his desk lay an array of photographs and files, but his gaze was fixed on one in particular—a picture of Peter Sutcliffe, the original Yorkshire Ripper. The image seemed to stare back at him, eyes that held a cold, mocking depth as if taunting him from beyond the grave.

George leaned back in his chair, his fingers drumming a steady rhythm on the wooden surface. The similarities between the current case and Sutcliffe's reign of terror were undeniable, and yet there was a divergence, a twisted evolution in the method that set this new predator apart. It was as if the killer was not only emulating Sutcliffe but trying to surpass him, to etch his own dark legacy into the annals of criminal history.

The silence of the room was oppressive, filled with the weight of unspoken questions and elusive answers. George's mind raced, analysing and reanalysing every detail, every piece of evidence they had gathered. The taunting letter, the coded messages, the meticulously replicated murders—they were pieces of a sinister puzzle that he was determined to solve.

Sutcliffe's picture seemed to follow him, the eyes almost alive with a nasty glint. George could practically hear the whispered challenge, a spectral voice from the past urging him on, testing his resolve. It was a psychological game, a battle of wits that stretched beyond the physical realm into the dark corridors of the human psyche.

George's thoughts were interrupted by the soft chime of the clock, marking the late hour. Time was slipping away, and with each passing moment, the killer was out there, a shadow moving in the night. George felt a surge of determination, a renewed sense of purpose. He would not be taunted, not by Sutcliffe's ghost, nor by the new Ripper who sought to follow in his footsteps.

He stood up, his movement decisive, and began to pace the room, his eyes once again scanning the array of files and photographs. There had to be a connection, a clue that they had overlooked. The killer was meticulous, leaving nothing to chance, and that very precision might be his undoing.

As George reviewed the evidence, his mind began to piece together a profile, a portrait of a killer whose desire to emulate Sutcliffe was driven by a deeper, more sinister motive. It was not just about the killings; it was about the message, the legacy. This new Ripper didn't just want to be another name in the annals of crime; he wanted to overshadow Sutcliffe himself.

The realisation sent a shiver down George's spine. They were dealing with someone whose ambition was as dark as it was boundless, a predator whose thirst for infamy knew no limits.

George returned to his desk, his resolve like steel. He would delve into the mind of this killer, understand his motives, and predict his moves.

* * *

Later, George succumbed to the weight of exhaustion, his mind drifting into the murky realm of sleep. However, rest was elusive; his subconscious was a battlefield, echoing the shadows of the case that consumed his waking hours.

In his dream, he found himself in his office, a sense of foreboding hanging in the air. The room was dim, the only light emanating from his desk lamp, casting an eerie glow on the walls. Papers were strewn across his desk, but among them lay a new letter, one he hadn't seen before. It was from the killer, its presence in his dream a sinister intrusion.

George's hands trembled slightly as he picked up the letter. The words were written in a jagged, haunting script, each stroke of the pen a deliberate mark of malice. As he read, the letters seemed to dance and twist on the page, forming a cryptic puzzle that taunted his mind.

"You've missed something, George," the letter read, its tone mocking. "Look closer. The answer is there, hidden in plain sight."

George's heart pounded in his chest, a sense of urgency propelling him forward. He scanned the letter, his eyes darting over each word, each phrase, searching for the elusive clue he had missed. The room around him felt oppressive, the walls closing in as if the very air was charged with the killer's evil presence.

He could hear the killer's laughter, a disembodied echo that filled the room, mocking his efforts. "You can't stop me, George. You're always one step behind."

The dream shifted, the room morphing into the crime scenes he had visited, the letter still clutched in his hand. The victims' faces flashed before him, their eyes pleading, their voices a silent scream for justice. George felt a surge of determination, a resolve to end this nightmare, to bring the killer to justice.

But the letter remained a riddle, its secrets shrouded in shadows. George felt a growing frustration, a sense that the key to the mystery was just beyond his grasp. He poured over the letter, the words blurring and reforming, a maddening puzzle that refused to be solved.

As the dream continued, the scenes changed, the letter leading him on a twisted journey through the darkest corners of his mind. The streets of Leeds, the faces of his team, the eyes of the killer—they all merged into a kaleidoscope of fear and obsession.

And then, just as suddenly as it had begun, the dream shattered, dissipating into the ether of his subconscious. George awoke with a start, his breath ragged, his heart racing. The room was dark, the silence of the night a stark contrast to the chaos of his dream.

He lay there momentarily, trying to catch his breath, the remnants of the dream lingering like a spectre in his mind. The letter, the message, the taunting words—he'd figured it out.

* * *

In a room shrouded in darkness, lit only by the flickering glow of a single lamp, the copycat sat hunched over a cluttered desk, his obsession manifesting in every fevered movement. The walls around him were plastered with photos and documents, a macabre collage dedicated to the Yorkshire Ripper murders. His eyes, wide and unblinking, gleamed with a maniacal intensity as he pored over each piece, relishing every detail with a twisted glee.

The room was a sanctum of his dark fascination, a shrine to the legacy he was determined to perpetuate. Stacks of old newspapers, weathered and yellowed with age, lay scattered around him, alongside police reports and photographs of the Ripper's victims. Each image, each article, was a piece of the puzzle he was meticulously assembling in his mind.

He traced his fingers over the photos, whispering names like incantations - names that had once sent shivers down the spines of the residents of Leeds. The copycat's lips curled into a smile, a grotesque parody of joy. He was more than just a follower; he was the Ripper reborn, his spawn, the keeper of a dark flame that he intended to burn brighter than ever before.

His gaze fell upon a map of Leeds, pins and strings creating a web of past crimes. He leaned in, his breath quickening as he plotted his next move. Each location held a story, a memory of terror that he was eager to rekindle. He imagined the streets, the fear, the chaos he would unleash, and it filled him with a perverse sense of power.

The clock on the wall ticked away the hours, but time held no meaning in his hunger. He sifted through the documents, absorbing every word, every detail. He was meticulous in his planning, determined to not only emulate but surpass his idol. Every step, every act had to be perfect, a tribute worthy of the name he had taken for himself.

As he delved deeper into the night, his plan took shape, a sinister blueprint for the continuation of the Ripper's work. He envisioned the headlines, the panic, the admiration he would command. In his twisted psyche, he was not a mere copycat; he was the next chapter in a saga of horror, a worthy successor to the throne of fear that Sutcliffe had once held.

The room around him felt alive with the echoes of the past, the whispers of the victims mingling with the ghostly presence of the original Ripper. In this hallowed space, the copycat felt a communion with his dark predecessor, a shared purpose that transcended time and death.

His fingers lingered on a particular photograph, a scene of one of the Ripper's crimes. He studied it with a fanatic's zeal, noting every detail, every nuance. It was a scene he would recreate, a homage that would reignite the terror that had once gripped the city.

The copycat leaned back in his chair, his mind a whirlwind of plans and fantasies. He could almost hear the whispers of approval from the shadows, the spectral nod of the Ripper himself. He was no longer just a man; he was a legend in the making, a nightmare poised to descend upon Leeds once again.

He was the Ripper reborn, and his reign of terror was just beginning.

Chapter Eighteen

The morning winter sun barely penetrated the thick clouds over Leeds as Detective Inspector George Beaumont entered DCI Alistair Atkinson's office. The air was tense, charged with the urgency of their ongoing investigation. Atkinson, seated behind his desk, looked up, his expression a mix of anticipation and weariness.

"Sir, I need to send a team to the old playground on Reginald Street in Chapeltown," George said, his tone firm, leaving no room for doubt about the importance of this request.

Atkinson nodded slowly, his eyes searching George's. "Reginald Street? What's led you there?"

George took a deep breath, the weight of his findings heavy in his mind. "It's the coded message in the killer's letter. One word stood out: 'Innocent.' It's a direct reference to Jayne McDonald."

Detective Constable Jay Scott, who had accompanied George, interjected with a puzzled frown. "Jayne McDonald? Why does that name ring a bell?"

George turned to him, his gaze steady. "Jayne was just 16 years old when Peter Sutcliffe murdered her. Her death marked a turning point in the Ripper's pattern. Until then, his victims were primarily known sex workers. Jayne's murder shattered the illusion that he only targeted certain women. The media and police dubbed her an 'innocent victim.'"

Understanding dawned in Jay's eyes, a grim realisation of the implication. "So, you think this killer is retracing Sutcliffe's steps, targeting locations with significant historical value to the original cases."

"Exactly," George affirmed. "Reginald Street could hold a clue, maybe something we've overlooked. This killer is meticulous, leaving breadcrumbs for us to follow."

Atkinson leaned back, his expression contemplative. "Alright, George. I trust your judgment. Organise a team. But be discreet. We can't afford to start a panic."

George nodded, a silent acknowledgement of the delicate nature of their task. He turned to leave, his mind already racing with the possibilities of what they might find.

As they walked back to the Homicide and Major Enquiry Team floor, Jay Scott seemed deep in thought, grappling with the gravity of their investigation. "So, this killer isn't just copying Sutcliffe. He's weaving a narrative, drawing connections to the original murders."

George glanced at him, his face a mask of determination. "That seems to be his game. It's a psychological ploy, a way to instil fear and assert control. But it also means he's leaving us a trail. And we're going to use it to stop him."

Arriving at the task force room, George quickly briefed a team of uniformed officers, instructing them on the sensitivity and importance of their mission to Reginald Street. He emphasised the need for a thorough but unobtrusive presence, aware that the eyes of the community, still haunted by the shadows of the past, would be upon them.

* * *

The evening sky was a deepening shade of twilight as Detective Inspector George Beaumont prepared to leave the station. The day had been long and arduous, filled with the meticulous piecing together of evidence and theories and setting up the Reginald Street team. He stepped into the cool air of the station car park, his mind still churning with the details of the case.

As he approached his car, a sense of unease prickled at the back of his neck. The car park was unusually quiet, the usual bustle of officers coming and going having dwindled as the evening wore on. George fished for his keys, his senses heightened, alert to the stillness around him.

Suddenly, a figure emerged from the shadows, swift and silent as a predator. Before George could react, the figure, masked and ominous, lunged at him. A flash of metal glinted in the assailant's hand - a knife aimed straight at George.

Instinct took over. George sidestepped the initial attack but not quickly enough to avoid the blade entirely. It sliced into his arm, a sharp burst of pain that jolted him into action. Adrenaline surged through him as he recalled his boxing training, skills honed in his youth now resurfacing in this moment of peril.

The assailant, undeterred, advanced again, but George was ready. He pivoted on his foot, delivering a swift, powerful punch to the assailant's chin. The impact sent the attacker stumbling back, the mask slightly askew, revealing nothing but a pair of cold, determined eyes.

For a moment, the assailant seemed to consider their options; the knife still clutched in their hand. But the sound of approaching footsteps from the station caused a moment's hesitation. Seizing the opportunity, the assailant turned and fled into the darkness, disappearing as quickly as they had appeared.

George stood there, heart pounding, his breath coming in ragged gasps. His arm throbbed with pain, blood seeping through his sleeve. With shaking hands, he pulled out his phone and dialled 999.

"This is DI Beaumont. I've been attacked in Elland Road station car park. The assailant... it could be the Ripper. He's fled the scene. I need backup and an ambulance, now!"

His voice was a mix of pain and urgency, the realisation of the encounter setting in. He had come face to face with the West Yorkshire Ripper, the very shadow they had been chasing, and had narrowly escaped.

As officers poured into the car park, lights and sirens cutting through the night, George allowed himself to be ushered into a waiting ambulance. His mind was a whirlwind of thoughts, the encounter replaying over and over. The Ripper had been bold enough to attack him at the station, a move that reeked of desperation or overconfidence.

In the ambulance, as the paramedics tended to his wound, George's thoughts were not on his injury but on the case. The encounter, though brief and violent, had provided a crucial insight. The Ripper was becoming more daring, more unpredictable. And that meant he was either close to achieving his goal or close to being caught.

As the ambulance doors closed, taking him away from the scene, George's resolve hardened. This attack was a message, a declaration of war. And he was ready to respond. The Ripper had made it personal, and George Beaumont would not rest until he had brought this monster to justice.

The night closed in around the ambulance as it sped away, but inside, George Beaumont was a beacon of determination, a hunter now more than ever focused on his prey. The game had changed, and the stakes had been raised, but so had George's commitment.

* * *

Detective Inspector George Beaumont lay on the hospital bed; his arm bandaged, a dull ache resonating from the wound where the knife had pierced his flesh. The air was thick with the antiseptic smell of disinfectant, a soothing balm to the adrenaline and fear coursing through his veins just hours earlier.

Dr Kapoor, a seasoned physician with a calm demeanour that belied the urgency of his work, stood beside George, examining the dressing on his arm. "You were lucky," he said, his voice measured and reassuring. "The blade missed the major arteries. You'll need to rest this arm, though. No strenuous activity for a while."

George nodded his mind only partially on his injury. His thoughts were racing, replaying the attack, dissecting every moment for a clue, a sign of who the assailant might have been. The idea that the West Yorkshire Ripper had been bold enough to strike at him, a detective, was alarming and illuminating.

Outside the room, two police officers stood guard, their presence a silent testament to the severity of the situation. The possibility that the Ripper might attempt to finish the job was a threat they couldn't ignore. George's role in the investigation had painted a target on his back, a reality that was now starkly evident.

Isabella rushed in, dishevelled, her hair a cascade of untamed worry. In her arms, little Olivia sobbed, her tiny body shaking with each cry. Isabella's eyes, red-rimmed and frantic, found George's, a storm of relief and fear crashing in their depths.

"George, thank God you're okay," she breathed out, her voice a trembling whisper. Olivia reached out, her tiny hands grasping for her father.

George's heart clenched at the sight, a surge of guilt washing over him. "I'm okay, love," he reassured, his voice a strained effort of normalcy. He gently touched Olivia's hand, a weak smile on his lips.

Isabella moved closer, her gaze intense. "You need to step away from this case, at least until you're better," she pleaded, her voice thick with unshed tears. The fear of losing him was palpable in every word. "Please."

George shook his head slowly, a stubborn set to his jaw. "I can't, Izzy. I've rattled the killer. He's feeling cornered, making mistakes." His voice was firm, a testament to his unwavering dedication.

Isabella's eyes brimmed with tears, her frustration and fear spilling over. "What about us? What about Olivia?" She gestured to their daughter, still clinging to her. "And Jack." She paused. "You can't keep putting yourself in danger."

George reached out, his hand gently caressing Isabella's cheek. "I know, and I'm sorry. But I have to see this through. For everyone's safety." His gaze was unwavering, reflecting the turmoil within.

Isabella slumped into the chair beside the bed, defeated, her shoulders shaking with silent sobs. Sensing her mother's distress, Olivia quieted, her small face buried in Isabella's neck.

Dr Kapoor finished his examination, offering a small, reassuring smile. "You should get some rest, Detective. Your body needs to heal."

George managed a wry smile in return. "Rest seems to be in short supply these days, Doctor. But I appreciate your concern."

As Dr Kapoor left the room, George's gaze drifted to the window, the night sky outside a canvas of darkness pierced by the occasional star. The attack had been a clear message from the Ripper, a taunt that he was always one step ahead. But it had also been a mistake. In his arrogance, the Ripper had exposed himself. But that only made him more dangerous.

George turned to Isabella; the room was heavy with unsaid words, the air thick with the weight of George's decision. He watched his family, a painful realization dawning on him. His pursuit of justice was a double-edged sword, protecting others while endangering his own.

As Isabella's sobs subsided, George whispered a promise, more to himself than to her. "I'll be careful. I swear." But even as he said it, he knew the path he'd chosen was fraught with peril.

* * *

The door opened, and Detective Constable Jay Scott entered, his expression a mix of concern and determination. "How are you feeling, boss?"

George shifted slightly, his arm protesting the movement. "Been better, Jay. But I'll live."

Jay nodded, pulling up a chair. "I bought you some sweets

but ended up eating them on the walk over." He grinned. "Sorry."

George grinned and asked, "Any news on the investigation?"

"We're combing through the CCTV footage from the station. We might get a lead on who attacked you. And the team's still working on the coded message. We're getting closer; I can feel it."

George's eyes hardened with resolve. "This attack... it's a sign that we're closing in on him. He's getting desperate, making mistakes."

Jay's gaze was unwavering, a reflection of his own commitment to the case. "We'll get him, boss. He won't get away with this."

Detective Sergeant Luke Mason's footsteps echoed through the corridors of the hospital, his pace quick and determined, a sense of urgency propelling him forward. News of George's attack had reached him like a shock wave, unsettling and unexpected. The usually composed Mason now battled with a tide of emotions, chief among them a pang of gnawing guilt for not being there when his superior, his mentor, was attacked.

As he reached George's room, flanked by police officers, Luke paused, taking a deep breath to compose himself. The door swung open silently, revealing George lying on the hospital bed, his arm bandaged but his eyes alert, the ever-present glint of determination undimmed.

"George," Luke began, his voice tinged with a mix of relief and self-reproach. "I should have been there, son. At the station. I should've—"

George raised his hand, cutting him off. "Luke, this isn't on you. We couldn't have predicted this. The Ripper is becoming more bold, more direct."

Luke pulled up a chair beside the bed, his expression troubled. "How are you holding up?"

George's gaze shifted, a flicker of vulnerability crossing his features before being swiftly replaced by resolve. "I'm alright. But this attack... it's a clear message. He's not just killing at random any more. He's targeting the investigation. Targeting us."

The weight of George's words hung in the air, a chilling realisation of the stakes they were up against. The Ripper had escalated from a shadowy predator to a direct aggressor, bringing a personal and immediate danger they hadn't faced before.

Luke's jaw clenched, a determined fire kindling in his eyes. "We'll tighten security at the station, at our homes. We won't let him get another chance."

George nodded, but there was a lingering concern in his eyes. "It's not just us, Luke. It's our families. If he's bold enough to strike at a police station, what's stopping him from going after our loved ones?"

The possibility hung between them, unspoken but deeply understood. The nature of their work had always carried risks, but now those risks were starkly personal, the threat a shadow that loomed over their private lives.

Luke leaned forward, his voice firm. "We'll protect them, George. We'll do whatever it takes. We're not just dealing with a killer; we're dealing with a monster. But he's made a mistake. He's brought the fight to us, and that's where we'll end it."

George's expression hardened, the familiar steely resolve returning. "You're right. He thinks he's scared us, weakened us. But he's only strengthened our resolve."

The room was silent momentarily, the two detectives lost in their thoughts, each contemplating the path ahead. The attack had been a seismic shift in the investigation, a game-changer that had brought the danger right to their doorstep.

Luke stood up, his stance one of unwavering support. "I'll coordinate with the team and make sure everyone's on high alert. We'll catch this bastard, George. We'll bring him down."

George, about to say something to Luke, winced at his wounds. The attack in the station car park had left more than physical wounds; it had struck a chord of fear that George rarely acknowledged.

Luke, sensing the gravity of George's mood, leaned in closer. "George, what's going on? Talk to me."

George's gaze was distant, his voice barely above a whisper. "Isabella and Olivia, they're my world, Luke. And then there's Jack with Mia in East Ardsley... If he's bold enough to strike at me in a police station, what's stopping him from going after them?"

Luke could see the turmoil in George's eyes, the internal battle between the seasoned detective and the concerned family man. "George, we'll put protection on your family, on all our families. We won't let him get to them."

George nodded slowly, but the worry lingered. "I know the measures we'll take, Luke. But knowing how this killer operates, how he thinks... It leaves a knot in my gut. We need to end this, and soon."

Luke's stance was unwavering, his voice firm with conviction. "We will, George. We're closing in on him. This attack, it's a sign of desperation. He's trying to throw us off, make us scared. But we won't let him. We'll turn this around on him."

George's gaze finally met Luke's, a flash of the old determination sparking in his eyes. "You're right. We can't let fear dictate our moves. We need to use this, use what he's given us. He's getting sloppy, and that will lead us right to him."

Luke nodded, the bond between them more than just professional; it was a bond forged in the fires of countless cases, a mutual understanding and respect. "I'll get back to the station and ramp up the investigation. We'll increase surveillance and go over everything again. He won't slip through our fingers."

As Luke turned to leave, George's voice stopped him. "Luke, keep an eye on them for me, will you? Isabella, Olivia, Jack... Just until this is over."

Luke turned back, his expression solemn. "You have my word, George. They'll be safe."

With that, Luke left the room, his mind already racing with plans and strategies. The attack on George had been a wake-up call, a stark reminder of the stakes they were playing for. But it had also been a mistake on the killer's part, a misstep that they would use to their advantage.

George lay back against his pillow, his thoughts on Isabella, Olivia, and Jack. The risk had never felt so personal, so close to home. But he knew he had a team he could trust, a team that would do everything in their power to bring this nightmare to an end.

Chapter Nineteen

Detective Inspector George Beaumont entered the Incident Room, his arm in a sling but his demeanour as formidable as ever. Upon seeing him, the team fell into a respectful silence, their gazes reflecting a mix of relief and renewed determination.

"Listen up," George began, his voice cutting through the tension in the room. "Our move to guard Reginald Street, it hit a nerve. We've clearly rattled our suspect."

He paused, surveying the room, his eyes locking onto each task force member. "This attack on me, it's a sign. We're closing in, and he knows it. Nearly killing a cop? It's a desperate move. It shows he's feeling the pressure of our manhunt."

Detective Sergeant Luke Mason, standing to the side, nodded in agreement. "It's reckless. It's not like the calculated moves we've seen before. He's losing his composure."

George leaned against the table, wincing slightly from the pain in his arm. "Exactly, Luke. And that means he's more likely to make mistakes. We need to capitalise on this. Increase patrols and keep a close watch on the key areas we've identified. I want eyes everywhere."

Detective Constable Jay Scott, his brow furrowed in concentration, spoke up. "Boss, if he's feeling cornered, he might escalate and become more unpredictable. We need to be prepared for anything."

George met Jay's gaze, a flicker of approval in his eyes. "Good point, Jay. We'll adjust our strategy accordingly. Everyone needs to be on high alert. This is the point where he's most dangerous."

The team members exchanged determined looks, a silent agreement passing between them. They were a united front, each aware of the stakes and ready to face whatever challenges lay ahead.

"We've got him on the back foot now," George continued, his voice imbued with a steely resolve. "He's made this personal, and we're going to use that. He thinks he can intimidate us, throw us off the scent. But all he's done is strengthen our resolve."

Luke stepped forward, his expression one of unwavering support. "We'll comb through every piece of evidence again, look for anything we might have missed. He's getting sloppy, and that's going to lead us right to him."

George gave a curt nod. "We need to keep the pressure on. He's vulnerable now, more likely to slip up. But we also need to be cautious. He's already shown he's dangerous and unafraid to take extreme measures."

The DI scanned the room, his gaze settling on each team member. "As we piece together the timeline, we need to consider every angle," George said, his voice steady and commanding.

It was then that Constable Andrew Finch, seated at the edge of the table, leaned forward. "Sir, if we cross-reference the locations of the recent crimes with the original Ripper's patterns, there's an overlap that hasn't been explored yet," he suggested, his tone measured but assertive.

George paused, considering Andrew's input. The constable's observation was unexpectedly perceptive, linking aspects of the case to bring new insights to the forefront. It was as if Andrew had been contemplating the connections deeply, seeing patterns others had missed.

"Good point, Andrew," George acknowledged a hint of surprise in his voice. "Let's have the analysts look into that. It could give us a new perspective on the killer's movements."

As the meeting continued, George found himself periodically glancing at Andrew. The constable's suggestion had been more than just a routine observation; it was as if he had an intuitive understanding of the killer's mind.

Soon the room buzzed with activity as the team sprang into action, each member keenly aware of the heightened danger and the need for swift, decisive action. George watched them, a sense of pride mingling with the weight of responsibility. They were a skilled team, and he trusted them implicitly.

As the meeting dispersed, George's thoughts turned to Isabella and Olivia, the worry for their safety a constant hum in the back of his mind. He knew the team would do everything in their power to protect them, but the fear remained.

* * *

Standing at the head, George unveiled the latest breakthrough in the case—a piece of evidence that directly linked the current string of crimes to the original Ripper's methodology.

"As you can see, the way the victim was positioned," George explained, pointing to a crime scene photo, "matches exactly with one of the Ripper's 1975 cases."

The team leaned in, examining the photo. It was a gruesome echo of the past, the signature of a killer recreating history. Amid the murmurs, George noticed Finch standing slightly apart. The profiler's eyes were locked on the photo, his face momentarily betraying a reaction that was out of character—a flicker of recognition, a shadow of distress.

George paused, his attention subtly shifting to Finch. "Mark, anything to add to the profile based on this?"

Finch seemed to snap out of his brief reverie, composing himself quickly. "It's... meticulous. This isn't just imitation; it's a homage. The killer is intimately familiar with the original cases." His voice was steady now, but George couldn't shake the image of that initial, unguarded expression.

The briefing continued, but George's mind was partially elsewhere, mulling over Finch's reaction.

As the team dispersed, Finch approached George. "I'll go over the archives again, see if there's anything we missed," he said, his tone back to its usual professional timbre.

George nodded, a thoughtful look on his face. "Good idea. Keep me posted."

Later, Beaumont stood before the array of screens displaying CCTV footage from the Leeds crime scenes.

George's gaze was intense, his eyes moving methodically over each frame of the footage. Then, something caught his attention—a minute detail that could easily have been overlooked. "Pause it there," he commanded, pointing to a figure captured on the screen.

The room fell silent as all eyes focused on the image. Shadows partially obscured the figure, but there was no mistaking the distinctive pattern on the shoes. A chill ran down George's spine. "Those shoes," he said, his voice steady despite the surge of adrenaline. "I've seen them before. On the attacker in the car park."

A murmur of realisation swept through the room. It was a breakthrough, the first time they had visual confirmation of the Ripper on film.

Detective Sergeant Luke Mason leaned forward, his eyes narrowing. "That's him, then. The Ripper. He's getting bolder, slipping up."

George nodded, his mind racing with the implications. "This is significant. We've got him on camera now. We need to enhance this image and get a clearer view. He's no longer just a shadow; he's becoming tangible."

As the team sprang into action, analysing the footage, enhancing images, and cross-referencing details, Profiler Mark Finch, who had been quietly observing, spoke up. "George, this attack, it's more than just a slip-up. It's a message. The culprit considers you his main adversary. This is becoming personal." He grinned. "It's all about the chase for him now, isn't it? The thrill of being pursued, the art of staying one step ahead."

The room grew still, the weight of Finch's words settling over them. George felt a cold resolve forming within him. "Then we'll use that," he said. "If he's focusing on me, he might get careless. We can exploit that."

Finch nodded, his expression grave. "Be cautious, George. This kind of personal fixation can escalate quickly. He's trying to get under your skin, throw you off balance."

George met Finch's gaze, a steely determination in his eyes. "Let him try. We're close now, closer than we've ever been. He's feeling the pressure, and that's going to lead to his downfall."

The team worked with renewed vigour, the footage offering a new avenue of investigation, a new piece of the puzzle to fit into place. George watched them, a sense of pride mingling with the urgency of the hunt.

* * *

George Beaumont, leaning over the shoulder of Detective Sergeant Yolanda Williams, watched as the enhanced CCTV footage flickered on the screen. In the grainy video, there was the elusive shadow they had been chasing—the suspect, captured for the first time. It charged the Incident Room with a palpable sense of anticipation.

"Back it up, zoom in there," George instructed, his voice a low command. The image on the screen expanded, the figure becoming more defined. A man, average height, build obscured by a heavy coat. His face was half-turned, a partial profile in the dim light of the streetlamp.

Candy Nichols, standing beside George, leaned in closer. "That's him, sir. Has to be." Her voice was a mix of triumph and tension.

George straightened, his mind racing with possibilities. "Let's get this image out to all units. Someone must recognise him."

The team sprang into action, each member fuelled by the breakthrough. Copies of the suspect's image were disseminated, a net cast wide across the city. George watched them, a sense of urgency driving his every move. The game had changed; they were no longer chasing a ghost.

"Set up checkpoints, focus on the area around the last

sighting," George ordered, his gaze fixed on the screen, the suspect's image burned into his memory.

* * *

Detective Sergeant Luke Mason and Detective Constable Jay Scott faced the man from the CCTV footage, Arnold Buxton. Upstairs in his office, George Beaumont watched the live link; his eyes narrowed in concentration. The man, nervous and fidgety, was an image of worry under the harsh lights.

"I swear, I was just walking home," the man stammered, his gaze darting between Luke and Jay. "I didn't even know about the attacks until you brought me here."

Luke leaned forward, his voice steady. "Your shoes, they match the ones seen on CCTV. We're told they're unique, with only a hundred sold worldwide. How do you explain that?"

The man's reply was a mix of frustration and fear. "They're just common shoes, aren't they? I bought them at the market. Well, outside, near the bus station."

In his office, George rubbed his chin, a nagging doubt creeping into his mind. The evidence was circumstantial, too convenient. His phone buzzed, and he glanced at the message from Candy. She and Tashan were out confirming the man's alibi.

Minutes later, another message came through: "Alibi confirmed. He was at his brother's birthday party. Dozens of witnesses."

George's heart sank. Another dead end, a red herring. He picked up the phone and called Mason. "Let him go, Luke. It's not him."

The disappointment was palpable in Luke's sigh as the call

ended. They had the man leave, his relief contrasting the detectives' frustration.

In the aftermath, the team reconvened in the Incident Room, a sombre mood hanging over them. George stood at the front, his gaze sweeping over his team.

"We were wrong," he admitted, his voice tinged with fatigue. "This was a red herring. Our suspect is still out there."

The room was silent, the weight of their unfulfilled task a heavy shroud. Candy and Tashan returned, their expressions mirroring the sentiment in the room.

"We'll start again," George said, his voice gaining strength. "Review everything from the start. There's something we're missing, and we'll find it."

As they dispersed, returning to their desks, George remained behind, his eyes fixed on the city map peppered with pins and strings. The suspect was clever, but George knew that even the most careful criminals made mistakes.

George Beaumont sat hunched over the sprawling case files that had become his world. The clock on his home office wall ticked past midnight, a silent witness to his relentless pursuit. In his hand, he held two co-codamols, a defiance of the doctor's orders. The pain in his arm was a constant reminder of his encounter with the Ripper, but it was a pain he chose to ignore. There was no time for rest, not when they were this close.

As he popped the pills into his mouth, swallowing them dry, there was a knock on his door—Isabella. His heart twinged with a mix of love and guilt, knowing what she would say.

"George, please," Isabella's voice was laced with worry and exhaustion. "You need to rest. You were nearly killed. You can't keep doing this to yourself."

George rubbed his temple, feeling the weight of her words. "Isabella, I can't. Not now. We're so close to catching him. The Ripper is scared; he's making mistakes. I need to be there."

There was a pause, and when Isabella spoke again, her voice was strained with unshed tears. "I'm scared too, George. Scared for you. You're not invincible. What if he comes after you again? What about Olivia?"

George closed his eyes, a wave of emotion threatening to overwhelm him. "I know love, I know. But think about the victims, the families torn apart by this monster. I have a duty to stop him. To make sure no one else suffers."

Isabella's voice broke a mixture of frustration and fear. "And what about our family? Your duty to us? Olivia needs her father, and I need... I need you."

George's resolve wavered, the image of his daughter's smiling face flashing in his mind. But then the faces of the victims returned, their silent pleas for justice echoing in his ears. "I need to end this, Isabella, for all of us. Once he's caught, I promise I'll take time off. We'll go away, just the three of us."

He could hear her breathing, a quiet sob muffled by her hand over her mouth. She turned, and as she was about to shut the door, she said, "Just... just come back to us, George. In one piece, please."

"I will," George whispered, the promise of a fragile thread in the darkness.

George turned back to the files, his mind a tornado of leads, theories, and strategies. The medication dulled the pain from his wound, but the mental strain was relentless. He poured over the CCTV footage, the photos, the notes, searching for the missing piece, the key that would unlock the door to the

Ripper's capture.

Outside, the night was still, but in George's world, the storm was raging. He was a man on the edge, driven by a maniacal obsession to catch a killer who had brought terror to the streets of Leeds.

And the stakes had never been higher.

Chapter Twenty

The office was quiet except for the low hum of the computer. George Beaumont and Candy Nichols were hunched over a profile document, the words blurring into a psychological map of their elusive killer. The room was bathed in the pale light of the screen, casting long shadows across their focused faces.

"This guy, he's meticulous, almost obsessive in his methods," George noted, his finger tracing a line of text.

Candy leaned back, her eyes thoughtful. "It's like he's trying to communicate something with these crimes, sir, a message or a legacy."

George nodded, his mind racing with theories. "A legacy of violence, like he's picking up where Sutcliffe left off."

Candy tilted her head, a new idea forming. "You know, it makes me think about the impact of family secrets, sir. How sometimes, the sins of the father are inherited in ways we can't see."

George paused, considering her words. "You mean like a cycle of violence passed down?"

"Exactly, sir," Candy replied. "Maybe our killer is living out some twisted family legacy. Something ingrained, hidden deep within."

The idea hung in the air, a new angle to consider. George

felt a chill run down his spine. The notion that their killer was acting out some inherited compulsion added a layer of complexity to the case.

"We need to dig deeper into his background," George decided, his voice firm. "Uncover any family connections that might be driving this."

Candy nodded, her mind already sifting through potential avenues of investigation. "I'll start with the old case files, see if there's any familial link that was overlooked."

* * *

Under the cloak of night, Detective Inspector George Beaumont traversed the dimly lit streets of Chapeltown, a place heavy with the echoes of a dark past. The area, once a notorious haunt of the Yorkshire Ripper, held an eerie stillness as if concealing secrets in its shadows. George's steps were measured, his senses heightened to every sound, every movement around him.

The pain in his arm, dulled by medication, was a constant reminder of the danger that lurked, yet his resolve was unwavering. He knew the risks of walking these streets alone, especially given the current climate of fear. But this was where the investigation had led him, to the heart of darkness, in search of the new Ripper's lair.

Dressed in plain clothes, he blended into the night, his eyes scanning the ageing buildings, the narrow alleys, and the deserted parks. He moved with purpose, his mind replaying the case files, the victim profiles, and the killer's patterns. With its grim history, Chapeltown seemed a likely place for the Ripper to hide in plain sight.

Every now and then, George stopped, his gaze lingering on a particular spot, a doorway, a window, a stretch of road. He was searching for something out of place, a sign that might lead him to the killer. The Ripper was meticulous and cunning, but George knew even the most careful predator left traces.

The night air was chilly, carrying whispers of the past, of terror that once gripped these streets. George felt a shiver run down his spine, not from the cold but from the realisation of the evil that had once prowled here and the evil that was emerging again.

As he walked, his thoughts drifted to Isabella and Olivia, the worry for their safety a constant ache in his heart. He knew he was walking a fine line, balancing his duty with the need to protect his family. But stopping the Ripper was the only way to truly keep them safe.

His phone vibrated in his pocket, a silent reminder of the world beyond these streets. He ignored it, his focus solely on the task at hand. This was not a time for distractions but a time for hunting.

George's keen eyes caught a flicker of movement in a narrow alley. He paused his instincts on high alert. Slowly, he approached, his hand resting on the concealed spray at his side. The shadows seemed to shift, to whisper secrets of the night.

He entered the alley, his footsteps echoing off the walls. At the end of the ginnel lay a discarded pile of rubbish, but something about it seemed deliberate, a camouflage. George crouched down, his fingers probing the debris, realising there was a door behind the garbage.

His heart pounded in his chest, a mix of adrenaline and caution. This could be it, the lair of the Ripper, hidden in the streets of Chapeltown. He hesitated for a moment, weighing the danger of proceeding alone. But the chance of discovering the Ripper's hiding place was too significant to ignore.

George took a deep breath, opened the door and stepped into the narrow passage, his senses on high alert. The air was musty, the darkness almost tangible. He moved forward, each step a descent into the heart of the Ripper's world.

As he navigated the narrow passage, the walls seemed to close in around him. He could feel the presence of the Ripper, a malignant force that had brought fear and death to the streets of Leeds.

But Detective Inspector George Beaumont was not a man to be deterred by fear. He was the hunter, and he was closing in on his prey.

Suddenly, a flicker of movement caught George's attention. In the periphery of his vision, a figure seemed to be following him, blending into the shadows with an almost spectral quality. George's pulse quickened, his instincts screaming that this was no coincidence. Could it be the Ripper, stalking him, toying with him in this macabre game of cat and mouse?

Without hesitation, George turned and gave chase. His footsteps echoed off the walls of the narrow backstreets, a rapid staccato in the night's silence. He glimpsed the figure ahead, darting through the labyrinth of alleys, a wraith in the darkness.

The chase was intense; the stalker was always just out of reach, always just a shadow ahead. George's breath came in laboured gasps, his injured arm throbbing with each movement, his bad leg struggling to propel him forward. The backstreets of Chapeltown were a maze, and his quarry knew them well, slipping through the night like a ghost.

Then, as suddenly as it had begun, the chase ended. The figure vanished into the darkness, leaving George alone in the empty street, his heart pounding, his body aching with the exertion and pain. He stood there, his chest heaving, a mix of frustration and realisation dawning on him. Had it been the Ripper, leading him on a wild chase, revelling in the sport of it?

The pain in George's arm flared, a sharp reminder of his physical limits. He cursed under his breath, realising the folly of chasing shadows alone, injured. It was time to head home, to regroup and plan the next move in the light of day.

As he turned to leave, a figure emerged from the shadows, a resident of Chapeltown, cautious yet curious. The man, middle-aged and weathered by life, approached George tentatively. "You're him, aren't you? The detective hunting the Ripper?"

George caught off guard, nodded warily. "I am. Why?"

The man shuffled his feet, his gaze flicking around the empty street. "I've seen something odd these past few nights. A man lurking around, always late. Doesn't belong here. Thought it was nothing at first, but with all that's happening…"

George's interest was piqued, and the pain was momentarily forgotten. "Can you describe him?"

The man hesitated, struggling to find the words. "He's always hooded, keeps to the shadows. But there's something off about him, something menacing. I see him near the old textile mill, down by the canal."

The DI pulled out his phone, and the man pointed to where he'd seen the figure.

A new lead, a glimmer of hope in the darkness. George's mind raced with the possibilities. With his voice firm with a newfound determination, he said, "Thank you…"

"Duncan. Duncan Smith," he said and then disappeared back into the shadows of Chapeltown.

George knew what he had to do. Despite the pain and exhaustion, the hunt was still on. He would follow this new lead and explore every possibility.

Chapter Twenty-one

Detective Inspector George Beaumont sat across from a local, a woman whose eyes held the weariness of one who had seen too much. The café in Chapeltown, with its faded wallpaper and the soft hum of a distant radio, felt like a world away from the chase and chaos of the night.

The woman, named Helen, clasped her hands tightly on the table, her knuckles white. George observed her with a keen yet gentle gaze, understanding the courage it took for her to come forward.

Duncan Smith's info hadn't revealed anything, but in canvassing the area, Helen had made herself known to the police.

"Helen, you mentioned you saw something on the night of Abigail Trent's murder. Can you tell me about it?" George's voice was soft and encouraging.

Helen took a deep breath, her eyes flickering with the memory. "It was late, well past midnight. I was up, couldn't sleep. I saw a man outside, just standing there in the shadows. He was... watching something."

Her voice trembled slightly, and George nodded, prompting her to continue.

"I didn't think much of it at first. But then, the next day, when I heard about the murder..." She trailed off, visibly shaken.

George leaned in, his tone reassuring. "Did you see where he went? Or did you notice anything unusual about him?"

Helen nodded slowly. "He met someone, another man. They talked, and then the second man walked off towards the old industrial area. The first man, he stayed, still watching."

The information was a revelation. Two men collaborating on the night of Abigail Trent's murder. It suggested a level of planning and local involvement that they hadn't considered before.

George's mind raced with the implications. "Did you get a good look at either of them? Anything that could help us identify them?"

Helen shook her head regretfully. "It was too dark, and they were too far. But I remember the first man was tall, broad-shouldered. There was something about him, an air of... control."

George scribbled notes, his thoughts already on the next steps. "Thank you, Helen. This information could be crucial. You've been incredibly brave."

As he stood to leave, Helen's voice stopped him. "Detective, this place, Chapeltown, it's been through so much. We just want peace."

George met her gaze, his expression solemn. "I understand, and I promise you, we're doing everything we can to bring this to an end."

Outside, the cold air of Chapeltown felt sharp against George's skin. The puzzle was becoming more complex, layers unfolding that hinted at a deeper conspiracy. The suspect may have had local help, an accomplice to aid in covering his tracks. It was a disturbing development, one that required a shift in their investigation.

George's phone buzzed – a message from Luke. He glanced at the screen, his resolve hardening. The team had actually found something at the old textile mill, a potential lead. It was time to act.

* * *

Detective Inspector George Beaumont strode into the Incident Room, a renewed vigour in his step despite the evident weariness etched on his face. His team, a mix of seasoned detectives and younger officers, turned their attention to him, sensing the urgency of the moment. The walls, adorned with maps and photographs, bore silent testimony to the grim task at hand.

"Everyone," George began, his voice cutting through the chatter, commanding the room with his presence. "We've had a breakthrough. Based on information from a Chapeltown resident, we're looking at the possibility of two individuals working in tandem – two Rippers stalking Leeds."

A collective murmur swept through the room, a mix of surprise and realization. The idea of two perpetrators brought a new dimension to their investigation, a complexity that both intrigued and alarmed them.

Detective Sergeant Luke Mason leaned forward, his expression intense. "Two of them? That could explain the discrepancies we've noticed. Different patterns, different MOs."

George nodded, his eyes scanning the room. "Exactly. Our witness saw a meeting between two men on the night of Abigail Trent's murder. One stayed behind, likely the killer, while the other, possibly an accomplice, left the scene."

The team absorbed this information, the wheels turning in their minds as they considered the implications.

Detective Constable Jay Scott, his brow furrowed in thought, spoke up. "So, we're dealing with a partnership. But what's their endgame? Is it just about causing terror, or is there something more?"

George paced in front of the task force, his mind racing with strategies. "That's what we need to find out. This changes our approach. We're not just hunting a lone predator any more; we're dealing with a pair, possibly supporting each other's activities."

The room was charged with a palpable sense of determination. George's revelation had lit a fire under the team, a shared resolve to unravel this new mystery.

Mason said, "Be careful though, son, this could be a game to them, a twisted form of camaraderie. One killer inspiring the other, perhaps even competing. We need to disrupt their dynamic, throw them off balance."

George stopped pacing, turning to face his team. "We take the fight to them. Increased patrols, more surveillance. We squeeze their operating space. Make them feel the pressure. If they're working together, they'll communicate, and that's where we'll catch them."

Luke nodded, already formulating plans. "We'll coordinate with uniformed officers, get more eyes on the street. We'll re-examine the crime scenes and look for any evidence of a second person."

The team sprang into action, energised by the new direction of the investigation. George watched them, a sense of pride swelling in his chest.

* * *

Detective Inspector George Beaumont stood alone in the Incident Room, surrounded by the stark reminders of the terror that had gripped Leeds. The walls were adorned with images from the crime scenes, each a gruesome tableau of the Ripper's handiwork. The air was heavy with the silent screams of the victims, their final moments captured in chilling detail.

George's gaze moved methodically over each photograph, his mind working like a machine, dissecting every angle, every clue. The brutality of the scenes was not just a display of violence; it was a message, a signature left by a killer who revelled in the fear he created.

He reached into his pocket, pulling out the co-codamol. The pain in his arm had flared up again, a throbbing reminder of his recent brush with death. He hesitated momentarily, aware of the doctor's orders, but the need to dull the pain and keep his mind sharp outweighed his concern. He swallowed the pills dry, a grim determination setting in.

"They won't get the better of me again," he muttered under his breath, his voice a low growl of defiance.

The Ripper had become his obsession, a spectre that haunted his every waking moment. George knew the killer was out there, watching, waiting for the next opportunity to strike. The question that plagued him was where. Where would the Ripper choose for his next act of violence?

Each crime scene had been carefully chosen, each location holding significance in the killer's twisted mind. George's eyes returned to the photographs, searching for a pattern, a clue that might reveal the next target.

As he studied the images, a sense of unease crept over him.

The Ripper was escalating, becoming more daring with each attack. The pattern suggested a crescendo, a final act that would be even more horrific than the last.

The clock on the wall ticked relentlessly, marking the passage of time in a room where time seemed to stand still. George felt a surge of frustration, the elusive nature of the Ripper's plan gnawing at him. He had to anticipate the next move and get ahead of the killer.

His phone rang, jarring him from his thoughts. It was Luke Mason, his voice urgent. "George, we've got something. A lead on the second man spotted in Chapeltown."

George's pulse quickened, a flicker of hope igniting in the darkness. "I'm on my way," he said, his resolve hardening.

As he left the evidence room, the images of the crime scenes burned in his mind, a grim reminder of what was at stake. The city was counting on him, his team was counting on him, and he would not let them down.

The night outside was a shroud of shadows, but George Beaumont was a beacon of determination, cutting through the darkness.

Chapter Twenty-two

The dim glow of the streetlamp cast long shadows on the pavement as George Beaumont and his partner Luke trudged through Chapeltown's underbelly. The evening's chill seemed to claw through their coats, seeping into their bones. They were a pair often seen but rarely noticed, their presence in the neighbourhood as typical as the graffiti staining the old brick walls.

Their lead was a wisp of a rumour, a second man, a shadow within shadows, seen only by the untrustworthy eyes of Chapeltown's insomniacs and night crawlers. They moved with an almost predatory purpose, gazes sharp, dissecting the alleyways and derelict doorways where danger loved to lurk.

George's mind was a swirling vortex of facts, theories, and hunches.

"Rat spotted him here, by the chippy," Luke's voice cut through the silence as they neared the said location, a greasy spoon now closed and silent as a grave.

"Rat sees a lot of things," George murmured, scepticism lining his words as his eyes scanned the area. He crouched, fingers grazing something metallic, a discarded can perhaps, a remnant of daily life ignored by most. But not by him. He examined it, his touch gentle, almost reverent.

Luke watched, his breath forming clouds in the cold air, his own instincts on high alert. "Could be nothing," he suggested, though the tense line of his shoulders belied his casual tone.

"Could be everything," George countered, standing up. His gaze followed the trajectory of a cat as it slinked across the street, its silent steps mimicking the stealth they attributed to their elusive quarry.

They moved on, steps synchronised, their ears straining for the sounds of the city's secrets. A shout in the distance, the clatter of a bin knocked over in a nearby alley, the soft sobbing of someone who had found their end at the bottom of a bottle. They catalogued each noise, each whisper of movement, every scent that the wind carried.

Their path led them to a pub, its windows frosted with years of neglect, the laughter and music inside discordant with the sombre mood that clung to the detectives. They exchanged glances, a silent conversation passing between them before they pushed through the door.

Inside, the racket was almost tangible, the stench of stale beer and sweat assaulting their senses. They split up, George approaching the bar while Luke mingled, their presence a disturbance in the pub's ecosystem. George's eyes were flinty as he made his request, the barman's nervous glance toward the back room not going unnoticed.

"Trouble?" Luke queried upon return, his voice a low murmur meant only for George's ears.

"Maybe. He's twitchy. Knows something," George replied, his words clipped as he nodded toward the barman.

They edged closer to the back room, the crowd's murmurs behind them fading into a dull roar. A sudden crack of a pool cue against a ball from the room ahead made them pause. They exchanged another look and, without a word, pushed open the door to confront what lay beyond.

There, amidst the haze of cigarette smoke and the stench of fear, tension palpable, stood their man—or so they believed. His eyes, wide with the instinctual knowledge of a cornered animal, met George's.

George stepped forward, authority radiating from him, a silent command for the man to stay put. But the suspect bolted, knocking over chairs in his wake, his panic infectious.

The chase was on.

The suspect's escape erupted into chaos, a visceral burst of adrenaline that turned the cramped back room into a turbulent arena. He was desperation incarnate, his movements erratic and wild, fuelled by the raw instinct to survive. Chairs toppled beneath his flailing arms, crashing to the floor with sounds splintering the smoky air.

George's hand reached out, fingers grazing the fabric of the suspect's coat, but it slipped away like a spectre in the night. He cursed under his breath, the word lost amidst the cacophony of shouts and curses from the startled patrons.

Luke was quicker, despite his age, and as he vaulted over the obstacle of fallen furniture, his eyes locked on the fleeing form. The suspect's foot caught on a snaking power lead, and for a heartbeat, he stumbled, his silhouette framed by the garish light of the exit sign.

Recovery was immediate, a testament to the cornered man's desperation. He burst through the back door, slamming it behind him with a resounding bang that seemed to echo the pounding of their hearts.

Outside, the fugitive's breath came in ragged gasps, his shoes pounding against the cobblestones, a staccato rhythm in the night's quiet. George and Luke emerged seconds later, the cold air slicing into their lungs as they pursued the fleeting shadow.

The suspect weaved through the maze of narrow alleyways, his familiarity with the terrain evident. He ducked under clotheslines, his form a blur against the backdrop of grimy walls and the detritus of urban decay.

"Split up!" George commanded, the order slicing through the night as they approached a fork in the alleys. Luke nodded, veering left as George continued straight, their separate paths part of a strategic gambit to outmanoeuvre their quarry.

The chase was not silent; the suspect's heavy breathing was a beacon for the pursuing detectives, a metronome that paced their own accelerating heartbeats. George's experience painted a mental map of the escape routes, predicting the suspect's moves with uncanny accuracy.

As the gap closed, the suspect's panic swelled a tangible thing that seemed to fuel his reckless speed. He risked a glance back, eyes meeting George's determined gaze, and in that split second, the chase's endgame was clear.

With the law's relentless stride on his heels, the suspect made a final desperate turn into a blind alley, his fate sealed by the high walls that loomed like silent judges. Trapped, he turned to face his pursuers, the fight and flight of his escape extinguished, replaced with the stark realisation of his capture.

George closed in, his posture unyielding, each step measured—the predator having cornered its prey. His eyes, sharp and calculating, never left the suspect's face, reading the flickers of fear, the subtle shifts of weight, the tension in his shoulders. George's experience told him that these moments were critical, a blend of psychology and timing.

He kept his distance, giving the suspect no cause for a rash move. "Easy now," George's voice was firm, a low timbre that filled the alley, "Don't make this harder on yourself."

The suspect, panting, his back pressed against the cold, unyielding brick, eyed the narrow ledges of the windows above him—too high to reach, a futile thought. His chest heaved, his gaze darting to the side, where Luke would soon appear to block any thought of escape.

George flicked his hand, a silent signal, and from the corner of his eye, he saw Luke's form materialise at the alley's entrance. They had practised this dance of silent communication; partners synchronised without words.

Reaching slowly to his belt, George produced a set of hand-cuffs, the metal glinting in the scant light, an unspoken promise of the suspect's immediate future. He tossed them to the ground halfway between them, a psychological ploy. "Cuff yourself," he ordered, his tone leaving no room for negotiation.

The suspect's eyes fell to the cuffs, a symbol of his lost free-dom, and for a moment, he appeared to consider resistance. But the fight had left him, the reality of his situation settling in like the cold. With trembling hands, he complied, the click of the cuffs resounding with finality.

George stepped forward, his movements deliberate, radi-ating authority. He patted the suspect down with practised hands, ensuring no hidden threats remained. "What's your name?" he asked, though he already had a good idea—their intel had been solid.

Silence hung for a moment before the suspect muttered a name, confirming George's suspicions.

With the suspect now secured, George allowed himself a brief moment of respite, his breath visible in the chilly air. His mind was already racing ahead to the interrogation, to the pieces of the puzzle this man would help put together.

"Let's walk," he said, his voice steady, guiding the suspect out of the alley with a light touch on the shoulder, ensuring that the man's dignity remained intact despite the circumstances. It was a small thing, but for George, it mattered.

Chapter Twenty-three

George and Luke settled into the familiar routine in the
interview room at Elland Road Police Station. The room was
bitterly cold, a by-product of a heating system that struggled
against the Yorkshire winter. Or that's what they told the
suspect.

The real reason was that they'd turned off the heat intentionally.

They wore their coats indoors, an unspoken statement of
solidarity with the suspect who shivered across from them.

George's fingers curled around a steaming cup of coffee,
the warmth seeping into his palms. He watched the suspect,
noting the way his breath puffed out in white clouds, the way
his arms wrapped around himself in a vain attempt to retain
heat. Compassion was not lost on George, despite the years
and the scars. He slid a second cup across the table, a small
mercy in the frigid room.

The suspect's hands, though cuffed, managed to grasp the
cup, a silent nod of thanks as he drew the warmth into his
chilled bones.

Luke, his silver hair lending him a distinguished air, observed the man with an intensity that belied his years. His
accent, though tinged with the tones of Leeds after four

decades, still carried the undercurrents of his Lancashire roots. It was a subtle reminder that he, like the suspect, had once been an outsider here.

"Let's start at the beginning," Luke's voice was softer than George's but every bit as commanding. "Tell us why you were running."

The suspect hesitated; his breath fogged the air, his body tensed against the biting cold, and his eyes flitted between the two detectives. George leaned forward, his expression unreadable. "You know how this goes," he said. "The sooner you talk, the sooner we all get out of this cold room."

His eyes darted to George, then back to Luke, seeking an ally or perhaps a reprieve. "I—I was scared, that's all," he stammered, the cup in his hands rattling against the tabletop.

"Scared of what?" George's inquiry sliced through the room as he rested his elbows on the table, cup forgotten.

The suspect's gaze dropped, his voice a low murmur, barely audible over the chattering of his teeth. "It's not... it wasn't what you think. I ain't done nothing wrong."

Luke's voice softened a gentle coaxing that belied the critical nature of the question. "We've been through this dance before. You run; you look guilty. So, what's the truth?"

The suspect's hands clenched the cup tighter, a lifeline in the freezing room. "Look, I just heard someone coming, got spooked, right? Thought it was someone else, someone I've been trying to lay low from."

"And who might that be?" George asked, his pen poised above his notebook, ready to document the next piece of the narrative.

The suspect's eyes met George's, a flicker of earnest fear within them. "I owe money, a lot of it, to some very nasty blokes. They said they'd... do things, you know? I thought you were them."

George's face remained impassive, though his mind raced, evaluating each word for truth. "What things? Be specific."

The suspect swallowed hard, his Adam's apple bobbing. "Said they'd hurt me, make an example out of me. I've seen what they do to people who don't pay up."

"And running into an alley was your best plan?" Luke's eyebrow arched, scepticism clear.

A bitter laugh escaped the suspect, his breath a puff of white. "In retrospect, not my brightest moment, no. But fear doesn't exactly make you think straight, does it?"

George nodded, jotting down the last of the suspect's words. "No, it doesn't. But it often leads you right back to the truth, one way or another." George's eyes remained fixed on the suspect, his voice carrying the weight of his next question. "Where were you on the nights of the Chapeltown murders?" George gave the dates and the times.

The suspect's shiver wasn't from the cold this time; it was from the gravity of the accusation. He set the coffee cup down with a clink, his voice a thread of sound. "I was with my mum, I swear. She's been sick, cancer. I look after her, nights especially."

Luke's expression softened fractionally. "Can anyone confirm that?"

"There's a nurse, comes in the evenings to help. She leaves late, she'll tell ya I was there," he said quickly, earnestly, his eyes pleading for belief.

"And the other nights?" George pressed, not allowing any room for ambiguity.

The suspect leaned back, his cuffed hands wringing. "It's

always the same. If I'm not at the pub trying to scrape together what I owe, I'm home with her. You can check, ask the barman, ask the nurse. They'll tell ya."

George noted his response meticulously. "We will. What's the nurse's name?"

"Jenny, Jenny Wills. She works with the local care service." His answer came fast, the details perhaps too crucial to be fabricated on the spot.

"And the pub?" Luke chimed in, his pen at the ready.

"The Broken Crown, up in Chapel Allerton. Ask anyone there; they know me."

Luke scribbled down the information and closed his notebook with a snap; the interrogation segment concluded for now, but the investigation was far from over. He stood and stretched, his movements echoing in the quiet room.

"We have what we need for now," George announced, his voice betraying a hint of weariness. The suspect looked up, hope mingling with fear in his eyes. George stood then as well, the notebook in his hand a testament to the night's work. "The sergeant outside will sign you out," George assured, his tone not unkind. "But if these alibis of yours don't pan out, you're in a whole lot of shit. Understand?"

* * *

In the Incident Room, a map of Chapeltown sprawled across one wall. The room was abuzz with the white noise of concentration, the occasional ring of a phone punctuating the steady hum. Officers and detectives were gathered in small groups, some sipping coffee, others discussing the nuances of their latest cases. The atmosphere was casual, but the undercurrent of the ongoing Ripper investigation was ever-present.

In one corner, Constable Andrew Finch was engaged in an animated conversation with a couple of junior officers. His voice, tinged with a passion not commonly heard in these walls, carried across the room.

"It's the lack of closure in the original cases that's always bothered me," Andrew said, his hands gesturing emphatically. "Sutcliffe's reign ended, but so many questions remained unanswered, so many threads left untangled."

Detective Inspector George Beaumont, passing by with a cup of coffee, paused to listen. Andrew's words were more than just professional interest; there was an enthusiasm in his tone, a frustration that seemed deeply personal.

One of the junior officers nodded, absorbing Andrew's words. "It's like he's still haunting Leeds, isn't it? A shadow over the city."

"Exactly," Andrew replied, his eyes intense. "And now, with this new Ripper, it's like we're reliving that nightmare. We can't let this one go unsolved. We owe it to the city, to the victims."

George moved on, Andrew's words echoing in his mind. The constable's sincere interest in the Ripper's history was becoming more apparent, his emotional investment in the case unusually profound. While it could be attributed to a young officer's zeal, George's instincts suggested there was more beneath the surface. The DI headed over towards Luke who was stood flanking the Big Board.

George's eyes were narrowed in thought, his fingers tapping an impatient rhythm on the tabletop. "What do you know about Finch?" he asked Luke.

"Good officer, apparently, why?"

"We're missing something," he muttered. "This is like trying to complete a jigsaw with half the pieces missing." He nodded towards Andrew. "He seems competent."

Luke, his silver hair catching the light, nodded in agreement. "Maybe it's time we bring in a fresh pair of eyes, eh?" he suggested, crossing his arms. "Someone who can see the patterns we're too close to see."

George looked up, the beginning of a conciliatory smile on his face. "You think we should include Andrew more?"

Luke shook his head. "Mark Finch," he said, the name carrying the weight of countless solved puzzles. "He's the one we need."

Before George could reply, the door to the Incident Room swung open, and DC Jay Scott strode in, his hair perfectly coiffed, a stark contrast to the severity of the room. Behind him, DC Tashan Blackburn followed, his striking blue eyes scanning the room until they settled on George.

"Boss," Jay began, his voice carrying a note of respectful urgency, "we've checked the suspect's alibis."

"And?" George prompted, his gaze shifting between the two younger detectives.

Tashan stepped forward. "Sir, they check out. The nurse corroborates his story, and the barman at The Broken Crown vouched for him too."

Luke blew a low whistle, "Well, that's that then. Back to square one."

George's expression was stoic, but the gears in his mind were turning rapidly. Without a word, he pulled out his phone, the weight of the case pressing down on him.

Just as he was about to dial, Jay added, "If there's anything else we can do, just say the word, boss."

George offered a curt nod, "Thank you, both of you. Good work."

The room fell silent as George dialled the familiar number, each ring echoing slightly in the tense atmosphere—finally, the call connected.

"Mark, it's George. We're in a bind here," he said, his voice a blend of frustration and resolve. "Can you meet me at the Drysalters? We need your help."

A murmur of assent came from the other end of the line, and George ended the call with a decisive click. He looked up, meeting Luke's eye. "Let's hope Mark can shine a light on this mess."

* * *

The Drysalters pub nestled just around the corner from Elland Road Police Station, its facade, a tapestry of weathered bricks, bore the mark of decades, a silent witness to the ebbs and flows of the city's heartbeats. The sign that hung above the door, creaking on its hinges, featured the local football team, faded but proud.

Inside, the pub was a cavern of warmth, the air thick with the scent of alcohol and the rich, earthy aroma of decades-old wood. The floors were a patchwork of tiles and scuffed wooden boards, worn smooth by the passage of countless patrons. Brass fixtures and dim, yellow lighting gave the space an inviting and forgiving glow, casting gentle shadows across the array of booths and tables scattered haphazardly around the room.

The bar itself was a long, solid structure of dark oak, polished to a shine from years of use, the surface a landscape of nicks and scratches, each a story in itself. Behind it, the shelves were stocked with various spirits and liquors, the glass bottles reflecting the light like jewels in a miner's trove.

In the corners, the murmur of conversations filled the air, a symphony of local accents and laughter. Regulars occupied their unofficially assigned seats, their presence as much a part of the pub as the furniture. The atmosphere was one of unpretentious camaraderie, a place where troubles could be drowned or at least shelved for the duration of a pint.

Overhead, the ceiling was a patchwork of wooden beams, some still showing the tree's original grain, others darkened by the smoke of a thousand cigarettes smoked back when the air inside was a fog of tobacco. The walls were adorned with black and white photographs of Leeds through the ages, the faces of long-gone patrons smiling down upon their modern counterparts.

"So you'll do it?" asked George, taking a sip of his pint.

"Aye," the Scotsman said.

"Thank you," said George.

Finch gave a grim nod. "It's the least I can do." Then Finch's expression turned sombre. "It's going to be difficult though."

"I know."

Finch took a long draft, gathering his thoughts. "I think I've probably said this before, but I imagine celebrity plays a role. The Ripper became a legend, a dark celebrity. This copycat clearly seeks to emulate that infamy."

Beaumont nodded solemnly, turning over the unnerving theories in his mind. There were too many. And the bastard had taken four innocent lives already: Cosima Winfrey and Tabitha Arrand from Bradford, and Abigail Trent and Emily White from Leeds.

* * *

Later, the two men sat across from each other in Finch's cramped university office, surrounded by stacks of faded case files and dusty books. Finch opened a bottle of 15-year-old Balvenie whiskey, pouring two glasses.

"This reminds me of home," Finch said solemnly. George nodded and sipped, feeling the warm burn in his chest.

Together, they began poring over the original Ripper files he'd printed out at the station. George was struck by how ordinary the victims seemed in these aged photos, everyday women frozen forever at their violent fate. He lingered on a crime scene depicting the Ripper's sixth mutilated victim. "Hard to believe this bastard once walked free."

Finch gazed at the horrific image sadly. "Aye. Which is why we must stop this impersonator." He opened another file, this one containing the eerily ritualistic fourth murder from 1977.

"I remember Mum telling me how hysteria gripped Leeds after this one," George recalled. "She was safe in Scotland."

"You ever thought about asking your dad about—"

"No," George interrupted. He was surprised. George had never heard his friend ask about that bastard before. Changing the subject, he said, "You seem really invested in this, Finchy."

Finch nodded solemnly. "Aye, I am."

"Why?"

"Sutcliffe is the reason I do what I do."

George was surprised the Yorkshire Ripper was the person who initially drew Finch to study criminal psychology. "I didn't realise the case inspired you to pursue the field."

Finch nodded. "My mum was only a teenager then, eighteen or nineteen, and fled to Scotland over fear of being killed."

George said nothing. Finch wasn't one to talk about his parents' pasts. In fact, when he thought about it, George didn't know anything about Finch's parents.

"I became obsessed with the reason I was born in Scotland and not England and became obsessed with understanding the root causes of such evil. What flaws in one's humanity allow them to commit such atrocities? You know?"

George nodded as Finch gestured at the gruesome photos. "Understanding monsters like the Ripper became my driving purpose. To find meaning in the senseless violence." He shrugged. "Mum helped me. She was in the thick of it all."

Beaumont processed this quietly. He had always known Finch possessed brilliant insight into the criminal mind. Now, he understood that his mother's traumatic experiences honed his friend's skills.

Finch opened another file, this one for victim Barbara Leach, Sutcliffe's eleventh known slaying in 1979. "This murder sparked a surge of national panic. That's when mum left, with me in her stomach."

Studying the ritualised evisceration wounds, Finch pointed out symbolic and meticulous elements clearly meant to shock and terrorise. "Our copycat seeks to channel that same malevolent power. His intimate knowledge of these murders implies a deep obsessive connection."

George felt uneasy at the thought of someone so enthralled by gruesome slaughter. What fetid secrets lurked in this killer's past to drive him down such a dark path?

Finch seemed to read his thoughts. "Of course, we must be wary of fully conflating this new killer with his grisly inspiration. He may reverence the Ripper's infamy, but different experiences and different psychoses shape his motivations."

George frowned. "I don't understand all your lecture talk, Finchy."

Mark grinned, and George realised it had been the first grin his mate had given him for a while. "I just mean we need to be wary that we don't shape this copycat into an actual ripper because the copycat's experiences and psychoses are different." He paused and locked eyes with George. "We're not looking for Sutcliffe."

George nodded, and Finch added, "If we move too rashly, seeing only Sutcliffe's shadow, we may overlook crucial details that actually individuate this unique offender. Do not let the past blind you to the present evil before us. That would be a mistake."

George nodded and said, "Point taken."

"That bastard died of COVID in 2020; he's not roaming the streets, OK?"

"OK." George appreciated his friend's wisdom to avoid confirmation bias. Still, studying these historical horrors foreshadowing the recent murders stirred a powerful, unsettling feeling. It was like a lingering evil was invading Leeds once again.

But the DI shook off the ominous sensations. Whatever darkness had spawned this new Ripper impersonator, together they would drag it into the light.

The cycle of violence ended now.

Finch poured Beaumont another finger of whiskey before raising his own glass.

"To catching this bastard," Beaumont toasted.

Chapter Twenty-four

The following morning, the bustling Incident Room fell silent as Professor Mark Finch stepped up to address the task force. All eyes were on the criminal psychologist as he prepared to deliver his profile of the elusive killer haunting Leeds.

"Thank you all for welcoming me as a consultant on this crucial case," Finch began, hands folded calmly behind his podium. "As you know, understanding the devious mind we are dealing with is key to stopping his deadly spree."

He clicked a remote, the projection screen filling with gruesome crime scene photos. "Examining the ritualised aspects of the murders and the intimate knowledge of historic Ripper killings, I believe we are seeking an organised, highly intelligent offender."

Finch's piercing gaze swept the room. "Do not expect this man to make mistakes. He has planned every brutal staging meticulously to achieve maximum infamy and chaos."

Changing slides, Finch continued. "Now, you may assume this imitation suggests a sexually motivated sadist, as was true of Sutcliffe himself. However, I believe this man harbours a different underlying drive—the desire for power through fear and legend."

The screen was filled with images of the growing media

hysteria around the case. "Our killer meticulously resurrects the Ripper's infamous slayings to feed off the resulting public terror, like an emotional vampire. He craves infamy, not carnal release."

George flinched at the word, 'vampire.'

"Are you OK, George?"

"Carry on, Mark," George said, not wanting to share with his mate the awful dream he'd had on Halloween.

Finch folded his arms grimly. "This is a cunning psychopath who views the original Ripper's mythic status as a blueprint for his own eternal celebrity. Murder is simply the means to an end—the pathology of a malignant narcissist."

"In English, please, Professor," said DC Scott.

Finch locked eyes with Jay. "The killer wants to become famous himself."

"Then why copy Sutcliffe?" asked Jay.

"I'll get to that later, DC Scott, but for now, may I continue."

Jay blushed as he nodded his head.

"Do not expect mercy or empathy from this subject. He will kill and maim without hesitation to further his delusional quest to become a living legend."

Letting the profile sink in, Finch softened his tone. "I understand the immense pressure you all feel to stop this monster quickly. But hastiness leads to mistakes. Remain vigilant and organised—that is how we will outwit this ruthless adversary."

He clicked the projector again, showing the growing memorial for the victims. "Finally, I ask you to remember it is not legends we seek justice for, but real human lives cut tragically short. This man may mythologise murder, but we must not lose sight of the tragic cost, or else his warped narrative prevails."

Finch opened the floor to questions. The seasoned detective sergeant, Luke Mason, raised his hand. "You believe the killer has no personal motive beyond attention and power?"

Finch nodded. "So far, I see no evidence of an underlying emotional trigger like revenge. But we must let the evidence guide us. If such clues emerge, I will reassess accordingly."

After fielding more queries, Finch concluded. "I hope this profile provides some clarity in the hunt ahead." He smiled. "And don't hesitate to use my expertise as needed. Stopping this imminent threat is most important."

He gathered his notes and caught George's eye with a subtle nod. They would speak more on identifying any suspects fitting the profile he had outlined.

* * *

The amber glow of a single desk lamp illuminated the organised chaos of case files and crime scene photos scattered across George's office. He leaned back pensively in his chair as Professor Finch sat across, nursing a coffee.

George valued Finch's insight and trusted intuition, honed from decades of studying disturbed minds like their elusive Ripper impersonator.

George pointed to the photo of the latest victim, mutilated just as Sutcliffe had done back in the day. "So you said our suspect's intimate knowledge of obscure Ripper crime details implies a deep obsession, right? But where does it come from?"

Finch considered this, slowly turning his mug. "The meticulous recreations suggest a strong personal connection to the original murders. Perhaps he views this as avenging old wounds somehow."

George frowned. "We've looked into the victims' surviving family members, and we have nothing." The possible familial link binding this new killer to the Ripper's past atrocities was a chilling thought indeed.

Finch nodded and tapped a photo showing the latest Chapeltown murder scene. Then, he placed an image of the Manor Street scene where Sutcliffe killed Emily Jackson in '76. "Now, the copycat couldn't kill anybody on Manor Street now simply because of the industry around it, but look at the similarities."

George did. Other than being nearly a mile away from each other, the two places were almost identical.

"So," said Finch. "Note how he specifically chose famous kill sites, locations seared into the public consciousness, even if they're nearly identical rather than the actual places."

"But surely he'd want to kill his victims in the same places Sutcliffe did?" asked George.

"I'd agree with you, but this man is not stupid. Whilst I believe the places hold special meaning for him, he's clearly intelligent enough to realise killing somebody on Manor Street would end his tyranny."

George's brow furrowed as he pondered Finch's theory. "So you're suggesting we avoid the actual places Sutcliffe killed but look at places similar?"

"Yes and no," Finch said. "Remember, this isn't an exact science." George narrowed his eyes, but Finch continued. "I think we should investigate Leeds residents who grew up surrounded by the pall of these murders. Who absorbed the tragedy and failures through local lore. Bitterness festered over decades may have spawned this cathartic outburst of violence."

"English, Finch. Or even Scottish," George said with a grin.

"Sutcliffe created a generation of people who are bitter against the police, bitter against prostitutes, and bitter against dark-haired men with full beards." Finch paused. "There's been four murders already."

"Maybe he'll stop there," George said, a hopeful look in his eye.

"I doubt that, mate," said Finch.

Nodding, George replied, "I'll get Mason and the others tracing connections between prior victims, current victims, and current persons of interest. With your criminal profile as a guide, hopefully, we flush out candidates."

* * *

The dusty air of the basement archive at Elland Road station made Finch cough as he followed Detective Inspector Beaumont inside. Rows of metal shelving held cardboard boxes crammed with ageing case files and other evidence relics from the West Yorkshire Police's storied history.

"Just over here," George said, leading Finch to a section marked 'Yorkshire Ripper' in faded marker. He retrieved one box labelled 'Ripper-Physical Evidence' and laid it on a table.

Finch felt a morbid fascination gazing upon these decaying pieces of such a dark chapter. "Are you sure I'm allowed access to these materials, George?"

"Normally no," George replied. "But with lives hanging in the balance, I convinced Atkinson we need you hands-on with any artefacts that could shed light on our suspect's psychology."

George carefully opened the box lid. "Some physical traces from the Ripper investigation were preserved for ongoing analysis. Since you're creating the offender profile, I thought you should examine anything that could provide insight from the original murders."

Peering inside, Finch saw rusted screwdrivers encased in plastic, their dull edges still flecked with dried blood. Tufts of hair and fabric taken from victims and scenes. A haunting array of the Ripper's ghastly trophies, preserved for posterity.

One item gave Finch pause —a letter penned by the killer himself, intended for his US cheerleader girlfriend Crystal Smithies. Contained in that box were the teddies and Valentine's Cards Sutcliffe had sent to her.

"May I?" Finch gestured to the letter.

"Of course. I thought it might intrigue you," George replied. "And here's the letter Smithies sent to get that reply from Sutcliffe."

Handling Sutcliffe's letter delicately, Finch scrutinised the deranged scrawl conveying smug satisfaction at having such a young, beautiful girlfriend, despite being imprisoned for mutilating women. Finch could practically feel the evil arrogance radiating from the page.

Mark placed the letter down gently and picked up Smithies'. After a moment Finch asked, "Have you read this bit, George?" He was referring to a section of the letter where Smithies wrote her dismay that they couldn't be together, blaming the English police for locking him up.

"If you turn Sutcliffe's letter over, Mark, you'll see his reply to Smithie's dismay."

Finch snatched the letter up immediately, and turned it over. "Jesus Christ!"

"I know."

"He's gloating how he thwarted police, elevating his intellect."

"What a prick," said George.

Finch handed the letter back. "He suggests at the end the police were like mice in his cat-like grasp." He shook his head. "How ridiculous."

"It's true though. He got away with it so easily for so many years."

Finch nodded. "Thanks for showing me this, George. It's motivated me."

"I'm glad," the DI said as he gently returned the artefacts to their box. It was strange to think the owner of such innocuous objects once played the leading role in an evil that still haunted Leeds today. That somewhere in this evidence might lie some clue echoing down the decades to unmask the latest Ripper incarnation.

Finch met George's steady, resolute gaze. "We'll find him."

George nodded, hefting the box as they moved to leave. "Until he makes a mistake, we have to keep digging for any insight into the dark mind we're dealing with. And you've been bloody invaluable on that front already, mate."

"It's the least I can do, George," Finch replied sincerely.

Chapter Twenty-five

Isabella poured two steaming mugs of coffee and smiled. Professor Finch sat across their kitchen table, looking wearier than his usual scholarly self after another long day aiding George and the Ripper investigation.

"Thank you, love," Finch said graciously as she set the coffee before him. "I'm craving caffeine."

Isabella smiled kindly, handing the other mug to her fiancée George as he joined them.

Finch noticed the shadows under George's eyes and how his fingers anxiously drummed the tabletop. Isabella looked exhausted, too. This case was taking its toll on them both.

"I hope George hasn't been keeping you up too late with his theories," Finch said to Isabella, adding sweetener to his coffee. "He gets rather obsessive."

"It's not me." George raised his brow, then grinned. "Olivia isn't sleeping too well."

"What's your excuse, Beaumont?" Finch asked.

"It's the price of chasing evil, I'm afraid, mate," George replied. He knew sleep would elude him until the Ripper was stopped. "Been like it forever."

Isabella sighed, taking George's restless hand in her own. "Yes, I know. I just worry for you." She turned to Finch.

"George looks tired, doesn't he?"

Finch nodded. "He does." He turned to George. "It's because he insists on doing everything instead of delegating."

"He's right, George," Isabella said.

George let out a long sigh. Eventually, he said, "Christ, if I'd have known you two were going to get on at me, I'd have said no to this."

Isabella squeezed George's hand tightly and said, "We just bloody care for you."

George softened, giving her a grateful squeeze.

"You're driving yourself to exhaustion trying to find this monster."

Finch's expression turned solemn. "I've researched the Ripper extensively, as you know, and Izzy's concern is wise, George." He paused. "There was massive strain put on good officers and their families when the original Ripper's shadow darkened Leeds."

The mention of that horrific era brought a haunted look to Isabella's eyes that surprised Finch. When she spoke, her voice was taut with old pain. "I don't remember it, but my grandma does." Isabella's maternal grandparents lived in Middleton, and whilst no murders happened in the area, Isabella's grandmother was terrified to go out. "She was really good friends with Emily Jackson. Emily lived in Miggy before moving to Churwell with Sydney. My grandma said she was gutted when Emily was killed. Made the fear more real."

Finch was nodding, a resolute look in his eye.

Isabella glanced away, reluctance warring with buried grief for her grandma. George shifted closer in silent comfort. After a moment, she continued softly. "She might be a good person to speak to, my Grannie-Annie. She even once thought my grandad was the Ripper, you know. Because he was the spit of Sutcliffe." She paused. "Looked a bit like you, Mark. You know, the dark hair and dark beard. He was a lorry driver, too." Izzy grinned. "She once said she was going to call the Ripper line and grass him in, but when Emily had been killed, my grandad had been at home with her all night." She shrugged. "Women were paranoid back then."

Isabella dabbed her eyes with a napkin. "I don't know why I'm getting so emotional when it's nothing to do with me."

Finch, overwhelmed by sorrow and sympathy, placed his hand on Isabella's shoulder and squeezed. "This is exactly what the copycat is trying to achieve."

* * *

George sat hunched in his chair, his phone to his ear. "You're sure about this, Luke?" the DI asked.

"As sure as I can be, son," Mason replied. "I'll email the files over now."

George thanked Mason and rang off before clicking the keys and opening up his email. They'd received a tip on the Ripper line about a 53-year-old man named Isaac Briggs, a social outcast living on the fringes of Leeds' rougher Chapeltown area.

Finch occupied the leather chair opposite, swallowing the last of his coffee. George handed him a printout, and Mark immediately started reading. He loved nothing more than working into the wee hours, fuelled by caffeine and determination. But tonight's revelations felt different. More exciting.

"Briggs certainly fits aspects of our offender profile," Finch said. "Shunned loner, petty criminal history, deep-seated

180

rage toward the world." He picked up his mug and, realising it was empty, immediately set it down.

George grinned. He hated it when that happened.

"The trauma is quite apparent in his psyche profile from the hospital," Finch explained.

George nodded slowly, skimming the disturbing details of Isaac's disturbed childhood. His mother, Rebecca, was a destitute prostitute crippled by drug addiction who sold her body to survive on Leeds' gritty streets. She was murdered in 1976 by an unknown client, leaving 6-year-old Isaac orphaned and damaged.

"It says here Rebecca Briggs frequented the same seedy red light district the Ripper culled victims from," George noted ominously. "You don't think..."

Finch's expression was grave. "It's possible she crossed paths with Sutcliffe in that sordid underworld. Perhaps there was even one who got away." He leaned closer, lowering his voice. "Isaac could be the Ripper's own spawn."

A heavy silence hung between them as George absorbed the disturbing theory. The idea of Sutcliffe's descendant being raised in squalor, left to rot mentally and carry on his father's savage legacy in bitterness...it made a twisted sort of sense. "I'll look into it."

Finch nodded.

"We'd need to DNA test Briggs against the Sutcliffe sample on the DNA Database to be certain," George said. But circumstantially, at least, the broken man fit the right demented profile.

Finch nodded slowly, fingers steepled in thought. "I say we bring him in. Now that we have a name, we must investigate every thread. Even if it leads to dire truths." His jaw was set, steeling himself.

George understood his friend's dread. Neither wanted to believe a second generation of Sutcliffe's evil could haunt Leeds, but if Briggs was their copycat, then great.

"I'll have Uniform pick Briggs up first thing tomorrow," George said. It was late, and he was shattered. He walked Finch out, clasping his hand. "Get some sleep, mate. Be at the station early tomorrow."

Finch nodded and then returned to the solitude of his car.

George watched, observing his streets as he waved bye to Finch.

An evil lurked out there; an evil George needed to stop.

And soon.

Chapter Twenty-six

The fluorescent lights of the interview room seemed excessively bright as Detective Inspector George Beaumont sat across from Isaac Briggs, the surly outcast they'd brought in for questioning. So far, the man had refused to speak beyond terse denials, staring sullenly at the table that separated them.

"For the last time, Mr Briggs, where were you eight days ago, Thursday around midnight, when Abigail Trent was murdered?" George asked evenly, though his patience was wearing thin.

Briggs just grunted and crossed his arms. "Told you already, I was at the pub until midnight. Then went home. Didn't kill nobody."

"And last Sunday when Emily White was murdered?"

"I already told you I didn't kill anybody."

George studied the man's rough features and dishevelled appearance. He certainly fit the profile of an antisocial loner harbouring deep-seated rage, the kind of fractured psyche susceptible to lashing out through violence. But without evidence, it was all circumstantial.

"We know your childhood was... troubled," George continued carefully. "Losing your mother so young in such a traumatic way. It couldn't have been easy."

Briggs' lip curled at the mention of his past. "You don't know shit about my life. Just leave me alone already."

Sensing he'd hit a nerve, George pressed further. "Records show your mother worked the same streets the Ripper hunted his victims on. Is it possible she had a... connection to Peter Sutcliffe?"

Briggs slammed his fist on the table at the name, making George jump. "Don't you say his filthy name! My mum was no whore!" He jabbed an accusatory finger. "Think you coppers can come 'round accusing me just 'cause of where we lived? You know nothing!"

Briggs slumped back, fuming but seemingly spent by the outburst. George leaned forward calmly. "A simple DNA test would clear up any uncertainty. If you consent, we can conclusively rule you out as a Ripper descendant and move forward."

The suggestion only ignited Briggs' anger once more. "So that's your big theory, eh? Think I'm that bastard's evil spawn back for revenge?" He spat on the floor. "I don't have to prove shit to you pigs. So fuck off!"

Realising any further questioning was useless, George suspended the interview and exited, frustration mounting. Briggs was hiding something; he was sure of it. But without evidence or a confession, there was little he could do.

Stopping by his office only increased George's aggravation, finding it empty save for a note from DCI Atkinson: 'Gone to the performance review meeting. We'll discuss Briggs later.'

Useless suits were pushing paperwork while a killer roamed free. George muttered a curse and headed straight for Atkinson's office, barging past the protesting secretary.

"Sorry to interrupt sir, but we need to act on Briggs now,"

George said brusquely, ignoring the other shocked officials. "He's uncooperative and volatile. I think it could be him."

Atkinson rubbed his temples angrily. "For God's sake, Beaumont, control yourself! We'll discuss this later."

But George refused to let it rest. "With your permission, sir, I'd like to establish surveillance on Briggs. Get a warrant to search his residence. I know if we just dig deeper..."

"Enough!" Atkinson snapped, then caught himself with a glance at his colleagues. In a lower voice, he added, "You need evidence before such measures, George, you know that." He sighed. "And you lack the evidence. We'll talk soon. Now, please, let me return to this meeting."

Chastened, George reluctantly departed and returned to his office, the urge to slam his fist into the wall nearly overwhelming.

* * *

The streets were still cloaked in morning darkness as George Beaumont and his team gathered outside the dilapidated row of houses. Thanks to a hastily acquired warrant, they were finally able to search the reclusive outcast's residence for evidence tying him to the Ripper copycat slayings.

Donning Kevlar vests emblazoned with the West Yorkshire Police crest, the heavily armed unit approached the front door. George nodded to Mason, who pounded loudly. "This is the police! Open up!"

Only silence responded. Mason tried again, bellowing a final warning. He signalled the battering ram team forward when there was still no reply.

With two powerful swings of the 'Big Red Key,' the reinforced door splintered open. An AFO crossed the threshold first, weapon drawn and torch piercing the gloom. "Clear!" came shouts from the other rooms, confirming no people were present. Considering Briggs was locked up at the station, George didn't think there would be, but he knew you could never be too careful.

George surveyed the squalor and stench of stale cigarettes that assaulted them. "Tear this place apart," he ordered brusquely. "I want anything that might hint Briggs is our guy."

He proceeded to the cluttered bedroom, watching with distaste as Luke rifled through soiled clothes and fast food bags stacked haphazardly around the stained mattress Briggs called a bed. It seemed doubtful they'd find anything linking him to the murders amidst such squalid chaos.

George was about to move on when a small cardboard box tucked behind the bed caught his eye. Retrieving it, he gingerly lifted the lid. Inside lay a collection of newspaper clippings about the original Yorkshire Ripper murders, along with crime scene photos and memorabilia. Had Briggs obtained confiscated case evidence?

Luke looked over his shoulder, wrinkling his nose at a Polaroid of a smiling Sutcliffe. "Guy's a proper Ripper devotee. But this doesn't prove he's our impersonator."

George had to agree. As disturbing as Briggs' twisted shrine was, the lack of links to the current murders meant it could be just a dark obsession—no concrete connection.

Continuing the search, George entered a dingy back room crowded with electronics and exercise equipment. One wall immediately drew his gaze—it was plastered in collages glorifying the Ripper's notorious rampage.

"Jackpot," Mason muttered. "Now there's the bloody proof of his demented fixation."

George moved closer, scrutinising the grisly displays. He recognised replicated Ripper murder scenes, taunting messages scrawled in red paint, and news clippings arranged in malignant tributes. The graphic shrine clearly betrayed Briggs' reverence for Sutcliffe's hideous legacy of terror.

"Call Lindsey and her team and ask her to bag all of this for evidence," George said. While this sick homage confirmed Briggs' obsession, it again fell short of putting him at the scenes of the new killings.

George cursed under his breath. He had been so certain Briggs was their man. That searching his lair would produce the final damning piece to cement his guilt. Instead, they only had proof of a deranged fixation, not a homicidal tendency.

He surveyed the room again rapidly, desperate for any scrap that could justify holding Briggs for longer. But found nothing beyond the ample evidence of loosely regulated psychiatric care.

As the team finished cataloguing the disturbing paraphernalia, George had no choice but to concede this raid had been another dead end. The thought of letting Briggs walk free to continue obsessing over the Ripper turned his stomach. But he lacked solid justification to hold him.

Bitterly resigned, George gave the order to pack up their efforts and depart.

* * *

George was just climbing into his car to head back to the station, frustration simmering after the fruitless raid on

Briggs' residence when his mobile rang. He checked the caller ID—it was DC Jay Scott, one of his most eager young detectives.

"Jay, please tell me you have good news," George answered wearily. "The search of Briggs' place turned up nothing solid as our killer."

"Well, boss, we just got an anonymous tip on the hotline that sounds promising," Jay replied, sounding excited. "The caller said we should look into storage units rented by Briggs over in Armley. Reckons that's where he keeps his real dark secrets."

George's pulse quickened. This could be just the break they needed. "Good work, Jay. Get a team out to that storage facility immediately."

Hanging up, George sped towards Armley. His mind raced faster than the car—what 'secrets' might Briggs have felt the need to hide away in a remote storage locker? The thought sent a chill down his spine.

Twenty tense minutes later, George arrived at the self-storage depot, a nondescript warehouse lined with rolling metal doors. Jay and the others were already there waiting, a manager having shown them to Briggs' unit.

George approached the locked door. He nodded to Luke who snipped the padlock with bold cutters. Together, they hauled the creaky door up, revealing stygian darkness within.

Torches in hand, they entered cautiously. Sweeping his beam around, George made out an old freezer chest and other innocuous household items. Nothing overtly sinister.

Moving deeper, behind some paint-stained drapes, the light glinted off something metallic—Tools. Hammers, screw-drivers. George caught his breath. It was just like the Ripper's.

"Christ," Luke muttered. "His bloody stash. And is that..." he trailed off, reaching into the toolbox to withdraw a sealed evidence bag. Inside was a bloodstained hammer.

Cold certainty seized George. "Our boy's trophy collection. Kept hidden away but close enough to revisit." It was the confirmation he'd desperately needed. Briggs was their killer.

Sensing what George was thinking, Mason said, "That looks too old to have been used recently, son."

"You think this hammer belonged to Sutcliffe?" asked George, and Luke nodded.

Jay spoke up nervously. "But how did Briggs get actual tools from the original evidence archives? You don't think...?"

George understood the unsettling implication. The idea of a corrupt officer secretly feeding Briggs artefacts of the killings turned his gut. How deep did this depravity spread? He turned to Scene of Crime Manager Lindsey Yardley. "Bag all of this up for me, please, Lindsey." Tersely, he looked at his team and added, "We need definitive proof Briggs wielded these on recent victims. And trace where in the fucking hell he acquired such items."

As the tools were catalogued as evidence, George's mind churned furiously. The question of police corruption aside, these trophies of terror buried among Briggs' other possessions confirmed the man's guilt beyond doubt. He was their Ripper successor. He had to be.

George had to act fast before Atkinson decided to pull the plug and have Briggs released.

Chapter Twenty-seven

The task force combed through every scrap of evidence related to the recent murders. At a desk in the corner, DS Luke Mason scrutinised crime scene evidence, searching for any clues they might have overlooked.

One series of bloody markings on a victim's torso gave him pause. He waved over George and Professor Finch. "Take a look at this odd symbol carved here. And there's similar ones on the other bodies." He shuffled through more images.

"Could be some kind of satanic ritual stuff," Mason suggested. "Might explain the brutality and precise mutilations if he's trying to perform some sort of dark ceremony."

George stroked his bearded chin, considering the theory. "We did dismiss the occult angle early on. But you're right, these repeated symbols can't be coincidence. Good spot, Mason."

He turned to Finch. "What do you make of this, Finchy? Some type of ritualistic motivation perhaps?"

Finch gazed at the photos with a clinical detachment. "An intriguing observation but premature to draw conclusions from, I'm afraid. Remember we must not clutch at mystical explanations when more pragmatic psychological motives likely drive this offender."

Mason looked crestfallen as Finch continued. "Beyond the obvious occultist trappings, I see little evidence that our suspect's core psychopathology derives from some supernatural fixation. The pragmatic enactment of these murders speaks to concrete violent compulsions, not otherworldly delusions."

Finch tapped one photo. "See how the cuts follow a meticulous pre-planned design, indicating conscious intentionality. Not the deranged flailing of an occult ritual."

He sighed. "I understand the temptation to ascribe this evil to forces beyond comprehension. But the vast majority of ritualistic killers still operate on internally coherent—if warped—psychological needs accessible to analysis."

Mason shook his head. "With all due respect Professor, you find it easier to accept this level of cruelty as part of some bloke's rational thinking?"

"Sadly, aye," Finch replied. "The human psyche has limitless capacity for the rationalisation of evil acts when fuelled by trauma or pathological urges. We need not turn to phantom mystical motivations to comprehend the incomprehensible."

Finch saw Mason was unconvinced and softened his tone. Finch added, "You raise a valid point worth keeping on the table. But right now, the evidence better supports a concrete psychological process driving these calculated killings over vague spiritual ones. Still, we must stay open to all possibilities."

He turned to George. "I suggest focusing the investigation on identifying any past trauma or pathological tendencies that could have spawned these homicidal compulsions. The occult trappings may be part of a delusion, but they are not the prime motivator." He paused. "Did you look into bitter, traumatised local men who may have festered obsessive hate of the notorious failures around the original murders?"

George had nodded and said, "We did," remembering Candy Nichols as she approached him, a stack of files in her hands. "I've been looking into local forums and chat rooms about the Ripper. A few names keep popping up, people with an unhealthy interest," she had said.

George remembered taking the files, his eyes scanning the pages. He'd said, "Good work. Let's dig deeper into these individuals."

Satisfied with Finch's assessment, George called Candy over and asked her if she dug deeper into the individuals.

"I did, sir, but found nothing other than a slightly morbid obsession with Sutcliffe."

"Understood," he said, dismissing Candy. He turned to Mark. "We'll keep digging into his background and upbringing. Something twisted him to admire the Ripper's fame. We just need to discover what."

The pair continued examining the uneasily ritualised crime scenes, seeking more mundane human monsters over supernatural ones. Finch was right, or so George thought. They weren't looking for Freddie Harman any more, but somebody else. Somebody worse.

But Mason eyed the ominous symbols warily, unconvinced darker forces weren't at play. For now though, he had a job to do, and orders to follow.

* * *

The persistent hum of the printer provided background noise as George finished typing up his report on the recent evidence found in Briggs' storage unit. His biggest concern was the implication that stolen Ripper artefacts had made their way into the suspect's hands, likely with help from someone on the force.

A knock at his open door made George look up to see DCI Atkinson filling the frame, his expression unreadable. "My office. Now."

With a sinking feeling, George gathered the report and followed Atkinson down the hall. Once inside, with the door closed, the DCI wasted no time. "This memo about possible evidence tampering. You actually believe an officer aided and abetted the Ripper copycat?" His tone walked the line between incredulous and furious.

George stood resolute. "With all due respect, sir, how else could Briggs have obtained actual murder weapons and artefacts from restricted evidence lockers?" He dropped the report on Atkinson's desk. "I can't ignore what's in front of my eyes."

"What's in front of your eyes, Inspector, is circumstantial conjecture," Atkinson replied coldly, picking up the report. "You accuse your own based on the ravings of a deranged suspect." He sat back heavily with a shake of his head. "Consider what you're implying here, Beaumont. A conspiracy within our own walls? It's not just your career on the line, but the reputation of the entire West Yorkshire Police."

George frowned but bit back against further argument. He had expected resistance but not outright disbelief over such compelling evidence.

Atkinson continued sternly, "I understand this is frustrating, but you need to get some perspective. What seems the obvious solution may simply be the easiest for your mind to accept." He leaned forward. "If you go voicing wild conspiracy theories without proof, you will only undermine the public's faith in our ability to catch this maniac."

With no choice but to accept his superior's rebuke for now, George adopted a more conciliatory tone. "You're right, sir." He took a breath. "I still think you should discreetly assign undercover officers to investigate, though."

Atkinson considered this before nodding reluctantly. "Fine. I'll put a small team on it. But only because I trust you believe this is best for the case, misguided as I feel it may be. I expect you to accept whatever their findings turn out." His stare bored into George, daring further dissent.

"Of course, sir. Thank you for understanding." George's mind was already analysing how to pursue the truth covertly if this internal investigation proved a dead end. The Ripper seemed to inherently breed mistrust and paranoia.

Departing Atkinson's office, George felt the creeping sensation of forces arrayed against him—superiors, the killer himself, and possibly even fellow officers. But his grim determination only grew.

When he reached his office, the tension in the air was palpable. "There's been another murder, boss," said Jay.

* * *

As he approached the taped-off alley, the stench burning George's nostrils told him all he needed to know. Another life was brutally extinguished.

After being signed in at the cordon and donning his protective gear, George headed towards the body. CSI was mulling around.

Kneeling down, George examined the body of a middle-aged

man. His throat was viciously slashed, and abdominal wounds evoked the Ripper's signature mutilations.

SOC Manager Lindsey Yardley appeared with a plastic exhibit bag containing a wallet.

"The victim's name is Frank Pearson, from Harehills."

The name tickled something in George's memory. George nodded to Jay, who pulled out his mobile. Five minutes later, he told his boss, "Boss, Luke says the victim has a rap sheet for petty theft and extortion. Suspected muscle for Schmidt's outfit."

George's eyes widened as it clicked—Frank Pearson was an enforcer for Schmidt, one of those at his house the day George had threatened them.

"Our killer's escalating," George said grimly. "Shifting from impersonal female targets to a more personal one. This was an execution." He studied the vicious neck wound. "He dies slowly, painfully. This was personal, sending a message."

Jay looked uneasy. "Sounds like mob retaliation. But using the Ripper's MO to do it? Maybe there's a copycat of our copycat now, boss?"

"That's a very good point, Jay," George said as pathologist Dr Ross arrived.

Dr Christian Ross knelt down beside the body, careful not to disturb the scene. The veteran pathologist's eyes narrowed as he analysed the precise slashes and openings carved into the corpse.

After a period of intent scrutiny, Ross rocked back on his heels with a sigh. "Well, there's no doubt in my mind this is the same offender as our other Ripper copycat murders. The abdominal mutilations match his distinctive style and apparent skill with a blade flawlessly."

He gestured to the gaping wounds. "See here the same methodical, almost surgical incisions. And the tearing of internal organs adheres to the same deliberate pattern. This is clearly the Ripper copycat's handiwork again."

George absorbed this grim confirmation with a nod. "So we can definitively tie this scene to our primary suspect rather than a random impersonator."

"Without question," Dr Ross replied. "The precision adheres too closely to be anyone but the same killer." He shook his head ruefully. "A sadistic talent seems to be developing a taste for more... creative renditions." He pointed at the abandoned leather armchair. "Especially if you consider that."

"What do you mean?" asked George.

"The body was found hidden under that." Christian cleared his throat. "None of your Ripper victims were hidden; they were exposed and posed purposely."

George frowned and saved that titbit of information for later. "You're sure this is the work of the same killer?"

Christian nodded, and Jay looked uneasy at the implication their target was escalating into further horrific theatrics. But George remained focused on the facts.

"This victimology departure still feels deliberate," George said. "Our profile suggests a controlled psychopath. Could the copycat be trying to lead us astray?"

Ross nodded. "You may be right, George. The meticulous methodology remains, even if applied to a new canvas. Evolving, rather than devolving." He straightened up with a groan. "I'll know more once we open him up."

George nodded thoughtfully, mind racing to discern this latest twist in the shadows. If the Ripper was intentionally shifting focus to execute known criminals, it could imply a deeper strategy than random madness. He turned to Jay. "I suppose this ties our copycat directly to organised crime after all."

Jay looked sceptical. "You really think he's eliminating criminal targets disguised as the Ripper, boss?" asked Jay.

George said, "That or he's trying to distract us from his true purpose."

"Why go through all that theatrical trouble, though?"

"He's probably trying to invoke the Ripper's terror in their underworld." Then George realised. "This crime syndicate is weaponising our killer's infamy, his lore, as psychological warfare on their own streets."

He was now convinced their perpetrator was carefully cultivating the Ripper's mythology to obscure his true purpose— underworld executions for an underground organisation. It made him realise they needed to interview Piers Keaton, Schmidt's second-in-command. "We need to shake down Schmidt's crew hard, rattle their cages. See who they've pissed off enough to pretend to be the Ripper and take out Pearson."

"Won't be easy, boss," Jay cautioned. "They'll never admit a rival took out their guy."

"Doesn't matter," he said firmly. "I won't be deterred or intimidated from catching this killer." He clasped Jay's shoulder.

* * *

Piers Keaton sat slouched insolently across from George in the interview room. His bruised face evidenced their brutal arrest days prior. But if it bothered Keaton, he didn't show it.

"Let's cut to the chase, Mr Keaton," George began evenly,

setting a photo of Frank Pearson's mutilated body on the table. "This man was found dead in Ripper fashion. One of your known associates."

Luke fixed Keaton with an uncompromising stare. "Why would someone want to send good old Franky off in such dramatic style?"

Keaton didn't even glance at the grisly photo, snorting derisively. "No comment. Don't know nothing about it."

"Is that right?" George allowed a hint of menace to enter his tone. "Because it seems someone went through a lot of trouble to make sure you lot understand this killing as more than your average underworld bust-up."

With exaggerated bewilderment, Keaton replied, "Underworld? What you on about, Inspector? I'm just a legitimate businessman, me." His insolent sneer made George's fingers itch to smack it off.

"There's already been three other victims preceding Pearson," George pressed on. "Young women stalked and savaged by an impersonator of the Yorkshire Ripper you lot unleashed."

At the provocative accusation, Keaton leaned forward, eyes narrowing. "You best watch your mouth, pig. Don't go making wild claims you can't back up."

Sensing the blow to Keaton's ego hit home, George doubled down. "Those are the facts. We know this Ripper kills on behalf of your boss, Schmidt. Carrying on the real Ripper's infamous work for your benefit."

Keaton shook his head, laughing derisively. "You're mental, you are. Talking about Rippers and whathaveyou. And for my benefit?" His scoffing denial only convinced George more of the truth. "I'm just a businessman."

"The Yorkshire Ripper copycat," George said coldly, "is one of your pet psychos doing hits, isn't he? But now you've lost control of the beast you collared. He's killed one of your own. Why?"

At this, Keaton bolted up furiously. "I already told you lot I don't know shit about any bloody Ripper! You deaf or just stupid?" His chest heaved with barely contained rage.

Finished playing games, George rose slowly and planted both palms firmly on the table, leaning down to fix Keaton with a molten stare. "That murder was a message meant for you. For all Schmidt's thugs who thought they could employ a myth to their ends without consequences."

George enunciated each word deliberately. "But your attack dog is off the leash now. He's coming for his own masters next. Tick tock."

He pushed off the table and headed for the door, pausing to drive home the implicit threat. "You can't control what you've unleashed. And we won't stop it from devouring you all. Especially Schmidt."

Keaton lunged against his cuffs as George exited. "You're a dead man walking, Beaumont! You just signed your death warrant, threatening him like that! Do you hear me?"

But George was already striding down the hall, Keaton's muffled tirade fading behind him. The brazen defiance only affirmed they were on the right track. Now, it was just a matter of applying pressure until someone in that viper's nest cracked and gave up the Ripper.

Luke hurried to catch up. "Do you really think it's wise to rile them up like that, son? Could be dangerous."

Chapter Twenty-eight

The neon lights of the grimy bar cast distorted shadows across the hunched forms of the intoxicated patrons within. Keeping his head down, George wove through the seedy crowd, DC Jay Scott trailing close behind. They were deep in the pulsating underbelly of Leeds' notorious criminal underground, following a slim lead.

Choosing an empty booth, George slid in while Jay went to get drinks. As he waited, George surveyed the room discreetly, trusting his street-honed instincts to identify underworld players who might have useful information.

But these desperate souls seemed mere addicts and petty thieves, oblivious to larger machinations in the city's corrupt hierarchy. George needed an insider, someone with their ear to the ground and rumours of the street.

Jay returned hurriedly, drinks in hand. "Think I spotted our man, boss. Back corner by the loo. I recognise him from when I worked the streets as a PC."

George followed Jay's discreet gesture towards a thin, nervous man in a threadbare trench coat nursing a pint. It took a moment before recognition clicked—Clarkie, a strung-out but oddly resourceful small-time drug peddler George had leaned on before. If anyone knew the word of Leeds' streets, it was him.

Leaving Jay to nurse their drinks, George sidled up to the booth. "Evening Clarkie. Fancy seeing you here."

Clarkie's head jerked up, eyes already darting for escape. But George's imposing presence made him think better of it. "Inspector… I already told your lot everything I know about the Chinatown heroin ring. It's Schmidt, and I don't know nothing else!"

George shook his head. "I'm not here about Schmidt today," he lied. "I wanted your take on these Ripper copycat killings, actually."

At that, Clarkie seemed to withdraw even further into his coat. "Don't know nothing about that mess," he mumbled shakily. "I steer well clear of psychos like that."

"Oh, come on," George pressed. "Word on the street is these slayings might be tied to certain… business interests in the city. The kind that values discretion." He gave Clarkie a knowing look.

The sly informant hesitated, then seemed to come to a decision, gesturing for George to lean closer. "I don't know details, you understand. But rumour is this 'Ripper' is some kind of underworld enforcer." His voice dropped to a whisper. "Killing on behalf of some very dangerous people."

George's pulse quickened—finally, a solid connection to organised crime. "These dangerous people—we talking about the Schmidt syndicate?"

But Clarkie was done talking. "I've said enough. Now, I'd appreciate you leaving me to my business, Inspector. And forgetting this conversation ever happened, aye?"

"Pearson is dead, Clarkie. Killed by this Ripper." George paused, allowing Clarkie to process what the DI had just told him.

"What?"

George nodded. "If the Ripper is working for Schmidt, why would he kill one of his own?"

Clarkie said, "I don't know. Honest." His nervous gaze warned against further questions.

George weighed pushing harder before deciding he'd gotten all he could for now. He slid some cash into the man's hand whilst they shook and, with a subtle nod, returned to Jay just as their informant scurried out into the night.

"He basically confirmed the Ripper copycat is a contract killer for a Leeds mob but didn't say which one," George explained tersely. "Seems they're using his MO to terrify and intimidate while hiding behind the hysteria."

Jay shook his head in disbelief. "Bloody hell, boss. If true, this goes deeper than we ever imagined."

George's eyes narrowed, thoughts racing about how to leverage this bombshell lead. Finally, confirmation the murders were more than a deranged impersonator's obsession. It was a wider conspiracy with influential players. But did he trust Clarkie?

No, of course, he bloody didn't.

This revelation changed everything about the case. The Ripper was still a phantom—but now one deployed deliberately by shadowy criminal forces. George had stumbled upon a deep web of organised evil with tendrils throughout Leeds' corridors of power.

He clapped Jay's shoulder firmly. "We need to unravel this syndicate link. Whatever clandestine deals are protecting our killer, we expose them. No one is above the law, understand?"

Jay nodded dutifully, though his eyes betrayed apprehension

at where this investigation was headed.

* * *

At the centre of the Incident Room that evening, George poured over files and criminal associations that might cement the theory of a contract killer using the Ripper guise as cover.

Across from him, Professor Finch leaned back with a sceptical glance. "George, we must be cautious of confirmation bias here. One mob hit dressed up as a Ripper kill does not necessarily implicate our primary suspect."

George didn't look up from his documents. "It's too coincidental, Mark. And Dr Ross confirmed it. Our Ripper is clearly connected to Schmidt's syndicate, intentionally invoking the Ripper to terrify. I'm convinced Pearson's murder proves he's their hidden enforcer, but what I don't get is why Schmidt took out one of his own."

Finch shook his head. "That's a wee bit of a leap, mate. What's more likely is organised crime noticed our killer's MO and mimicked it to conceal recent underworld killings." He tapped the folder decisively. "Our DNA evidence and victim profile analysis still points to a solitary sexual sadist fixated on emulating the historic Ripper, not some gang hitman."

Finally glancing up, George frowned. "Are you sure? The timing seems too convenient." He didn't want his best theory undermined.

"Aye, I am," Finch replied firmly. "Think of Abigail Trent and the meticulous staging, the care to precisely recreate every aspect of historical murders. That is not the work of gangsters covering their tracks, George, but of a pathological obsessive working towards his own twisted vision."

Seeing George's continued resistance, Finch softened. "I understand, mate; you feel the organised crime link may be a breakthrough. But don't lose sight of the behavioural evidence still pointing to our socially alienated culprit."

Finch slid the folder back. "However, if having a wee dig deeper into the victims' pasts might confirm or refute that theory, then do it."

George sighed, acknowledging the wisdom in Finch's analysis. He had to suppress the urge to latch onto the most convenient explanation rather than see the intricate case objectively. He was slowly turning into DCI Atkinson, and George berated himself for it.

"You're right, Mark. I need to stop jumping to conclusions either way until we get more solid intelligence." He tapped the personnel files of the three female victims killed so far. "I'll have our background team dig deeper into Cosima, Tabitha, and Abigail's histories and associations. With luck, we can determine if any mob ties are present."

Finch gave an approving nod. "A sound approach. A famous Criminologist once said, let the evidence guide you without bias in either direction."

They shared a grin. Finch's insight kept George's obsessive nature in check, stopping him charging headlong down blind alleys. Together, their contrasting talents made them an effective team seeking justice, not just straightforward answers.

* * *

The polished oak door of the residence swung open, revealing a bulky man with cold, appraising eyes. "Can I help you, gentlemen?"

George flashed his warrant card, as did Jay. "DI Beaumont and DC Scott, West Yorkshire Police's Homicide and Major Enquiry Team. We're here to speak with Mr Schmidt."

The guard's stare remained impassive. "Have you got a warrant?"

"Just a friendly chat today," George replied breezily, though his jaw was tight. "He knows me. We won't take much of his time."

The guard stepped aside after an interminable silence and obviously a message in his ear. "This way."

They followed him down a marble hallway lined with antique landscape paintings. The lavish décor spoke to one thing—old money. Lots of it. Likely dirty, knowing Schmidt's reputed dealings.

Entering a sunlit kitchen, George finally set eyes on the elusive kingpin himself. Jürgen Schmidt cut an elegant figure standing by his coffee machine, his silver hair and charming smile belying his notorious reputation.

"Detective Inspector Beaumont. To what do I owe the pleasure?" His accent was faintly discernible. "Coffee?"

George shook his head and gestured towards the living room. Schmidt nodded and led the way.

"Just had a few routine questions, Mr Schmidt," George began conversationally, settling into a leather chair opposite him. "Regarding recent violent incidents that we thought you might be able to help with."

Schmidt raised an eyebrow. "I'm afraid you have me at a loss. I'm merely a simple businessman." A sly twinkle was in his eye as if enjoying a private joke. "And it's very late."

George placed a graphic crime scene photo on the coffee table. "Let's skip the pretences, shall we? There have been multiple women slain and mutilated by an individual the media has dubbed the Yorkshire Ripper copycat."

He studied Schmidt intently for any reaction. "We have reason to believe this perpetrator has connections to organised criminal elements. Perhaps your own syndicate."

But Schmidt didn't even glance at the grisly photo, waving a dismissive hand. "I do not know what you insinuate, Detective Inspector. But I assure you neither I nor my legitimate business partners have any dealings with this madman."

His stare turned icy. "Now, I have been more than cooperative already. So, unless you have a warrant or evidence to the contrary, I must ask you to leave my private residence at once."

Knowing he had no grounds to push further yet, George adopted a more conciliatory tone. "Of course, apologies for disrupting your morning. However, if you do hear of anything related to these murders through the grapevine, please get in touch."

Schmidt simply smiled. "I admire your dedication, Inspector, misplaced as it may be. You seem very eager to connect these vile killings with me specifically. Now, why is that?" His smile held an unspoken warning—tread carefully.

George bit back his simmering retorts and stood abruptly. Clearly, this visit was pointless except to rattle Schmidt's cage. "Thank you for your time. We'll be in touch if needed."

The guard arrived to escort them out, and George turned. He said, "I'm very sorry to hear about Pearson, by the way. I know how close you both were."

Once outside, George cursed under his breath. Schmidt's smug denials only convinced him more of the crime lord's complicity. He just needed to find that one loose thread to unravel the whole filthy web.

Jay gave him a sympathetic look. "We'll get him eventually, boss. His kind always slips up eventually."

* * *

George tuned out the activity in the Incident Room, staring intently at the financial records and profile notes spread on the desk before him. The ruthless methodology of the copycat killer had to be rooted somewhere in these mundane details— if only he could spot the pattern.

A coffee mug appearing in his peripheral vision broke George's focus. He glanced up to see DS Mason leaning on the corner of his desk, steaming drink extended.

"Thought you could use the pick-me-up, son," Mason said, eyeing the piles of paperwork.

George gave a grateful nod, taking a long swig of sweet caffeine. "Cheers, Luke. Trying to unravel our suspect's motives through these financial statements, but it's a fucking pain."

Mason picked up a credit report flagged with missed payments. "Yeah, our four female victims all seemed to have money troubles mounting. And the offed gangster, Pearson, as well."

Studying the ledgers intensely, Mason's eyes lit up as a connection seemed to hit him. "You know, these Ripper killings could be debt-related. A clawback scheme."

Intrigued, George set down his mug. "How so?"

"Well, we know Schmidt's organisation loans out dirty cash at shark rates," Mason explained.

George nodded, thinking about dead footballer Paxton Cole.

Mason added, "When payments stop coming, they send a message by any means necessary. Make an example to keep the rest in line."

He gestured to the victim profiles. "If these were in deep to Schmidt's gang, offing them in brutal Ripper fashion covers the hit while spreading fear in the debtor community."

George leaned back, impressed by the inventive theory. It offered a logical link between the disparate slayings. And aligned with Schmidt's syndicate being behind the callous killings.

"It's possible," George said slowly. "We know Pearson was a low-level muscle in Schmidt's crew. If he got greedy and stole..." He rifled through more notes. "And Abigail Trent was behind on all her bills and her rent."

The pieces were coming together—a predatory lending scheme enforced by the lethal debt collector masquerading as the returned Ripper. It explained the viciousness meant to terrify debtors across Leeds.

Mason nodded enthusiastically, encouraged by George's interest. "We find out if Cosima or Tabitha owed the gang money, I bet this theory sings. It's all about power and control, son. The psychology fits."

But George hesitated, recalling Finch's warnings about confirmation bias. "Before we commit fully, let's run it by Mark first. Get his take if it aligns with the suspect's profile."

Slightly deflated, Mason agreed reluctantly. He was proud of his brainstorm, but had to concede Finch's academy-honed assessments carried weight. "Yeah, OK. You're right. A second opinion couldn't hurt."

Together they reviewed the clawback hypothesis, searching for more subtle ties between the victims' financial woes. If true, it hinted at human motivations just as chilling as the occult theories.

Greed and power reduced lives to commodities in the underworld, where the Ripper was just another grim debt collector. An avenue worth pursuing once Finch gave his input.

Chapter Twenty-nine

George sat hunched at his desk the following day, scrutinising the detailed background reports he had requested on the Ripper copycat's victims. Searching their histories for any thread connecting the women to Leeds' expansive underworld and the Schmidt syndicate.

Financials, employment records, known associates—it was all there. But so far, nothing jumped out to support the working theory of gang hits shrouded in the Ripper's infamy.

Cosima Winfrey's history of sex work traced a sadly familiar trajectory of substance abuse and desperation. But no concrete ties to criminal elements beyond street-level hustling. It was the same with Tabitha Arrand.

University student Abigail Trent showed no associations beyond college party circles. Her mounting bills showed her as desperate and vulnerable. But the motive for a professional hit remained unclear.

And living at home and having a decent job at a book shop, Emily White had zero debts to her name.

George sighed, leaning back to massage his tired eyes. Thus far, the victim profiles offered more questions than answers. His expectations of unmasking the killer's true purpose felt increasingly tenuous.

A soft knock at his open door made George swivel around. Professor Finch stood there clutching a distressing fax. The grave look in the profiler's eyes made George's pulse quicken anxiously.

"What is it, Mark?"

Finch stepped inside, gently closing the door behind him. "There's been another murder. The theatricality bears the Ripper's hallmarks, but..." He hesitated.

"But what? Spit it out, mate." George rose from his desk impatiently.

"It seems vicious and flamboyant beyond the previously organised kills," Finch continued carefully. "Ritualistic elements from the original Ripper slayings, but almost exaggerated. More...personal."

George narrowed his brows. "How do you know?"

"DS Mason showed me the crime scene images Lindsey Yardley sent over." He paused. "It's fascinating, though, isn't it? The precision indicates control, finesse even. The Ripper's evolving, becoming more confident."

George shot up and headed immediately into the shared office, seeking Luke.

When he found his old mentor, George's gut twisted as he studied the crime scene images. It was a dramatic display of blood and guts. Mark was right—the calculated mutilations had an edge of raw fury that felt distinct from the coldly methodical earlier murders.

"You believe this rules out our gang hitman theory?" George asked, trying to keep his voice neutral against the crushing disappointment.

"Aye." Finch spread his hands helplessly. "I'm afraid this level of violence supports our original profile of a lone sexual sadist. No professional would take such liberties if merely covering up an underworld killing." He paused. "And those cuts," he explained as he tapped the image, "are practically surgical. It's almost artistic in its execution."

Seeing George's frustration, Finch added gently, "I know you were invested in the organised crime angle, mate. And it's not definitively disproven yet. But this latest homicide shifts the behavioural evidence considerably."

George shivered as he stared down at the horrific images, damning them to hell for undermining what had felt like a significant breakthrough in the arduous case. But he couldn't deny Finch's clinical observations, even if they had chilled him to the bone. The ferocity on display spoke of twisted personal compulsions, not business.

Clenching his fists, George forced himself to step back and regroup rationally. "You're right, Mark. I let myself get carried away chasing the money trail. Clearly, this bastard operates by his own twisted logic."

* * *

The screech of sirens pierced the quiet residential street in Farsley as George pulled up to the latest ghastly scene courtesy of their elusive Ripper devotee. A young woman lay crumpled amidst backyard bushes, the brutal nature of her death abundantly clear even from a distance.

Climbing from his car, George steeled himself before donning his protective outfit and signing in. Then he approached the victim.

Her eyes were still frozen open in a horrific mix of shock, agony, and accusatory disbelief. He silently swore to give her justice.

"Evening, Detective Inspector. Hell of a scene your man's left for us this morning," said SOC manager Lindsey Yardley grimly. Lindsey had seen plenty of atrocities, but this spree strained even her composure.

George surveyed the carnage clinically. "What can you tell me so far, Lindsey?"

She indicated the deep abdominal wounds, scabbing over and clotted with soil. "Killed her right here using the same MO as the others. Hammer and Philips head screwdriver. Then the ritual disembowelling." Lindsey swallowed hard. "But he's really escalating as if in a fury."

Nodding sombrely, George examined the victim's discarded purse. "Any ID on her?"

"Name's Kerry Barlow according to her license," Lindsey replied. "Poor girl's only 22. Found some cash, so robbery wasn't the motive." She shook her head. "Just rage and madness, as far as I can tell."

George processed this dispassionately, refusing to dwell on the senseless loss of life. He had to maintain composure and catch her killer through reason, not anguish. Still, his heart went out to her loved ones, soon to be devastated like so many before them.

Footsteps announced the arrival of the pathologist, Dr Ross. The old, washed-out pathologist regarded the scene with a weary sigh. "No rest for the wicked or those who pursue them, eh, George?"

George gave the man's shoulder a sympathetic pat. "Once we catch this monster, we'll all rest easier, Dr Ross." He paused. "What's your initial assessment?"

Ross knelt gingerly beside the body. "Well, the precision of the cuts makes it abundantly clear this is our Ripper disciple again. He wanted us to know it was his handiwork beyond doubt." He indicated various incisions.

"The killer definitely knew the human anatomy well enough to keep her conscious for an extended period while inflicting maximum suffering." Ross closed the victim's eyes gently. "I'll know more once I get her on the table, but this does appear to be an escalation in savagery from his prior kills."

George suppressed a shudder at the thought of this shy university girl being ruthlessly tortured by a figure out of her grandparents' darkest nightmares. But Kerry would be the last if he had any say.

Taking one last sweeping survey of the scene, George committed every grim detail to memory.

* * *

When his mobile rang, George was halfway out of his Mercedes in the station car park. Still preoccupied with mulling over the Barlow crime scene, he answered without checking the caller ID.

"DI Beaumont."

"George, it's Lindsey Yardley. We've made a strange discovery you should know about."

George paused, interest piqued. "Go on."

"Our initial sweep of the victim's remains turned up several five-pound notes stuffed deep into the abdominal wounds. Not just left behind, but deliberately implanted."

Planting cash in injuries? George's pulse quickened. What sort of twisted message was that? "Appreciate the quick update, Lindsey. You may be onto something big here," he said, mind racing.

Rushing inside, George limped urgently through the lobby, ignoring the stabbing pain in his bad leg. He had to get upstairs and research Kerry's background immediately. A wild hunch was forming.

Bursting into the Incident Room, George made straight for the Big Board as detectives looked up in surprise. Catching his breath with difficulty, George scanned the photos rapidly until he found Kerry's driver's license.

There it was—her address was listed as Manchester, over an hour away. Why was a University of Leeds student from another city targeted by their Leeds killer? The cash suddenly made terrifying sense.

"Briefing. Now!" George barked. As the team quickly assembled, George explained the money discovery and its potential meaning. "Our Leeds Ripper murdered a girl from Manchester and intentionally left five-pound notes on her."

The implications sunk in, eyes widening around the room. Luke flipped through the slim file on Kerry. "Says here she was studying social psychology." He froze. "Barbara Leach studied social psychology."

George nodded, and Mason added, "Hold on, wasn't Jean Jordan—"

"Sutcliffe's sixth victim in 1977. A Manchester girl." George finished. It all clicked into place. The cash was the Ripper's trademark taunt about Jean's death.

He whirled to face the assembly. "Don't you see? The copy-cat is intentionally hunting victims that share characteristics with the original Ripper's victims." He slammed his fist on the Big Board angrily. "This bastard isn't escalating randomly. He's methodically recreating famous Ripper murders, step-by-step!"

The room buzzed with dismay at this chilling revelation. By mirroring infamous slayings, their target was elevating the deadly performance art, mocking police's inability to anticipate his next homage.

"Pearson's execution threw us off the scent, but Finch was right. This is about meticulous obsession, not organised crime," George admitted begrudgingly.

Luke shook his head in frustration. "Just when we think we have a pattern, this demented prick changes the game." He gestured helplessly to the board. "How do we predict where he'll strike next or who when he's just recreating random past murders?"

"I'm guessing they're not in order?" asked Jay.

George shook his head and said, "By studying those original cases more closely, we can predict." George's eyes burned with zealous purpose. "He's already alluded to Emily Jackson and Barbara Leach before. Now Leach and Jean Jordan this time. George paused. Sutcliffe didn't kill any men—"

"That we know of," interrupted Mason.

George conceded the point. "But Frank Pearson could be the copycat's nod to Yvonne Pearson."

"And his body was found under an old armchair in the alley," Mason explained.

"Jesus Christ," said Jay.

George turned to Jay. "What?"

"Wasn't Yvonne's body found hidden under a sofa?"

"Ah, so you have been listening," said George, and Jay nodded. "I want background reports on all confirmed and suspected Yorkshire Ripper victims from back then. There must be clues in their histories as to who our copycat will mimic next."

* * *

The video screen flickered to life, revealing a dim room at a Manchester police station. A burly detective chief inspector occupied most of the frame while a devastated couple clung to each other in the corner—Kerry Barlow's grief-stricken parents.

George's chest tightened with empathy. Breaking the horrific news never got easier, especially remotely. But he kept his tone gentle yet professional.

"Mr and Mrs Barlow, I'm so very sorry we have to meet under these circumstances. I'm DI George Beaumont of the West Yorkshire Police Homicide and Major Enquiry Team." He paused to let that sink in. No parent should have to endure this.

The DCI cleared his throat gruffly. "The Barlows have been fully briefed on what occurred, Inspector. Please, ask your questions so these poor folks can start grieving proper." His brusque tone held compassion underneath.

George nodded. "Of course. And again, our deepest condolences. I know words mean little right now, but Kerry's loss won't be in vain. We will find who did this."

Mrs Barlow emitted a strangled sob at hearing her daughter's name. George braced himself and continued. "I just need to ask some questions that may help our investigation. Take your time responding."

He glanced down at his notes, determined to get through this as quickly as possible for their sake. "Was Kerry aware of anyone in Leeds who might wish her harm? Any bad blood or dangerous affiliations?"

The couple shook their heads helplessly. "Our girl wasn't like that at all," Mr Barlow choked out. "She was bright, friendly... got on with everyone she met. Can't imagine anyone wanting to..." He broke down.

George gave them a moment before proceeding as gently as possible. "Did she owe money or have any financial issues that you know of?" Again, defeated, head shakes.

"Lastly, do you know if Kerry recently became involved with anyone new? A boy or girlfriend, colleague, or acquaintance who might know more about her activities in Leeds?"

But the grief-stricken parents had no insights to offer. Kerry hadn't mentioned anyone new in the months since starting university. They were at a total loss to explain the tragedy.

Realising he would get nothing more of use, George reluctantly concluded the painful interview. "Thank you again for speaking with me during this impossibly difficult time. We won't rest until Kerry's killer is brought to justice."

The DCI leaned into the camera. "You have my word too, Inspector Beaumont. This evil bastard will face Manchester's justice soon enough." His protective glower said he considered Kerry one of his own now.

George nodded his thanks before terminating the feed, the image dissolving into darkness again. Witnessing such raw devastation only strengthened his resolve.

Chapter Thirty

Detective George stepped up to the podium, jaw set and eyes blazing. In the wake of last night's brutal murder, he had called this emergency press conference to address the dangerous sensationalism fuelling the killer's bloody ego.

George adjusted the mic, gathering the righteous anger simmering within. "By now, you've all heard the tragic news of another young life cut short by the so-called 'West Yorkshire Ripper.' Kerry Barlow, from Manchester, only 22 years old."

He scanned the captive audience sternly. "While police pursue every available lead to apprehend this offender, I must address how your irresponsible reporting only feeds this spree and jeopardises further public safety."

Murmurs rose from the crowd, but George spoke over them. "Ever since the story broke, your headlines have focused on mythologising this murderer as an unstoppable spectral bogeyman back to haunt Leeds. Just like the original Ripper's reign."

Striding out from behind the podium, George jabbed an accusatory finger at the cameras and, recalling the phrases Mark had taught him, said, "This sensationalised narrative only emboldens the killer by fuelling his delusions of infamy.

You enable his body count through such dangerously amplified coverage." He shook his head. "In short, you're making him a celebrity, and you need to bloody stop!"

The reporters shifted restlessly under his damning scrutiny. George pressed on, volume rising. "So let me make this abundantly clear to any who might defend this shite reporting as free speech. If you glorify this maniac's exploits, ignoring the trail of real suffering left in his wake, then you share the guilt of every kill!"

His words hung heavy in the air. George's chest heaved with passionate conviction as he scanned the room. "So stop martyring the Ripper's legacy. Sutcliffe was a bastard! Everybody knows that! So, from now on, I expect sober, responsible updates on the investigation's progress, concentrating on the victims and giving them a voice, not fear-baiting drivel. Or I swear to God..."

Turning his fiery gaze directly into the main camera, George addressed the watching killer. "And you—if you're out there watching this, understand your days of roaming free are numbered." His voice was steel. "I don't care if you think you're Sutcliffe. I don't care if you want to be him. We see through your mask to the fragile coward beneath. And I swear to you, when we inevitably cross paths, you're mine!"

George leaned forward, eyes unblinking. "You're on borrowed time, Ripper!"

Straightening again, George concluded in a tone brooking zero dissent. "Let this serve as your one warning. The public limelight you crave will soon close in around you. And then you'll have my full attention."

With that ominous vow left chilling the air, George departed without fielding questions, leaving a trail of uneasy whispers in his wake. He didn't care if Atkinson or Smith reprimanded him for his threats. He meant every word.

The time for defensive reaction was over.

* * *

The Incident Room doors flew open as George stormed in, the rest of the task force swivelling to see the DI's stormy expression. Fresh from the press conference, George was in no mood for further frustrations. Tossing his coat aside angrily, he headed straight for the Big Board.

He whirled to face the room. "That bastard's out there, mocking us, and it's starting to really fucking piss me off!"

"Calm down, son," said Mason, putting a hand on George's shoulder.

"I just think we're wasting time chasing empty occult theories and organised crime dead-ends. We need to refocus on determining the real motive before the body count rises again!"

From his desk, DS Luke Mason threw up his hands defensively. "With all due respect, son, we've explored every conceivable angle on this nutter. No way to know which lead might crack the case."

"Well, we'd best figure it out soon," George shot back. "Because another girl will turn up ripped open while we spin our wheels, grasping at straws!" His shout echoed off the walls, making several constables wince.

Before the tension could escalate further, Finch interjected calmly. "George, your frustration is understandable but misdirected. Each person here wants justice and closure just as much as you." He ran his fingers through his thick beard.

"Trust me."

He moved closer, lowering his voice to almost a whisper. "Getting emotional and lashing out only breeds hostility among allies, George. We must stay methodical and unified moving forward."

Chastened, George ran a hand through his blond hair, wincing at the tender spot. "You're right, Mark. This case just has me so on edge…" He turned back to the room. "I'm so sorry. We're all tired and overextended. I do know how hard you're all working."

There were nods and murmurs of acceptance among the team. Taking a deep breath, George gathered himself. "Right then. Let's re-examine the victim profiles for any cross-connections suggesting an underlying pattern or motive."

But Mason wasn't ready to let it lie. "With due respect, son, we've been over their backgrounds half a hundred times now. There's no obvious rhyme or reason." He crossed his arms stubbornly. "Well, other than the fact that the two Bradford victims were prostitutes, and the three Leeds victims have a connection to Sutcliffe's victims, be it name or the course they were studying."

Before George could respond, Tashan added, "And we can't just ignore legitimate OCG aspects, sir. The killing of Frank Pearson raises valid questions."

Mason jumped on this. "Exactly! For all we know, the OCG angle could be the break we need—"

"Enough!" George's sharp tone cleaved the growing debate. "Mark is right; petty squabbling gets us nowhere. We need to refine our focus to the most probable motives." He met each person's gaze pointedly. "Understood?"

There were reluctant nods all around.

Placated, George moved to pour himself a strong coffee. He knew the team was just as shattered and desperate for a break as he was. Tempers were high, but they couldn't lose it when lives depended on them.

For now, they would look into Sutcliffe's known and suspected victims, systematically eliminate what they already knew, and build up a case.

And that meant using Finch and his clinical approach to steer the ship until the killer's motives came into focus through reason and deduction.

With caffeine coursing through his veins, George turned to his team and gave out orders.

* * *

The silence of the empty Incident Room at midnight was interrupted only by the rhythmic tapping of George's pen as he gazed up at the Big Board, bloodshot eyes tracing the web of head shots, crime scene photos, and truncated leads. So many paths explored, and yet the shadowy figure behind it all continued eluding his grasp.

Dropping the pen, George kneaded his throbbing temples. The long hours were taking their toll, both mentally and physically. He couldn't remember his last full night's sleep or meal that didn't come from the vending machine down the hall or the canteen. Even bathing had become sporadic.

But none of that mattered. Not when the Ripper's copycat was still roaming free out there, ready to claim his next innocent victim. George couldn't rest until Leeds, no Yorkshire, was finally free from that fear, once and for all. It was his duty.

With a weary sigh, he leaned back in his chair, listening to it creak under the shifting weight. How long had Finch warned him about burning out? But George hadn't listened then and couldn't afford to now. Not with the city's safety on the line.

His gaze drifted over the case details that he had already seared into memory despite the haze of exhaustion. The infernal puzzle consumed him even in fitful half-sleep, prodding at the frayed edges of sanity—an endless recursion of connections sought but not found.

Occult rituals, police conspiracies, organised crime debt collection, and links to Sutcliffe's murders. All provocative theories ultimately led nowhere but empty alleys and decommissioned warehouses. Just grasping at errant straws while the real pattern continued eluding them.

George blinked gritty eyes and forced his bleary focus back to the victim photos. There had to be some thread there that he simply wasn't seeing—some microscopic detail or hidden symmetry that betrayed the cold, precise logic in this bastard's rampage.

How long could a phantom remain untouchable? How many more broken lives and grieving families before this wraith took tangible form? George's fist clenched involuntarily at the thought.

His eyes bored into the latest grisly photo, wanting to reach through the daunting barrier of time and space and extract the secrets directly from the carnage. Something in the cruel ritual of death spoke to compulsion, not confusion. He only had to learn the language.

Somewhere out there in Leeds' sleeping neighbourhoods, the Ripper impersonator was surely planning his next performance, basking in the chaos he'd sown. But his reign of terror only strengthened George's resolve.

With obsessive determination bordering on fervour, he resumed cataloguing every element of the case, searching for the hidden logic that would force the killer from the comforting long shadows and into the harsh light. He would find the pattern, clawing sanity and sleep aside until he did.

* * *

The night wrapped around George Beaumont like a shroud as he trudged back to the sanctuary of his home, each step heavy with the day's unresolved burdens. Inside, the world softened, the sharp edges blurring into the warm embrace of Isabella, his fiancée. Her presence was a balm, soothing the raw edges of his psyche. With a sigh that seemed to release the weight of his investigations, he collapsed beside her, seeking solace in her arms.

In the softly lit room, their silhouettes merged a display of tranquillity amidst the chaos. Isabella's gentle breathing was a lullaby, luring him into a reluctant sleep. But rest was a deceitful companion that night.

As sleep deepened its grip, George's mind, a relentless detective even in slumber, conjured images too ghastly to face in the light of day. The scene unfolded with a chilling clarity: Isabella, the love of his life, in the cross hairs of the West Yorkshire Ripper. The dream twisted reality into a macabre dance, the Ripper a shadowy figure looming over her.

George, bound to the bed, muscles rendered useless, struggled against an invisible force. His arms, usually capable of fending off any danger, were now shackles of paralysis. He strained against the unseen bonds, his voice a prisoner in his own throat. The helplessness clawed at him, a beast with unforgiving nails tearing through the layers of his composure.

In this nightmarish realm, every detail was excruciatingly vivid—the cold glint in the Ripper's eyes, the sinister curve of his smile, the slow, deliberate movements that spoke of unhurried malevolence. Isabella's eyes, wide with terror, sought George, pleading for salvation he couldn't provide. Her silent screams echoed in his mind, a symphony of dread that he was powerless to silence.

The Ripper's hand moved, a conductor orchestrating a crescendo of fear. George's heart thundered against his chest, a desperate drumbeat in the oppressive silence of the dream. He wanted to shout, to break the chains of his paralysis, to leap forward and shield her from the impending doom. But his body betrayed him, a traitor anchored to the bed, a spectator in his own nightmare.

As the phantom blade descended, a shriek pierced the air— his name, a desperate invocation from Isabella's lips. It was the jolt that shattered the illusion, pulling him from the depths of his terror. He awoke with a start, a cold sweat clinging to his skin, his breath ragged, as if he had been running a marathon.

The room was still, bathed in the soft glow of the moonlight filtering through the curtains. Isabella stirred beside him; her brow furrowed in concern. "George?" she whispered, her voice laced with sleep and worry.

He reached for her, his hands trembling, needing the reassurance of her warmth, the confirmation that it was all just a figment of his tormented mind. "It's nothing," he lied, his voice barely a husk. "Just a bad dream."

But as he held her close, feeling the steady beat of her heart against his, George knew the truth. The Ripper wasn't just a threat lurking in the shadows of Leeds; he had invaded the sanctum of his mind, threatening the very essence of what he held dear.

Chapter Thirty-one

The morning dawned with a steel-grey sky, the kind that hung over Leeds like a foreboding omen. George Beaumont sat in his office at the station, the weight of sleepless nights etched in the lines of his face. His eyes, once sharp and probing, now mirrored the exhaustion that gripped him. The case files on his desk were a jumbled testament to the chaos that had engulfed his life.

A knock at the door jolted George from his reverie. DC Jay Scott stood at the threshold, a mix of urgency and apprehension in his eyes. "George, we've got something," he said, his voice edged with a tension that immediately put George on alert.

"What is it, Jay?" George asked, straightening up.

"A call from Roundhay. A neighbour reported hearing screams. She's certain she heard the word 'Ripper'."

The word hit George like a physical blow, its impact sending a surge of adrenaline through him. He was on his feet in an instant, the fatigue momentarily forgotten. "Let's go," he said, his voice a low growl of determination.

They moved quickly through the station, George's mind racing. Every scream, every cry for help, had become a personal affront, a challenge to his ability to end this nightmare. As they approached DCI Alistair Alexander's office, George's stride became more purposeful.

Alexander looked up as George barged in, his expression one of mild annoyance that swiftly changed to concern. "What's the urgency, Beaumont?" he asked.

"We need a raid team for Roundhay, now," George said, his words clipped and decisive. "There's been a report of screams and the mention of the Ripper. We can't afford to waste a second."

Alexander assessed George for a moment, then nodded. "I'll get it authorised. Go, but be careful. We can't afford any slip-ups."

George acknowledged with a terse nod and left. The drive to Roundhay was tense, each second stretching out tortuously. George's grip on the steering wheel was tight, his jaw set. Beside him, Jay Scott remained silent, the gravity of the situation hanging heavily between them.

Arriving at the scene, George's senses went into overdrive. The street was eerily quiet, the only sound the distant murmur of curious onlookers held back by police tape. The house in question loomed ominously, its windows like dark, unblinking eyes.

The raid team was already in position, a palpable sense of readiness emanating from them. George approached the officer in charge, a man named Sergeant Davies. "We need to go in now," George said, his voice carrying an authority that brooked no argument.

Davies nodded, signalling his team. They moved as one, a well-oiled machine of efficiency and force. George followed, his heart pounding in his chest, a mix of fear and anticipation coursing through him.

The raid team, a cadre of determination and steel nerves, swarmed the suspect's house in Roundhay. George Beaumont, at the helm, felt the familiar surge of adrenaline as they prepared to breach. The 'Big Red Key,' a sarcastic moniker for the battering ram, smashed against the door, its thunderous echo a herald of their arrival. The door gave way with a splintering groan, revealing the shadowed innards of the house.

Inside, the air was stale, heavy with the scent of neglect. Each step was cautious and deliberate. The team split, a practised dance of clearing rooms, their movements synchronised yet tense. George's eyes scanned every corner, every possible hiding spot. His mind was a maelstrom of scenarios, each more grim than the last.

Then, a sound pierced the silence—a muffled scream, faint but unmistakable, emanating from the depths of the house. It was a sound that set every nerve in George's body alight. He signalled the team, his hand movements sharp and decisive. The scream had come from the basement.

An AFO, an Armed Firearms Officer, weapon drawn and ready, took point as they approached the narrow staircase leading downwards. The steps creaked under their weight, a sinister symphony accompanying their descent into the unknown. George's hand hovered near his own weapon, his senses on high alert.

The basement was a cavern of darkness. The only light came from the beams of their torches, slicing through the gloom like searchlights. Dust motes danced in the air, disturbed by their intrusion. The muffled screams continued, now interspersed with sobs, a haunting melody of despair.

In the oppressive darkness, George's senses were acutely

heightened, every nerve tuned to the grim scene before him. There, under the feeble light of a single bulb, lay Sarah Wayne, a young woman whose terror-filled eyes spoke volumes. Bound, gagged and tied to a table, she was seconds away from a fate too ghastly to contemplate.

The assailant, a man with dark hair and a full beard, loomed over her, his intentions clear. The glint of a knife in his hand was like a flash of lightning, a harbinger of the storm to come. George's heart pounded in his chest, a drumbeat of dread and determination.

As the killer turned, sensing the intrusion, his eyes locked on George. There was a brief and electric moment where fear and resolve collided. Then, with a snarl of rage, the man charged, knife raised, his movements a blend of desperation and madness.

The AFO reacted with trained precision, his firearm a sudden, deafening presence in the claustrophobic space. Multiple shots rang out, echoing off the walls, each one a punctuation in the nightmarish sentence they found themselves in. The assailant stumbled, his momentum halted, then collapsed to the ground, bleeding but still clinging to life.

The immediate danger neutralised; George's focus shifted back to the woman. He moved quickly, his hands working to free her from her bindings. Her sobs filled the room, a soundtrack of relief and trauma. As she was carefully lifted from the table, George felt a wave of emotion he couldn't quite name. Relief, yes, but something else, too—a gnawing sense of unease.

With the basement now a crime scene, George turned his attention to the suspect. The owner of the house, a man they hadn't considered in their investigations. He lay there, a puzzle piece that didn't quite fit the picture George had been forming of the Ripper.

Kneeling beside the fallen man, George studied him, a maelstrom of thoughts whirling in his mind. Was this a breakthrough or a diversion? The man's breathing was laboured, his eyes fluttering open to meet George's gaze. There was something in that look, a depth of madness and despair that sent a chill down George's spine.

As an AFO called for backup and medical assistance, George stood up, his mind racing. This man, this unexpected piece of the puzzle, had thrown everything into disarray. George prided himself on his intuition, his ability to read people, to anticipate the moves of those he chased. But now, staring down at the suspect, he couldn't shake the feeling that he was missing something crucial.

Walking away from the scene, George's steps were heavy, and his thoughts clouded. The house, once just another building on a quiet street in Leeds, was now a landmark in their investigation, a turning point that raised more questions than it answered.

Outside, the night air was cold, a stark contrast to the stifling atmosphere of the basement. George stood there momentarily, allowing the chill to clear his thoughts. Sarah Wayne had been saved, a life pulled back from the brink. Yet, the victory felt hollow, tainted by the uncertainty that now clouded the case.

* * *

The suspect sat across from George Beaumont and Detective Sergeant Luke Mason in the interview room, his demeanour a blend of defiance and fear. The room, bathed in the harsh glare of fluorescent lights, felt like a stage set for a grim play, with George and Luke as unwilling actors.

The suspect, his dark hair dishevelled, his beard lending him a wild appearance, met George's gaze with a flicker of something akin to triumph. "Yeah, I attacked her," he confessed, his voice a husky whisper. "But I ain't your Ripper."

George leaned forward, his eyes narrowing. "Then why, exactly, did you do it?" he asked, his controlled calm belying the frustration simmering beneath.

The man's lips twisted into a semblance of a smile, a grotesque parody of amusement. "Sarah... she wouldn't give me the time of day. Always there in the pub, acting like she's too good for the likes of me." He leaned back, a shrug lifting his shoulders. "So, I figured... why not give her a real reason to be scared? The Ripper's a legend 'round here, innit?"

Luke's hands clenched into fists, the urge to leap across the table barely restrained. "You terrorised a woman, nearly killed her, just because she rejected you?" His voice was a low growl, the words dripping with disgust.

George's mind raced, analysing every word, every nuance. This man was a predator, but he lacked the cold, calculating demeanour of the Ripper copycat they were hunting. He was a different kind of monster, one driven by rejection and a twisted desire for control.

"You understand you're facing serious charges?" George pressed, his tone icy. "Assault, attempted murder... you're looking at a long time behind bars."

The man shrugged again, his eyes glinting with a disturbing nonchalance. "Whatever. I did what I did. Ain't changing it now."

George and Luke exchanged a glance, a silent conversation

passing between them. This was a dead end, a detour in their hunt for the true Ripper copycat. Frustration coiled tight in George's chest, a bitter taste in the back of his throat.

They wrapped up the interview, ensuring the man was securely locked up. But as they left the station, the weight of the encounter hung heavy on them. This was not the resolution they had hoped for, merely another dark chapter in the ongoing saga.

The drive to the hospital was a quiet one, each man lost in his own thoughts. The city passed by in a blur, the familiar streets now tainted with the knowledge of the horrors they concealed.

At the hospital, they found Sarah Wayne in a private room, her appearance a stark contrast to the frightened, vulnerable woman they had rescued from the basement. Bandages adorned her wrists, a physical testament to her ordeal, but it was the haunted look in her eyes that spoke volumes.

George approached her bed, his demeanour gentle, his voice soft. "Sarah, I'm George Beaumont, and this is Detective Sergeant Mason. We need to ask you a few questions about what happened."

Sarah nodded, her voice a fragile whisper. "I understand."

Chapter Thirty-two

George Beaumont stood before his team, a portrait of controlled frustration. The room was alive with the low hum of anticipation, each member of the team acutely aware of the gravity of their situation.

"The impersonator," George began, his voice steady but edged with a tinge of irritation, "gave us nothing of substance. He's a dead end, a distraction from our real target." His eyes swept across the room, meeting those of his team members. "Jay, Tashan, I need you to double-check the suspect's alibis. We can't afford to leave any stone unturned."

Detective Constables Jay Scott and Tashan Patel nodded, their expressions a mix of determination and concern. The room buzzed with a renewed sense of purpose as the team dispersed, each to their respective tasks.

Retreating to his office, George immersed himself in paperwork, the mundane task a stark contrast to the chaos of the investigation. Reports, statements, evidence logs - each document a piece of the puzzle that was the Ripper case, a mystery that seemed to grow more complex with each passing day.

Jay and Tashan returned an hour later, their faces etched with the weariness of their fruitless endeavour. "The alibis check out, boss," Jay reported, his voice tinged with disappointment. "He was where he said he was, except for the night of the attack."

George leaned back in his chair, a deep sigh escaping his lips. This was not the news he had hoped for. Every lead that turned cold, every dead end they hit, was a reminder of the Ripper's elusiveness.

"Thank you," George said, his voice low. "Keep digging. There has to be something we're missing."

The rest of the day passed in a blur of activity, the task force a hive of focused energy. George watched them, proud yet pained by their dedication. They were fighting a shadow, an enemy that seemed to slip through their fingers with annoying ease.

As the evening drew in, the office grew quieter, the team's energy waning under the weight of their unyielding task.

* * *

In his home, far from the relentless pace of the investigation, George Beaumont found no solace. The dining room, usually a haven of domestic tranquillity, was tonight a battleground of unspoken tensions. Isabella, his fiancée, watched him with a mix of concern and frustration.

"George, this obsession with the case... it's consuming you," Isabella said, her voice a gentle yet firm plea. "What if it's blinding you to the truth that's right there, in front of your eyes?"

Her words, meant to be a lifeline, felt like accusations to George. His jaw tightened, a wave of defensiveness rising within him. "This isn't an obsession; it's my job," he retorted, his tone sharper than intended. "The Ripper is out there, and I have to stop him."

Isabella's sigh was heavy, laden with worry. "I just don't want you to lose yourself in this."

George's response was a terse nod, the conversation a cul-de-sac of frustration and worry. Abruptly, he stood and left the room, his footsteps echoing his internal turmoil.

In his home office, a sanctuary of sorts, George sat at his desk, the familiar surroundings a cold comfort. His mind, a relentless detective, refused to rest. He pulled out the original Ripper case files, the pages worn by time and scrutiny. As he pored over them, a nagging sensation tugged at the edges of his consciousness.

There, in the margins of the evidence photos, in the barely noticeable discrepancies of the witness statements, were inconsistencies that had always been there yet had remained unexplored. George leaned closer, his eyes tracing each line, each word. Could these minute details, overlooked in the more significant chaos of the case, hold the key?

The photographs, monochrome memories of a horror long past, seemed to whisper secrets in the silence of the room. A footprint not quite matching the suspect's shoe size, a fibre out of place, a timeline that didn't quite add up. To the untrained eye, they were trivialities, but to George, they were screaming anomalies.

His mind raced, connecting dots that had lain dormant, drawing lines between what had been known and what had been assumed. The original Ripper, a spectre that had haunted Leeds for years, was a puzzle George had thought solved. But now, these inconsistencies painted a different picture that suggested a deeper, more convoluted narrative.

George's heart pounded a drumbeat of revelation and dread. Could they have been chasing a ghost while the real threat lurked in the shadows, unnoticed, unchallenged? The thought was a chilling one, a possibility that unravelled everything he thought he knew.

He stood up, a sudden movement borne of a need to act, to follow this new, uncharted path. The pieces of the puzzle were rearranging themselves, forming a new picture that George knew he had to pursue.

Pulling out his mobile, he dialled a number he knew by heart.

The line clicked, and then Mark Finch's voice, steady and calm, filled the room. "George, what's got you calling at this hour?"

George didn't waste time on pleasantries. "Mark, I've been going over the original Ripper evidence. There are inconsistencies, things we might have missed."

There was a pause, a moment of contemplation. "George, you know Sutcliffe confessed. He detailed everything," Mark replied, his tone a mix of scepticism and concern.

"I know, but what if there's more to it? What if we've been looking at this all wrong?" George's voice was a mixture of frustration and conviction, a man grasping at shadows in the dark.

Mark sighed, the sound crackling over the line. "George, you're one of the best, but you might be chasing ghosts." He paused. "The Ripper keeps slipping through the net, but he's certainly not a ghost. He's as real as you or me."

"What?" asked George.

"Sutcliffe's confessions were comprehensive. He had no reason to hold back."

"But what about the copycat? The one we're after now?"

George pressed his mind, a whirlwind of theories and possibilities. "Could there be some truth in his raving confessions?"

Another pause, longer this time. "It's possible," Mark conceded slowly. "Sometimes, within the twisted mind of a killer like this copycat lies a fragment of truth, buried under layers of delusion and obsession."

George leaned back in his chair, the weight of the case pressing down on him. "So, you're saying we shouldn't dismiss what he's been saying outright?"

"Exactly," Mark confirmed. "These types of individuals, they play games. They hide truths within their lies, like a twisted riddle. It's a part of their pathology."

George's hand tightened around the phone. "Alright. I'll dig deeper, see if I can sift through his confessions for anything that might be credible."

"Be careful, George," Mark warned, his voice lowering. "You're walking into a maze of madness with these types. Don't lose yourself in it."

The line went dead, leaving George alone with his thoughts. He stared at the files spread before him, each one a piece of the grotesque puzzle he was trying to solve. The copycat, a shadowy figure who had taken up the Ripper's mantle, was a complex enigma, one that seemed to defy logic and reason.

George's mind raced, piecing together fragments of confessions, snippets of ravings, looking for a thread of truth in a tapestry of lies. The words of the copycat, once dismissed as the ramblings of a madman, now took on a new significance. Could there be clues hidden within his twisted declarations?

He pulled out the transcripts of the copycat's interrogations, his eyes scanning the pages. Words and sentences jumped out at him, a chaotic jumble of thoughts and confessions.

Somewhere in this labyrinth of madness might lie the key to unlocking the mystery.

Hours passed, the night waning into the early hours of the morning. George's eyes grew heavy, his mind saturated with information. The words on the pages began to blur, merging into an indecipherable mass. But he pressed on, driven by a relentless need to find the truth, until he passed out.

Chapter Thirty-three

The frosty Headingley air was thick with the scent of decay as Detective Inspector George Beaumont surveyed the desolate waste ground near the Arndale Centre. A woman lay motion-less, her brown hair framing her face like a grim halo, her eyes staring vacantly into the oblivion that had claimed her. No ID, no clues to her once vibrant life—just another mystery in a spate of killings that mocked the living.

George's gaze was unwavering, his mind dissecting the scene with clinical detachment. He noted the lack of defensive wounds and the precise placement of the body—hallmarks of a predator who revelled in control.

"Morning, son," Luke's voice pierced the silence, a grim undercurrent running through it. "Candy's on the missing persons. She'll call us if there's a hit."

George merely nodded, his thoughts already racing ahead. Dr Christian Ross, the pathologist, knelt beside the victim, his brow furrowed in concentration. "George, it's him again," he said without preamble. "The replication of methods is textbook, almost obsessive."

Lindsey Yardley, crouched by a patch of undisturbed soil, added, "And he's meticulous. Leaves nothing behind. It's like chasing a ghost."

The Ripper's ghost, George, mused silently. He couldn't help but draw parallels to Jacqueline Hill—Sutcliffe's last known victim. The thought gnawed at him. Is this the end, or just a prelude to more bloodshed?

The squawk of his mobile interrupted his reverie. "DI Beaumont."

"Sir, it's Candy. We've got an ID—Carolyn Carson, 34, a primary school teacher. Reported missing by her husband this morning."

His heart sank—a life full of promise, snuffed out. She had been someone's joy, someone's compass. Now, she was a name in a case file, a blip in the Ripper's perverse game.

The wind picked up, carrying with it the echoes of a city too familiar with grief. George stood, his resolve hardening. This wasn't just about catching a killer any more; it was about halting a cycle of terror that had haunted West Yorkshire for far too long.

He turned to his team, his voice steady, commanding. "I want everything we've got on Carson. Friends, family, last known movements."

As the team sprang into action, George's phone again vibrated with a call from Candy. "Her husband's at home, sir. He's in pieces."

* * *

The narrow streets of Headingley, lined with their mixture of student lets and family homes, led George and Luke to an imposing Victorian house, its red brick facade a testament to a bygone era of affluence. George appraised the residence with a seasoned eye, noting the ornate stonework and the sprawling size. "How does a primary school teacher afford this kind of place?" he murmured, more to himself than to Luke.

Luke shrugged, his gaze following the wrought-iron fence that bordered the property. "Maybe the Carsons have secrets richer than we know."

Inside, Stevie Carson sat on a Chesterfield sofa, his eyes red and swollen, a portrait of grief that was all too familiar to George. The room was a stark contrast of old wealth, with its high ceilings and antique furniture, and the palpable desolation of a man who had just lost everything.

"Mr Carson, can you walk us through last night?" George asked, his voice even, his notepad ready.

Stevie's voice cracked as he began. "I was here, just here by myself," he said, his hands fidgeting with the hem of a frayed cushion. "Carolyn was out with the girls from school. Christmas do, you know?"

"And when she didn't come back?" George prodded.

Stevie's gaze flickered, avoiding George's probing eyes. "I called her. No answer. I thought... she'd gone on to a club. It wasn't like her, but..." He trailed off, his voice a thread of despair.

George pressed on, his questions sharp, calculated. "What time did you wake up this morning, Mr Carson?"

"Early, just after six. Still no sign of her." Stevie's words tumbled out, edged with panic. "Her phone was off. I called the school and her friends. Then Umi said they'd left around eleven."

George leaned in, his scrutiny intensifying. "And that's when you dialled 999?"

Stevie nodded, his fingers entwined tightly. "I was scared. The Ripper..." His voice was a hoarse whisper, the name itself a spectre in the room.

"Mr Carson, what do you mean exactly by 'home alone'?" George's question sliced through the tension.

Stevie hesitated, his eyes clouding with something that wasn't just grief. "Just that. Alone," he replied, but the hesitation spoke volumes.

Luke exchanged a glance with George, both sensing the undercurrents of something unsaid, a narrative hidden beneath the surface of Stevie's words.

George stood, his decision made. "Thank you, Mr Carson. We're very sorry for your loss. We'll be in touch."

They left the house, the echo of the closing door a sad note in the quiet street. As they walked to the car, George's mind raced with the discrepancies in Stevie's account, the pieces of the puzzle not yet aligning.

"Something's off," Luke said, echoing George's thoughts. "Since when does fear and worry make you sleep through the night?"

George grunted in agreement. "Let's get back. There are more pieces to this puzzle. We just need to find them."

* * *

George Beaumont crossed the threshold into the Incident Room, his mind already cycling through the myriad details of Carolyn Carson's case. Before he could address the sea of expectant faces, his phone cut through the tension.

"Lindsey? What have you got?" George's voice was steel, already braced for the unexpected.

Her reply came swift and clear, "Found a hair on the body. It's blond, George. Not black as we anticipated."

A muscle twitched in George's jaw. "Could be from one of her colleagues. Check with Umi Suzuki, the friend who last saw her. And keep this under wraps."

Ending the call, George surveyed his team, his gaze sharpening. "Listen up, we've—"

The click of the door, a minor yet insistent interruption, preceded the entrance of a civilian admin assistant, a letter clutched in her hands like a harbinger of ill news. She extended it towards George, her movements betraying her awareness of its ominous nature.

The room held its breath as George, cursing his bare hands, tore open the envelope. Inside, a sheet of paper—a taunt penned with a venomous flourish, aimed directly at him, at the heart of their investigation. The killer's words, a twisted jibe at their efforts, seemed to crawl across the page.

George's voice, when he spoke, was a controlled calm that belied the storm beneath. "Get this to forensics. Check for DNA, prints, anything."

As the letter was whisked away, George turned back to his team, his resolve unwavering despite the fresh wave of provocation. "This changes nothing. We're close, and he knows it. Now, let's get to work."

* * *

DC Jason Scott approached DCI Alexander Atkinson's desk, the latest murder scene's grisly details fresh in his mind.

"Sir, the Headingley scene," Jay began, his voice steady despite the images seared into his memory, "it's a mess. Carson, the victim, she was..."

Atkinson held up a hand, his expression grave. "I know, DC

Scott. I've read the report. This killer's turning the city into a charnel house." The DCI's eyes met Jay's, searching, probing. "Be careful, Jay. We're dealing with a mind that wants us to see patterns where there may be none."

Jay nodded, but confusion furrowed his brow. "Sir, about DI Beaumont—"

Atkinson leaned back, his chair creaking under the shift of weight. "I find it strange, Jay. Only George seemed to understand what I thought was a misleading clue." The DCI's tone was thoughtful, tinged with an unspoken caution.

Jay's stance shifted, a discomfort taking root. "You think there's a personal angle for the DI in all this?"

"I'm saying your DI has a knack for getting into the heads of people like the Ripper," Atkinson said, his words deliberate. "But yes, it's concerning. It creates an illusion of connection where there should be none."

The unvarnished implication of Atkinson's words hung between them—a trickle of doubt where trust should have stood firm. Jay's allegiance to George was unshakable, yet the seed of disquiet had been planted.

"I trust George," Jay said finally, his voice carrying a conviction that he hoped was contagious.

Atkinson's gaze softened slightly. "As do I, but this killer... he's making it personal, and that's dangerous territory. Stay sharp, DC Scott, and keep an eye on George. Sometimes, the hunter gets too close to the hunt."

Jay turned to leave, the weight of the DCI's words settling like lead in his gut. He understood the line they all tread, a tightrope between duty and darkness. The question now was whether George Beaumont could maintain his balance.

* * *

George and Luke delved into the files spread before them like cards dealt by fate. They were piecing together the life of Carolyn Carson, whose premature end had left more questions than answers.

"She's a local lass, born and raised in Middleton," Luke remarked, flipping through the dossier's pages, his tone methodical, just shy of detached.

George's hands stilled on a photograph, his senses tingling with a ghost of recognition. "Middleton?" he echoed, his voice betraying nothing of the sudden tightness in his chest.

Luke's eyes flicked up, keen and probing. "Yeah, same as you. Did you know her, George?"

George held Carolyn's picture closer, his scrutiny intense. "I don't know anyone named Carolyn Carson," he said, but his pulse quickened, the rhythm of his heart a dissonant beat.

Carolyn's eyes in the photograph, wide and expressive, seemed to hold a depth of unspoken stories. Was she familiar, or was the weight of the case conjuring phantoms of recognition?

Luke, with a detective's instinct, dropped another piece into the puzzle. "Her maiden name was Kelly. Carolyn Kelly."

A rush of memories flooded George's mind, unbidden, swift as an undertow. A brunette named Carolyn Kelly, laughter shared in the corridors of a secondary school, moments of teenage abandon before life had ushered them onto divergent paths.

The revelation hit with the force of a physical blow, a punch to the gut that left him momentarily breathless. He'd known a Carolyn Kelly. Dated her, even. But surely this wasn't the same girl?

A silence had fallen, a lull in the storm, as George grappled with the spectre of the past. "Kelly…" he murmured as if testing the name, feeling the weight of history in its syllables.

Luke watched him, a question unasked in his gaze. But George was a fortress of composure, his face an inscrutable mask. "Doesn't ring any bells," he lied, setting the picture down with deliberate care.

The lie sat uneasily in his stomach, a bitter taste on his tongue. He could not afford to reveal this thread of connection, not with Atkinson's scrutinizing eyes searching for any excuse to sideline him.

Carolyn Carson, née Kelly. The girl he once knew, now the woman whose life had been brutally snatched away. The thought was a thorn, sharp and unrelenting.

"We should focus on her recent years," George suggested, steering the conversation away from dangerous shores. "Let's not get sidetracked by coincidences."

Luke nodded, acquiescing, but George could tell he was not entirely convinced. It was a crack in the foundation of trust, and George knew the cost of such fissures.

The rest of the afternoon was spent in a dance of evasion and investigation, George carefully negotiating the line between past and present.

Chapter Thirty-four

Stevie Carson sat rigid, his solicitor at his side like a shield. George watched him, his gaze unyielding, while Luke hovered in the background, his presence a silent pressure.

Stevie's eyes, once wild with grief, now held a glimmer of something else—a resignation to truths untold. He drew a breath, the sound jagged in the silence.

"I wasn't home," Stevie's voice broke the stillness, quieter now, laced with a different fear. "I was with Nyala Edmonstone."

George leaned forward, his hands clasped on the table, his interest piqued. "The headteacher at Carolyn's school?"

Stevie nodded, a flush creeping up his neck. "Yes."

Luke shifted, his posture straightening as he registered the significance. "Your wife is dead, Mr Carson, and you were with another woman. Start talking."

The solicitor raised a hand, caution in his eyes, but Stevie spoke over him. "We were having an affair," he admitted, the words spilling out like a dam breached.

George's pen was steady as he took notes, his face betraying none of the storm inside. "Why lie about being home alone?"

Stevie's hands twisted in his lap. "I was supposed to be on my own Christmas do with the lads. I cancelled to be with

Nyala."

"And Carolyn?" George pressed, his voice sharpening like a knife's edge. "Did she know about the affair?"

A beat of silence, then a shake of the head. "No, she didn't. Nyala and I were careful."

Luke's snort was soft, but its disbelief rang clear as a bell in the room. "Careful doesn't change the fact that while your wife was being murdered, you were in another woman's bed."

Stevie's face crumpled, the façade of control slipping. "I didn't know. I swear, I didn't know."

George stood, his movement deliberate. "Your alibi, Mr Carson. It just evaporated. And now you're in a very precarious position."

Stevie's eyes darted to his solicitor, seeking an anchor as the tide turned against him. But George was already heading for the door, the weight of Stevie's confession heavy in the air behind him.

* * *

The primary school loomed silent and empty; the laughter and chatter of children long faded into the dusk. DC Jay Scott and DS Luke Mason approached the head teacher's office, where Nyala Edmonstone sat behind a desk cluttered with papers and children's artwork, the stark reality of Carolyn's demise a grotesque contrast to the innocence depicted in crayon and glue.

Nyala's face was drawn, eyes red, and her usual composed demeanour crumbled under the weight of tragedy and scandal. She looked up as they entered, her distress palpable.

Luke took the lead, his voice soft yet insistent. "Miss

Edmonstone, we need to confirm your whereabouts last night."

Nyala nodded, her voice barely above a whisper. "I was with Stevie. He was... with me until the early hours."

"And you were aware of Mrs Carson's Christmas outing with her colleagues?" Jay asked, his tone gentle but probing.

"Yes, of course," Nyala replied, her hands fidgeting with a paper-clip. "It's been a tradition for years." She paused. "I was supposed to go but cancelled at the last minute to be with Stevie."

Luke leaned in, his gaze steady. "Can you think of anyone who might have wanted to harm Carolyn?"

Nyala's breath hitched her distress a sharp note in the quiet room. "No, Carolyn was... she was loved. Everyone here adored her."

Jay exchanged a glance with Luke before continuing. "Miss Edmonstone, was your relationship with Mr Carson known to anyone else?"

She shook her head, a strand of hair falling into her face. "We were discreet. It was a private matter."

Luke's voice was gentle but firm. "We were advised to speak with Umi Suzuki. Can you tell us about her?"

Nyala hesitated, then released a slow breath. "Umi... she's one of our teachers. She and Carolyn were close, very close. If anyone knows more, it would be her."

Jay scribbled notes, the pen scratching across the paper. "Thank you, Miss Edmonstone. We'll be in touch."

* * *

Luke and Jay sat across from Umi Suzuki. Her posture was

rigid, a defence against the onslaught of questions and the tide of guilt that seemed to be drowning her.

"Umi, how was Carolyn on the night of the outing?" Luke's question sliced through the tense air, his voice a measured calm.

"She was... vibrant, full of life," Umi answered, her voice trembling. "Happy. We all were. It was a celebration."

Jay watched her closely, noting the strain around her eyes, the way her hands clenched and unclenched in her lap. "Did she mention any plans after the dinner?"

Umi shook her head, her gaze fixed on some unseen point on the desk. "No. She was going to catch a taxi home. She..." Her voice faltered, "She should have never been left alone."

The detectives exchanged a glance, a silent agreement passing between them not to reveal Stevie's alibi just yet. "Did she seem worried about anything? Anyone she might have been avoiding?" Jay asked, his inquiry soft but pointed.

"No, not Carolyn. She was open and friendly with everyone. She and Stevie were..." Umi trailed off, then added with a certainty that seemed to anchor her, "They were good together."

Luke's nod was almost imperceptible. They had to tread carefully, the knowledge they held like a loaded gun that could shatter the fragile veneer of normalcy Umi clung to.

"And after dinner, you all parted ways outside the restaurant?" Luke pressed, coaxing the timeline from her.

"Yes. We hugged, said our goodbyes. I watched her walk to the corner," Umi's voice cracked, "I should have stayed with her. I keep thinking..."

"What?" Jay leaned in, his voice a gentle prompt.

Umi's eyes met his, and in them, he saw a well of guilt that went deeper than mere survivor's remorse. "That maybe if I'd waited with her, she'd still be alive."

"We all do the best we can with what we know at the time, Umi," Jay said, his words a balm meant to ease the sting of hindsight.

"You said you watched her walk to the corner. Did you see her get into a taxi?" Luke's question pulled the narrative back into focus.

"No, I... I didn't. I assumed she would." Umi's admission was a whisper, a confession that seemed to sap her remaining strength.

* * *

The drive back from the primary school was a quiet one, the car's engine humming a steady undertone to the unspoken tension between Jay and Luke. It was Jay who broke the silence, his voice carrying an uncharacteristic hesitation.

"Do you trust the boss, Sarge?" he asked, his gaze fixed on the passing blur of Leeds' cityscape.

Luke's response was immediate, a reflex born of years of camaraderie in the force. "Of course I do. Why wouldn't I?"

Jay nodded a non-committal gesture that did nothing to quell the unease now evident in his posture. "Just checking," he murmured, his eyes returning to the window.

Luke's eyes narrowed, a seasoned detective's instincts kicking in. "Jay, what's this about? Spit it out."

But Jay was a closed book, his youthful features set in a practised mask of neutrality. "Nothing. Forget I mentioned it."

Luke wasn't convinced, the question mark Jay had placed

over George's trustworthiness gnawing at him. He made a mental note to confront George to clear the air of any doubts that might be festering within the team.

Upon their return, the station's usual bustle greeted them, but it was George's absence that resonated louder than the cacophony of ringing phones and clicking keyboards. Luke's concern deepened, a frown etching itself across his brow.

"Where's DI Beaumont?" Luke asked one of the officers passing by.

"Haven't seen him," came the distracted reply.

The response did little to ease the disquiet that had settled over Luke like a shroud. George's disappearance, coupled with Jay's cryptic questioning, left a bitter taste of anxiety that Luke couldn't shake off.

He decided there and then, as he scanned the room for any sign of George, that this was a matter he'd have to delve into. For the sake of the team, for the sake of the case, and for the sake of the trust that was the foundation of their work.

* * *

The living room of George Beaumont's home was alive with the sound of laughter, a stark contrast to the sombre tones of his professional life. Jack and Olivia tumbled around him, their giggles punctuating the air as George, the ever-stoic detective, transformed into a human jungle gym. His children's joy was infectious, and for a moment, the weight of the Ripper case lifted, replaced by the simple, unadulterated happiness of family.

Mia, Jack's mother, must have seen the shadows that the case had cast over George, not even arguing with him at his request.

From the kitchen, the aroma of tea wafted through the house, a homely scent that spoke of normalcy and comfort. Isabella moved about the space with a grace that belied the complexity of her thoughts, the clatter of pots and pans a soothing background symphony.

She paused, leaning against the door frame, her eyes resting on George. There he was, a man who faced down the darkest corners of human nature, now wearing a paper crown and a face painted with a child's clumsy artistry. Isabella's heart swelled, the corners of her mouth lifting into a smile that was both tender and tinged with sadness for the trials she knew he faced.

"Tea's almost ready," she called out, her voice a gentle sing-song that momentarily drew George's attention.

He looked up, his eyes meeting hers, the connection between them a silent exchange more potent than words. A quiet thank you, a silent promise, all conveyed in a single glance.

"Smells amazing, love," George called back, the term of endearment coming as naturally as breathing. His hands were gentle as he lifted Olivia into the air, her shrieks of delight a music that chased away the echoes of crime scenes and press conferences.

Isabella turned back to the stove, her movements fluid as she stirred and tasted. This was her domain, a place where she could express love in the most primal of ways—through nourishment and care.

The table was set, a mosaic of domesticity that stood in defiance of the chaos of the outside world. Plates were filled, glasses clinked, and for a while, the only detective work George had to contend with was deciphering the mystery of his son's storytelling.

This was the other side of George Beaumont, the side that wasn't defined by warrant cards or cases but by the laughter of his children and the warmth of the woman he loved. As they sat down to eat, the Ripper was a phantom banished to the shadows, kept at bay by the light of family and home.

Later, George and Isabella prepared for the night, the room around them a sanctuary sealed away from the world's cruelties. The laughter and stories from tea still lingered in the air, a bittersweet reminder of life's fragile beauty.

Isabella watched George as he readied for bed, noting the subtle ease in his shoulders and the softness in his eyes that had been absent for too long. "You seem... lighter tonight," she observed, her voice a tender murmur in the quiet.

George turned to her, a genuine smile playing on his lips. "Having Jack here, it's a reminder of what's good... what we're fighting for," he admitted, the lines of strain that often furrowed his brow now smoothed away.

Isabella reached out, her hand finding his, their fingers intertwining naturally. "And Olivia, she adores her big brother. Seeing them together, it's like a piece of the world is right."

He nodded, his gaze reflecting the soft lamp light, a rare tranquillity settling over his features. "It's more than right, Isabella. It's... I can't describe it, but I love it," he said.

In the quiet cocoon of their bedroom, they slipped beneath the sheets, the fabric cool and soft against their skin. As they drew close, the warmth between them was not just from the contact of bodies but the mingling of souls seeking solace in one another.

Isabella rested her head against George's chest, listening to the steady heartbeat that spoke of life's tenacious rhythm.

George's arm curled around her, a protective embrace that was as much about holding as being held.

As sleep drew them into its embrace, George's last conscious thought was gratitude for the respite of the evening. For the first time in what felt like an eternity, his mind did not wander to the dark corners where the Ripper lurked.

That night, as George drifted into slumber, the case did not invade his dreams. There were no shadowy figures, no whispers of violence. Instead, there was only the calming presence of Isabella, the soft breathing of his children, and the security of a happiness that was as close to peace as he could hope for in these turbulent times.

Chapter Thirty-five

The morning in East Ardsley was grim, the sky a steely grey, the air filled with a chill that seemed to seep into the very bones of the onlookers gathered behind the police tape. On Moor Knoll Lane, a patch of grassy wasteland had become a stage for horror, the latest act in a play that Detective Inspector George Beaumont wished had never been penned.

George's car pulled up, the engine cutting abruptly as he sat for a moment, wrestling with the gnaw of concern for Mia. With Jack safely at his side the previous night, Mia was alone, and with another victim on the green, his mind reeled at the possibilities. He checked his watch—Isabella wouldn't drop Jack off until noon, the hours stretching out like a tightrope over an abyss of what-ifs.

He stepped out, his strides purposeful as he approached Police Sergeant Greenwood. "Get your uniforms going door-to-door," he instructed, his voice steady despite the turmoil within. "Someone must have seen something."

Greenwood nodded, immediately dispatching his officers with a sense of urgency that matched the gravity of the situation.

George suited up, the Tyvek suit crinkling with every move-ment, shoe covers snapping against his heels, gloves sheathing his hands in latex, and the mask rendering his breathing into a muffled echo in his ears. As he approached the body, a silent prayer thrummed in his chest—let it not be Mia.

The corpse was still amidst the wavering grass, displayed with a deliberate care that spoke volumes of the killer's intentions. George's eyes traced the familiar horror of the scene, a scene grotesquely reminiscent of too many others. And then, recognition flickered in his gaze—not Mia, thank God, but a face that seemed etched in the annals of his memory.

Dr Ross' expression, grave beneath the mask, rose from his crouched position. "Same MO, George. He's consistent, I'll give him that."

George's nod was barely perceptible, confirming the familiar pattern a cold comfort. "Thank you, Doctor. Let me know when you have more."

Lindsey Yardley stood to the side; her kit laid out like a surgeon's tray, her focus absolute. "No ID on her," she reported, her voice muffled. "But I'm not finished. I'll be in touch with anything I find."

George's gratitude was a silent pulse in his chest as he watched her work, her meticulous nature a bulwark against the chaos of crime.

As he left the scene, the weight of the day already bearing down, George's thoughts were a whirlpool. The relief that Mia was safe warred with the knowledge that someone else had fallen prey to the monster they hunted. The familiarity of the victim's face was a puzzle piece that didn't fit yet, a niggling at the back of his mind that promised more sleepless nights to come.

* * *

The drive back to the station was a silent battle for George Beaumont, his mind a storm of fear and deduction. With each passing streetlight that flickered over the hood of his car, he saw the haunting image of the woman on the wasteland, her stillness a scream in the quiet of his thoughts.

Ellie Addiman. He couldn't shake the certainty of her identity. The New Forest Book Club organiser with a passion for mystery novels—another figure from his past, another life extinguished. The coincidences were piling up like accusations, and a cold hand seemed to grip his heart at the thought that the Ripper might be laying a breadcrumb trail right to his own life.

The urge to call Isabella was a visceral pulse in his chest, a need to hear her voice, to know she was safe. But he resisted, the phone a leaden weight in his pocket. He couldn't burden her with his fears, not when they were just maybes and what-ifs.

And then there was Mia, living her life just a stone's throw from where they'd found Ellie. His mind raced with the geographical implications, the proximity too close for comfort. But he forced the paranoia back. He was George Beaumont, the man who dealt in evidence and facts, not in the shadows of fear that tried to cloud his judgment.

He gripped the steering wheel tighter, knuckles white, as he navigated the labyrinth of Leeds' streets. This Ripper was playing a game of chess with human lives, and it seemed he was unwittingly cast as the opponent. But if the killer was indeed targeting the women from his past, what was the message? What was the connection?

The police station loomed ahead, a bastion of order and law. George parked his car with a precision that belied the turmoil within him. He sat for a moment, drawing in a deep breath, trying to cage the beast of dread that threatened to consume his rationale.

He couldn't call Isabella, not yet. To voice his fears would be to give them life, and he wouldn't—couldn't—do that to her. And as for Mia, he had to trust in the safety measures he knew she had in place.

Stepping out into the chill air, George set his jaw, the mask of the detective sliding into place. He would not fall prey to the Ripper's psychological warfare. He had a team waiting, a case to solve, and a killer to catch.

And so, with the ghost of Ellie Addiman's lifeless eyes etched in his mind's eye, George Beaumont walked into the station, the heavy doors closing behind him with a thud of finality. The game was on, and he would play his part until the end.

The solemn walls of the station held their breath as George entered, the air seemingly dense with unspoken truths. He found Jay waiting, a grim set to his jaw that told George all he needed to know before a word was even spoken.

"It's Ellie Addiman," Jay said, his voice low, handing over the report. "Jerry Khan, who lives by the football pitches in East Ardsley, reported her missing this morning."

George's face remained impassive, a blank canvas hiding the turmoil of recognition and fear. "Ellie Addiman," he echoed, feigning a detachment he was far from feeling.

Jay's eyes narrowed, a glint of suspicion flickering within. "Surprised you didn't recognise her, boss. Weren't you SIO when she was attacked?"

The implication hung heavy between them, a question mark that grew in size with every passing second. George's mind raced for a viable alibi, an excuse that would hold water under the scrutiny of his own team.

"I didn't," George stated, pushing down the rising panic. "The injuries... and my own accident at the time, it didn't click."

Jay seemed to consider this, his gaze lingering on George for a moment longer than was comfortable. "Alright, boss."

George nodded, his throat tight. As Jay walked away, somewhat appeased, George's paranoia swelled. The details were too precise, the connections to his past too acute for the Ripper to be anyone but an insider. Someone with intimate knowledge of his life, his career, someone who knew exactly where to strike to hit him where it hurt the most.

The idea that the West Yorkshire Ripper could be one of their own was a poison seeping into the very foundations of the station, of his trust. It was a notion so vile, so treacherous that it threatened to unravel everything George believed in.

In his office, George sat alone, the file on Ellie Addiman open before him, her smiling photograph a stark contradiction to the scene on Moor Knoll Lane.

* * *

The usual din of activity paused in the Incident Room as Police Sergeant Greenwood's firm knock sounded at the door. The man's silhouette was stiff, the lines of his uniform sharp against the glass pane. George looked up from his desk, his eyes meeting Greenwood's, reading the silent urgency in the sergeant's stance.

"DI Beaumont, got a moment?" Greenwood's voice cut through the buzz of conversations and ringing phones.

George nodded a subtle motion that held authority. "In my

office," he responded, betraying none of the anxious churn of his thoughts. But standing up and leading the way, his limp became more pronounced. It was a cold day, and George was struggling.

Once the door clicked shut behind them, the privacy of George's office enveloped them, a quiet bubble amidst the station's unending rhythm. "What's the problem, Greenwood?" George asked, his tone even expectant.

Greenwood leaned forward, his hands clasped tightly in front of him. "We've got three separate witness accounts. They saw a blond man with a limp on the wasteland last night."

George's pen was already moving across the notepad, the scratch of the nib a percussive echo in the room. "Descriptions? Anything distinctive?"

"They were vague on details," Greenwood admitted, his frustration evident. "But it's a lead. Some houses were dark, no answer. My team is still on it."

George's nod was thoughtful, his mind already racing with the possibilities this new information brought. "Keep me updated. Anything at all, Greenwood."

Greenwood stood, the promise in his posture resolute. "You'll be the first to know," he assured before exiting the office.

Alone now, George stared at the notes before him, the words 'blond' and 'limp' stark against the white of the page. It was a tangible clue in a case mired in shadows, and he felt the relentless pull of the chase. Whoever this man was, George knew he was one step closer to unmasking the Ripper.

* * *

Orange Tree Grove in East Ardsley was a stark contrast to the wasteland where Ellie Addiman's life had been brutally snatched away. The neat rows of houses with their manicured lawns spoke of a community untouched by the chaos that seemed to follow George like a persistent shadow.

He and Jay arrived at Jerry Khan's house, a modest semi-detached with toys strewn across the garden—a silent testament to the children who played there. Jerry answered the door, his face drawn, his eyes betraying a sleepless night.

George took note of the man's demeanour, a mixture of grief and the strain of sudden responsibility. "Mr Khan, we need to verify yours and Ellie's whereabouts last night," George stated, his voice soft but firm.

"I was here with her kids," Jerry replied, his alibi quick and confident. "Ellie went out with friends in Wakefield and said she wanted to celebrate her new independence." There was a touch of pride in his voice that didn't escape George's notice.

George remembered Ellie's ordeal, the accident that had almost robbed her of the ability to walk. "Celebrate?" he echoed, his mind working through the implications.

"Yeah, she's been using a stick for so long... Yesterday, she walked out that door without it," Jerry said, a slight smile breaking through his sorrow.

"Did Ellie have any enemies, anyone who might want to harm her?" George probed, watching Jerry's reactions closely.

Jerry shook his head, his certainty wavering. "No, but..." He hesitated, and then the name came out like a sigh. "She had a falling out with Jonah Grant a while back."

George's pen was already capturing the name on his notepad. "Can you tell me about Jonah Grant?"

Jerry's hands clenched, his knuckles whitening. "Old friend.

They had some stupid argument months ago. I don't know the details." He shook his head. "The argument started up earlier this week." He paused. "I wanted to knock his block off, to be honest with you."

"We'll look into it," George assured him, his mind already cataloguing the new lead. "Thank you for your cooperation."

* * *

George had barely settled into the hard plastic of his chair when Greenwood appeared at his door, his face etched with the strain of urgency. "Got something, DI Beaumont," he said, a clipped tone cutting through the room's hum.

George's eyes met his, a silent command for him to continue.

"It's Jonah Grant, who lives just off the wasteland. Blond walks with a limp," Greenwood reported, his voice low but clear. "Neighbours say he and Ellie were at each other's throats these past weeks."

A muscle in George's jaw ticked. "Jerry Khan mentioned him too. Reckons there was bad blood."

Greenwood nodded, his posture rigid, a soldier delivering intelligence that might turn the tide of battle. "Could be our guy, or at least he knows something."

George leaned forward, his fingers steepled, his mind already racing down the myriad of avenues this new information provided. "Alright. Pull Jonah Grant's records, everything. I want to know who we're dealing with."

With a sharp nod, Greenwood turned on his heel and strode away, leaving George in the wake of potential breakthroughs and the weight of responsibility that each brought. He scribbled a note to himself, the name Jonah Grant, a new beacon in the murky waters of the investigation.

The pieces were beginning to form a disturbing picture, each one a jagged shard of a mirror reflecting back at George.

Chapter Thirty-six

Jonah Grant's presence was sullen, an evident defiance emanating from his slouched posture. The room was silent but for the hum of the air conditioning and the occasional shuffle of papers as George and Luke prepared to pierce the veil of silence that Grant had wrapped himself in.

George reeled off the usual spiel.

"Mr Grant, can you account for your whereabouts last night?" George's voice was steady, the calm before the storm.

Grant's eyes flicked up to meet George's, a glint of something unreadable within their depths. "No comment," he replied, his voice a monotone that spoke of rehearsed rights and a lawyer's coaching.

Luke leaned in, his voice a sharpened edge. "Neighbours saw you arguing with Ellie Addiman recently. Care to explain why?"

Again, the exact two words fell from Grant's lips, a barrier as formidable as any wall. "No comment."

George's hands tightened into fists beneath the table, his frustration a rising tide. "We have witnesses, Jonah. They place you near the wasteland on the night Ellie was killed. We're not here to play games."

But Grant was a statue, his resolve not to speak a silent

challenge. "No comment."

The repetition was a metronome in the room, each 'no comment' a tick in the stale air. George's voice grew terse, his patience fraying. "Your limp, Mr Grant. It matches the description given by witnesses of a man seen fleeing the scene. How did you get it?"

Something flickered in Grant's eyes for a moment, but it was gone as quickly as it came. "No comment."

Luke's fingers drummed on the tabletop, a staccato rhythm against the obstinate silence. "Ellie's boyfriend mentioned you, Jonah. Said Ellie had a falling out with you. What was that about?"

Grant's gaze drifted to the mirror that spanned one wall, his face a mask. "No comment."

George stood abruptly, his chair scraping back with a sharp screech. He towered over the table, his presence dominating the small room. "You can sit there and say 'no comment' all day, but it doesn't change the facts. We will find out what happened to Ellie, and if you're involved, you're going down, Jonah."

Grant's chin lifted a silent, defiant jut. "No comment."

With a curt nod to Luke, George signalled the end of the interrogation. They had hit a wall, but it wasn't over. As they left the room, George's mind was ablaze with the next steps, the next strategies. This was chess, and Grant had made his move. It was time for George to make his.

* * *

Unsurprising, the Incident Room was a hive of focused energy, with officers navigating between desks laden with case files and ringing phones. George Beaumont stood amidst the organised chaos; his thoughts laser-focused on the elusive figure of the blond man with a limp.

"We need those witnesses brought in," George announced, his voice cutting through the din. "It's time for an ID parade, digital. Full body shots. We match the descriptions given."

Jay Scott, his features set in a determined line, nodded once, crisply. "I'll get on it," he said, already moving towards the door with the contained urgency of a man on a mission.

George watched him go, a sense of anticipation coiling in his gut. This was a step forward, a tangible action in a case that had been shadowed by intangibles for too long.

Jay's steps were swift and sure as he made his way to Atkinson's office, the weight of the task at hand a familiar presence in his stride. He knocked once and entered at the sound of Atkinson's gruff "Come in."

Atkinson looked up from a landscape of paperwork, his expression inquiring. "DC Scott, what is it?"

"Sir, DI Beaumont is setting up a digital ID parade for the witnesses—the blond man seen near the wasteland," Jay reported, standing at attention.

Atkinson's gaze held Jay's for a long moment, the wheels clearly turning behind his calculating eyes. "Include George in the line-up," he said finally, his voice even but with an undercurrent that hinted at the gravity of his command.

Jay's brow furrowed slightly, but he was too well-trained to question orders. "Sir? DI Beaumont is leading this investigation..."

Atkinson leaned back in his chair, interlacing his fingers. "And that's precisely why. Suspicion is a shadow growing longer with each passing day. If Beaumont is our man, the witnesses will tell us."

The directive hung in the air between them, fraught with implications that neither man voiced aloud. Jay's "Yes, sir" was automatic, but as he left the office, his mind raced with the ramifications of what they were about to do.

The digital line-up would be telling—either it would steer them closer to the killer or it would cast a damning light on one of their own. The thought was a shiver down Jay's spine, a disquiet that settled in his bones as he set about the task, the image of George now among those to be scrutinised.

* * *

A witness sat, their face taut with concentration. Images flickered across the screen, each one a life captured in pixels and potential suspicion. DC Jay Scott watched, a silent guardian of process and protocol, as the witnesses grappled with recognition and doubt.

The images were indistinct, designed to be so, a parade of similar features, builds, and hair colour. Among them was Jonah Grant, his features digitally rendered alongside a line-up of similarly blond-haired officers. And there, to Jay's unease, was an image of George Beaumont, his inclusion a secret edict from Atkinson.

Each witness took their time, which Jay appreciated. But he noticed each witness' eyes flickered between Grant and George and back again. Their uncertainty was a palpable force in the room, a current of confusion that Jay felt even from his vantage point.

"He's the one, I'm sure of it," one witness ventured, her finger hovering over the image of Grant. But her certainty wavered, faltering. "But the limp... it was more pronounced, like his," she countered, doubt seeping into her tone as she pointed towards George's image.

The second witness, a middle-aged man with a furrowed brow, shook his head. "It's hard to say. The night was chaotic, my memory... It's between these two."

The third witness, a younger man in his thirties, pointed straight at George. "It's him. I'm positive." He paused. "I watched with my binoculars." But then he paused again. "It could be him, though."

Jay frowned as he realised he'd pointed at Grant.

Their indecision was a knot that tightened with each passing moment, a noose around the neck of the investigation. Jay's thoughts were a whirlwind, Atkinson's directive echoing like a drumbeat in his mind.

With the identity parade concluded and the witnesses' statements collected, Jay found his steps leading him once again to Atkinson's office, the weight of the results a heavy burden.

Atkinson's expression was unreadable as Jay relayed the outcome. "They couldn't decide, sir. It's between Grant and DI Beaumont," he reported, a reluctance in his voice that he couldn't quite mask.

Atkinson's gaze was steady, unfathomable. "Keep this under wraps, DC Scott. For now, this information stays between us."

Jay's affirmation was automatic, but his thoughts were in turmoil as he exited the office. To suspect George Beaumont, a man he respected, a man who had become a legend in the force, was to question the very foundations of his world.

But orders were orders, and Jay's role was clear. The truth, however it unfolded, would have to wait. The seeds of doubt, once sown, would grow in silence until the time was right to bring them into the light.

* * *

The incessant ring of George's desk phone broke the cadence of his typing. He glanced at the caller ID, his pulse ticking up a notch as he saw Lindsey Yardley's name flash across the small screen. DNA results didn't call for pleasantries.

"DI Beaumont," he answered, his voice the definition of police brevity.

"DI Beaumont, we've got the DNA analysis back from the hair found at Headingley," Lindsey's voice came through, matter-of-fact yet bearing the weight of implication.

He braced himself, knowing well the duality of such calls— the bearer of breakthroughs or the harbinger of complications. "And?"

"It's a match for you, DI Beaumont," she stated, the words clinical and void of accusation, yet they hung in the air like a verdict.

A silence filled the space between them, a canvas for George's thoughts. "Lindsey, you know why that is. I was there, on the scene. It's protocol to have our DNA on the Contamination Elimination Database for this very reason."

There was a pause, an audible breath on the other end of the line as Lindsey processed the explanation. "Yes, of course. I understand. Just have to follow every lead, you know?"

"I do, Lindsey. Thanks for the heads-up." George hung up, his hand hovering over the receiver momentarily longer than necessary.

The results should have been a non-issue, routine even. But

in light of recent whispers, the shadow of suspicion seemed to stretch further with each passing day. George knew the science of it, the rationale. Yet, the cold grip of implication was indifferent to such logic.

He leaned back in his chair, his gaze distant. His own DNA at the crime scene was innocuous, a mundane fact tainted by the climate of doubt that seemed to be seeping into the very walls. It was a simple truth, now complicated by the complex web of this investigation—a web that, with each entanglement, felt more personal, more targeted.

* * *

As the day waned into the murky twilight of a winter Yorkshire evening, the police station began to empty, the bustle of activity dimming to the quiet hum of the night shift. George Beaumont remained, the glow from his computer screen casting shadows across his face as he perused the shared inbox, a routine task before the solitary drive home.

His cursor hovered over a new file, the label clear even against the stark white of the email background: Digital Identity Parade Results. A click, a moment's loading, and then the contents sprawled before him, the faces of potential suspects lined up like a modern-day rogue's gallery.

His heart rate spiked as his own full-body image came into view, sandwiched between the others. Anger, hot and fierce, coursed through him, a betrayal by protocol that he could not fathom. Witnesses would have seen him there, at the crime scene, and now his image was paraded among suspects?

Without a second thought, he summoned DC Jay Scott, his voice sharp as it rebounded off the shared office's walls.

Jay entered George's office, the door swinging shut with a click that sounded like a gavel. George stood, his stature dominating the room, his eyes two flints about to spark.

"Explain this, Jay," George said, his voice a dangerous calm before the storm, motioning to the screen.

Jay leaned in, his eyes scanning the images, realisation dawning. "I... Sir, I was following orders—"

"Orders?" George's voice crescendo, his control fraying. "My face and body in an identity parade when I'm the Senior Investigating Officer? What were you thinking?"

Jay's posture wilted under the barrage, his apology a stammer. "I'm sorry, sir. It was DCI Atkinson's directive. I didn't think—"

"No, you didn't think!" George's shout ricocheted off the walls, an erratic symphony of fury and disbelief. "You've compromised the entire investigation, Jay!"

Jay stood mute, his figure a study in regret, the apologies falling from his lips now ineffectual against George's wrath.

George's hands balled into fists, his following words a hiss. "You've let me down, Detective. Now get out."

Jay retreated, the door closing with a soft click that belied the fierce exchange. Alone, George slumped into his chair, the anger seeping out of him, leaving a residue of weary frustration.

He knew Jay wasn't to blame, not really. It was the game, the Ripper's game, twisting them all into pawns and players.

Chapter Thirty-seven

George Beaumont woke with a start, his heart a frantic drum in his chest. The remnants of a nightmare clung to him, tendrils of terror that he couldn't shake off as easily as the sweat that beaded on his forehead. He sat up, the darkness of the room a canvas for the replaying horror of his dream.

The realisation came to him as clear and cold as the dawn light that began to seep through the curtains. He was being framed. The pieces of this twisted puzzle were starting to fit together, forming an image he dreaded to confront. The very fibres of his being rejected the notion, but the evidence was like a neon sign flashing across the dark recesses of his mind.

It had to be the work of the Ripper, retaliation for the vice of investigation tightening around him. The pattern was too intricate, too intimate to be the design of an outsider. It pointed to someone who knew the ins and outs of police work, someone who could manipulate the scene, plant evidence, and guide suspicion.

George swung his legs out of bed, the motion brusque, fuelled by a volatile mix of anger and trepidation. The notion that the killer could be one of their own, a fellow officer, was more than just a breach of trust—it was sacrilege against the very creed he'd lived by all his career.

He moved through his morning routine mechanically, his thoughts a chaotic symphony, each strand playing a discordant tune. The coffee he made went cold, untouched as he stood at his kitchen window, staring out at a world that seemed suddenly unfamiliar.

The killer had to be someone with access, knowledge, and the audacity to dance with the law on such intimate terms. The profile was forming, a shadow taking shape against the wall of facts and evidence he'd built.

As George dressed, the weight of his warrant card was heavier than ever, a symbol of order now tainted by the grim farce playing out.

He needed to act, to take control of the narrative that was spiralling into chaos. The killer was close, perhaps closer than he'd ever been, hidden behind the guise of a protector. It was a bitter irony not lost on George as he locked his front door behind him, stepping out into the cool breath of the morning.

The drive to the station was a blur, the streets empty, the city still slumbering, unaware of the monster that walked among them. George's grip on the steering wheel was a lifeline, grounding him to reality as he navigated the labyrinth of his thoughts.

Today, he would have to look at his colleagues with a sceptic's eye, question loyalties, and demand unblemished truths. He would have to tread the line between suspicion and certainty with the precision of a tightrope walker.

But for now, as George parked his car and made his way to the station's entrance, his resolve was a fortress, his determination a shield.

The atmosphere in the station was thick with an unspoken tension, the air charged with a new, unsettling electricity.

George could feel the weight of every sidelong glance as he walked through the rows of desks, each wary eye that flicked in his direction a tangible manifestation of the Ripper's latest psychological warfare.

The usual morning greetings were truncated, the casual banter that typically filled the room now stifled. George's team, a unit that once functioned like a well-oiled machine, seemed to sputter and falter, the gears of trust gummed by doubt and suspicion.

He moved to his desk with a stoic grace, setting down his coffee cup—a cup that no one had offered to fill for him this morning. The sound seemed to echo, a gunshot of normalcy in the strained silence.

"Morning," he announced to the room at large, his voice a deliberate calm that belied the tightness in his chest. The response was a murmur of clipped acknowledgements, a symphony of uncertainty.

George sat, his fingers drumming a steady beat on the surface of his desk. He knew the looks, the whispers, were not personal—how could they be when a killer was toying with them so expertly? Yet, knowing did little to assuage the sting of isolation.

He could sense the questions that hung in the air, unspoken but as loud as any shout: Could George Beaumont, the bedrock of their department, the model of investigative prowess, really be involved? The Ripper's stunt had been cunning, undermining the team's unity with surgical precision.

As the morning wore on, the routine policing tasks were carried out with mechanical diligence. George's directives were met with hesitant compliance, the usual fluidity of their operations now clunky and uncertain. The team was a body second-guessing its mind; the connection between head and heart was momentarily severed.

At one point, George caught Jay's eye, the young detective's gaze quickly darting away, a mix of embarrassment and confusion written in the lines of his face. George gave a subtle nod, an assurance that needed no words, a silent vow that they would see this through together.

Lunchtime approached, and the team disbanded in small clusters, the unity of the communal table abandoned. George remained at his desk, the files before him a fortress against the siege of doubts.

He poured over the evidence, the crime scene photos, the witness statements, looking for the thread that would unravel the Ripper's shroud of anonymity. His focus was unbreakable, a lifeline thrown into the maelstrom of chaos that the case had become.

In the end, it was not the evidence that would break the case wide open but the unwavering conviction of the man who pursued it.

* * *

George sat across from his superior. The room was a stronghold of order, but today, disorder sat between them, an unwelcome guest.

Atkinson's scrutiny was as sharp as the crease in his trousers, his eyes boring into George with an intensity that had little to do with the files strewn across his desk. "Beaumont," he began, his voice measured, "this case is taking its toll, not just on you but the whole team."

George sat, his posture upright, betraying none of the

turmoil that churned within. "We're close, sir," he replied, a statement more of conviction than reassurance.

"Are we?" Atkinson leaned back, the chair creaking under the shift of his weight. "Or is this case leading us by the nose? I've seen strong detectives crumble under less."

The air between them thickened with the unspoken, with the weight of doubt and concern that Atkinson was tasked to both harbour and voice. "I'm not crumbling," George said, his tone even, his gaze unwavering.

Atkinson's fingers tapped a staccato rhythm on the desk, the sound punctuating the silence. "It's not a sign of weakness to admit the pressure is getting to you. Hell, George, you've been included in an identity parade. That's bound to rattle you."

George's jaw clenched, a micro-expression of defiance. "Rattled isn't broken, sir. I'm as committed to catching the Ripper as I was on day one."

"I know that," Atkinson said, his voice softening just a fraction. "But being committed isn't the same as being clear-headed. And with these stunts, the killer is pulling... it's personal. Too personal."

The DCI's words were like a mirror reflecting George's own fears back at him. The line between the hunter and the hunted had blurred, a dangerous shift in a deadly game. "If it's personal, that's because he's made it so," George countered. "But it won't cloud my judgment."

Atkinson stood, the movement an implicit conclusion to the conversation. "Just be sure, George. Because if you become the story, you can't tell it. And we need you telling the story, not starring in it."

George rose, the interview at an end, but the inquisition was far from over. As he left Atkinson's office, the glances from his team members were less wary than before, but the question in their eyes was the same as the one in Atkinson's.

He returned to his desk, the sanctuary of paperwork and procedure. But even as he delved back into the files, into the minutiae of the Ripper's cruel narrative, George knew that the line he walked was razor-thin.

* * *

That night, Isabella was in bed, and George's kitchen was quiet, but outside, a storm brewed—a media tempest that threatened to wash away the foundations of his reputation. As he sipped his coffee, the television screen flickered with the evening news, and with it, the visage of his own life under a microscope.

"New developments in the West Yorkshire Ripper case," the anchor woman's voice cut through the stillness, her tone portentous. "Questions arise over lead investigator Detective Inspector George Beaumont's methods and history."

The camera panned to a reporter standing outside the station, papers in hand, her words sharp as the morning chill. "Sources reveal that DI Beaumont's presence at multiple crime scenes has become a focal point of the investigation, bringing his past decisions and mental stability into question."

George's grip on the mug tightened, the ceramic cold against his skin. The report continued a relentless barrage of insinuation and half-truths. His history was picked apart, past cases dissected, each decision laid bare for public scrutiny.

The room seemed to close in on him, the walls papered with his life's work now echoing back the doubts of a public fed by sensationalism. The Ripper had found a new weapon in his arsenal—public opinion and it was just as sharp as any knife in his collection.

Footage rolled, clips of George at press conferences, his image spliced between scenes of crime tape and flashing blue lights. The narrative was clear: once the hunter, was he now the hunted?

They quoted psychologists, even dredged the barman George had spoken with last night, all to paint a picture of a man unravelling at the seams. "Is Detective Inspector Beaumont too close to the case? Too entangled in a web of his own making?" the journalist Paige McGuiness mused, her voice a velvet hammer driving the nails of doubt deeper.

George stood, his body a map of tension, the coffee forgotten. He turned off the television, the silence a sudden void where accusations had just been. The media had cast their lot, the dice rolling out over the airwaves to settle in homes across Leeds.

This was not just a leak but a calculated strike; information weaponised to undermine and isolate. And it was working. With each broadcast, the Ripper eroded the trust between George and the world he had sworn to protect.

Chapter Thirty-eight

As he readied himself for work that morning, the mirror reflected a man besieged. He straightened his tie with hands that refused to tremble, his eyes meeting his own gaze with a defiance that had carried him through the darkest of cases.

The TV was on again, a repeat of McGuiness' report from last night. This was his trial by fire, by public inquisition, but he would not burn. George Beaumont had faced down monsters before, real and figurative, and he would face this one, too.

He left his home, stepping out into a world that now viewed him with suspicion, the weight of the warrant card a reminder of the duty that propelled him forward. The media could question his methods, his past, and even his sanity, but they could not question his resolve.

The station would be a crucible today, the eyes of his team a jury he must convince anew of his innocence.

* * *

George's steps echoed down the corridors, a lone cadence amidst a symphony of hushed voices that fell silent as he passed. Each morning briefing, once a forum of spirited strategy, had become an exercise in isolation; his input met with polite nods rather than the collaborative enthusiasm of days past.

His desk, a once proud mess of active case files and urgent notes, now lay bare, the more sensitive documents conspicuously absent. The tangible evidence of his gradual exclusion from the lifeblood of the investigation was a silent siren that something was fundamentally amiss.

Even the most routine interactions seemed laced with doubt, colleagues pausing mid-sentence as he approached, their eyes flickering with an emotion that was not quite pity or fear but something in between. The unspoken question hung in the air: was George Beaumont the man they knew or the man the media painted him to be?

In this shifting landscape of trust, only Mark Finch remained steadfast, a lighthouse in the storm that had engulfed George's professional life. They sat in the quiet of George's office, the door firmly closed against the current of suspicion that flowed outside.

"George, you can't let this... bastard get in your head," Mark said, his voice a low rumble of conviction. "This frame job, it's designed to do just that—to isolate you, to make you doubt yourself."

George leaned back in his chair, the leather creaking under the weight of his burden. "It's working, isn't it?" he asked, the edge of his usual stoicism blunted by the relentless pressure. "The whispers, the decisions taken from my control—I feel like I'm on the outside looking in."

Mark leaned forward, his eyes sharp with a strategist's intensity. "That's exactly what he wants. But you're George Beaumont. You've pulled the truth from tighter knots than this."

There was a steel in Mark's words that forged a semblance of armour around George's resolve. "I keep going over it, Mark. The evidence, the leads... How did I miss it? How did we miss it?"

"Because he's good," Mark admitted, his respect for the enemy's cunning clear. "But not as good as you. This is a psychological play, a move to shake you. But you're not shaken, are you?"

George's eyes met Mark's, a flare of the old fire reigniting within their depths. "No. I'm not shaken. I'm pissed off."

A half-smile quirked at the corner of Mark's mouth. "That's the spirit. Now, we need to turn the tables. Start thinking like him—anticipate his moves, find the patterns. He's human, George. He'll slip up."

The room was a cocoon, shielding them for a moment from the storm of suspicion that raged beyond its walls. In the solidarity of old friendships and shared battles, George found a renewed sense of purpose.

"Alright," George said, standing, a newfound determination lifting his shoulders. "Let's go over it again from the top. This time, we're not looking for a suspect. We're looking for a traitor."

* * *

The night had settled over East Ardsley like a shroud.

Earlier, as if compelled by a force he could neither name nor resist, George found himself driving towards East Ardsley after work, his movements automatic, driven by the need to assure himself of Mia and Jack's safety. The drive to their house was a blur, his hands steady on the wheel while his heart raced with a thousand what-ifs.

He parked his Merc discreetly down the street, the engine's soft purr dying as he cut the ignition. The house stood serene in the silver wash of moonlight, a portrait of suburban tranquillity. Yet, to George's eyes, it was a stage set for potential tragedy, and he was the lone audience member watching the play unfold.

As minutes ticked by, his vigil unbroken, a figure emerged from the play of shadows and light. It moved with a deliberate attempt at nonchalance, a predator's mimicry of the innocent. George's pulse quickened, his training kicking in as he stepped out of the car, his every sense on high alert.

The figure seemed to sense his presence, its movements becoming more furtive, the pretence of innocence abandoned. Adrenaline surged through George's veins as he gave chase, his footsteps a silent drumbeat on the pavement.

But the figure was elusive, melting into the shadows with a practised ease that sent a chill down George's spine. He rounded a corner, his eyes straining in the darkness, but the stalker was gone, vanished as if swallowed by the night itself.

George stood alone in the quiet street, his breath coming in short, sharp gasps. His back and leg were killing him. Had it been real, or had his mind, wound tight with stress and suspicion, conjured the phantom of a threat from the ether of his fears?

He made his way back to the car, his mind a tumult of doubt and confusion. As he drove away, the rear-view mirror reflected a street empty of all but the echo of his pursuit.

The incident left him shaken, the lines between reality and the tricks of a mind pushed to the brink growing ever fainter. As George lay in bed again, the darkness seemed full of unseen eyes, watching, waiting.

* * *

Isabella watched George pace the length of the living room, his movements a manifestation of the turmoil that churned within him, his mind a prisoner to the case that had entangled their lives.

The man she loved was slipping away, unravelled thread by thread by the killer's insidious design. His eyes once filled with warmth, now held a haunted gleam, windows into the siege he was under. His sleep, when it came, was restless and brief, often interrupted by murmurs and gasps as he battled unseen demons in his dreams.

"George, this isn't like you," Isabella whispered one evening as they sat at opposite ends of the sofa, a physical distance that mirrored the emotional chasm growing between them.

"I know," George replied, his voice a roughened edge, "but I can't let up. Not when he's still out there."

Isabella reached out, her hand hovering over his, yearning to bridge the gap with her touch. "But at what cost? You're consumed by this... it's like you're chasing a ghost and becoming one in the process."

George's hand turned, fingers entwining with hers in a fleeting connection that offered a glimpse of the man he once was. "It feels like he's always one step ahead," he admitted a vulnerability surfacing in his eyes.

She pulled him closer, her embrace a harbour in the storm. "But you're not alone in this. You have a team; you have me."

His sigh was a release, a surrender to the comfort she offered. "I just need to end this, Isabella. For the victims, for us,"

George said, his resolve a tangible force.

Isabella held him tighter, but in her heart, fear blossomed like a dark flower. The man who always had answers, who always stood firm in the face of danger, was now the one in peril. The killer's scheme had woven itself into the very fabric of their lives, a dark tapestry that George was struggling to unravel.

The night had been punctuated by the glow of George's laptop coming from under his closed office door, the click of keys, and a staccato rhythm that countered Isabella's silent prayers for peace. She lay in bed, listening, a sentinel to his dedication, her own sleep sacrificed on the altar of his quest for justice.

The distance between them seemed to expand with each passing day, filled with the echoes of a life they once knew. Isabella clung to the hope that once the Ripper was caught, once the case was closed, she would have her George back. But the shadow that had settled over him was a foreboding omen, a sign that the man she loved might never fully return from the depths of the darkness he was so determined to conquer.

Chapter Thirty-nine

DCI Atkinson looked up from a landscape of case files as Mark Finch knocked and entered, his expression of weary inquiry. "Finch, what brings you here? Where's Beaumont?"

"It's about the Ripper case," Mark began, his voice low but firm. "I've been comparing the original investigation files with the current case. There are... parallels that suggest insider knowledge."

Atkinson's demeanour shifted, a sharpening of his features. "Go on," he urged, motioning to the seat across from him.

Mark laid the files on the desk, pointing to specific pieces of evidence. "These details here—they were never released to the public. The way the bodies were positioned, the... it's as if the killer is recreating scenes known only to those involved in the original case."

Atkinson leaned forward, his eyes scanning the information, the years of experience etched into his brow furrowing deeper. "You think this is an inside job? Someone with access to these files?"

"Aye. It's the only explanation that fits." Mark's conviction was palpable, a clear note of truth in a cacophony of lies and deception.

Atkinson sat back, the implications of Mark's discovery

settling around them like a shroud. "If you're right, we're not just looking for a killer. We're looking for a traitor."

Mark nodded.

"I need to tighten the circle, Finch, and you need to keep this close to the chest so I can root out this betrayal from within." Alistair paused. "You tell no one, OK? Not even Beaumont."

Mark went to speak, but Atkinson cut him off. "Just remember you're only a consultant, not a police officer."

Mark nodded. As he left the office, the gravity of the task was not lost on him. The police were no longer just hunting the shadow of a killer; they were searching for the shadow within their ranks.

* * *

The tension in Atkinson's office was palpable, the air thick with the unsaid. George stood rigidly across from his superior, a man he'd known for years, now a figurehead of authority and, potentially, the end of his career's greatest challenge.

"George," Atkinson began, his voice steady but not unkind, "I know you're a good copper, but I'm considering pulling you off this case."

The words hit George like a body blow, his mind reeling. "Sir, I—" he started, his voice betraying the barest hint of desperation.

Atkinson raised a hand, halting George's protest. "You're too close to it. It's affecting your judgment and your health. And the team... they're feeling it, too."

George's hands clenched at his sides, the fight within him rising. "With all due respect, sir, no one knows this case like I do. I've given everything to it."

"And that's precisely the problem," Atkinson said, his gaze unwavering. "You've given too much. It's not just your case, George. It's the department's, the city's. We can't have you spiralling out."

The word 'spiralling' echoed in George's head, a grim reminder of the whispers and doubts that had been circling him like vultures. "I am not spiralling. I'm on edge because there's a killer out there, and I'm so close to catching him."

Atkinson stood, his height commanding the room. "Catching him or chasing phantoms? Because from where I'm standing, it's getting hard to tell the difference."

George's jaw set, his resolve hardening. "Give me a chance to prove it. Let me stay on the case."

The DCI sighed, the weight of his decision clear in the lines of his face. "I'll give you 48 hours, George. But if there's no substantial progress, I'm pulling you off. For your own good."

The reprieve was a double-edged sword—time granted but with a guillotine's blade hanging over it. George nodded, his throat tight with unvoiced protests.

"Thank you, sir. I won't let you down," he said, his voice a low promise.

As George left the office, the station's usual cacophony of sounds seemed distant, as if he were moving through a tunnel. His mind was a whirlwind of activity, thoughts colliding and fusing in a frantic search for the thread that would unravel the Ripper's web.

Atkinson's warning had stoked the fires of urgency within him. He had two days to validate his worth, two days to keep the chase alive. And in this high-stakes game against a shadowy foe, two days felt like both an eternity and a fleeting moment.

The echo of Atkinson's ultimatum lingered in the air as George strode through the station, his every step a testament to a newfound resolve. The murmurs of his colleagues faded into a backdrop of white noise against the clarity of his singular objective. His mind was a whirlpool, but at its eye was a stillness, a resolve that bordered on the obsessive.

Back at his desk, George sat, the hum of the station's daily grind all around him, yet he was an island in the tumult. He booted up his computer, his fingers poised over the keys like a pianist ready to unleash a symphony. The screen came to life, a gateway to the answers he sought, the justice he was sworn to uphold.

He leaned into the monitor's glow, the files before him a labyrinth to be navigated, each click bringing him closer to the heart of the maze. He was aware of the cost, the personal toll this chase had exacted, but the price mattered little compared to the need for resolution.

"I won't quit," he muttered, a silent vow filling the space around him. "Not until this killer is where he belongs."

His eyes were hard, the green of them iced over with determination as he delved into the archives, revisiting witness statements, re-examining evidence, looking for the elusive thread that had danced just beyond his reach. Time slipped by, unnoticed, as George worked, piecing together the fragments of a puzzle only he could complete.

The station clock ticked past hours, but George was oblivious to its passage. He was a man possessed, driven by the image of the Ripper who haunted his waking hours and stalked his dreams. He could feel the pressure of the ticking clock, Atkinson's deadline hanging over him like the sword of Damocles, but it was no match for the pressure he placed on himself.

His phone buzzed with calls and messages of concern from Isabella, but George silenced it, his focus unbreakable. She, too, was part of the cost, their future collateral in his crusade against the darkness. But he had made his choice, and there was no turning back.

Night fell, and the office grew quiet, the day shift long gone, the night crew too embroiled in their own duties to notice the still figure at the desk. George's eyes never wavered from the screen, his mind piecing together a picture that was slowly coming into focus.

He would not be deterred by whispers, by threats to his standing, or by the threat of his removal from the case. The killer would be brought to justice, and no cost was too great, no sacrifice too large.

Chapter Forty

Morning light filtered through the blinds of George Beaumont's office, slicing the dimness into stark bands of light and shadow. The station was waking up, the early buzz of activity slowly swelling as officers began their day. George, however, had been there since dawn, his presence an unyielding constant amidst the ebb and flow of police work.

He reached for his phone, the device feeling oddly cumbersome in his hand as he dialled Mark Finch's number. The line rang each tone a beacon of hope that today might bring some semblance of clarity, some whisper of insight from his most trusted confidant. But the hope withered with each unanswered ring, dissolving into the dull ache of concern.

Voicemail greeted him, impersonal and cold. "Mark, it's George. Call me as soon as you get this." His words were measured, the undercurrent of urgency restrained but palpable. He replaced the handset with deliberate slowness, his gaze lingering on the phone, willing it to spring to life with a return call.

The silence that followed was oppressive, the unresponsiveness from Finch uncharacteristic and troubling. George's mind raced through possibilities, each more disquieting than the last. Mark was the linchpin of his strategy, the one person who seemed to understand the darkness they were facing. His silence was a void that George couldn't afford.

George stood and began to pace the confines of his office, each step a punctuation to his racing thoughts. The clock on the wall ticked, a metronome to his mounting frustration. He paused by the window, staring out at the city that was just beginning to bustle with life, oblivious to the drama unfolding within the walls of the station.

The Ripper was still out there, and now Mark Finch, the one person who had stood by George without falter, was unreachable. It was a complication that George didn't need— not when every fibre of his being was stretched to its limit, not when the sand in the hourglass of Atkinson's ultimatum was rapidly dwindling.

He returned to his desk and flicked on his computer, the screen's glow a harsh contrast to the ambient light of the office. If Finch weren't going to come to him, he'd delve into the files once more. Perhaps there was something he had missed, some clue that would unlock this whole case and blow it wide open.

As the system whirred to life, George's fingers danced across the keyboard, his eyes scanning the influx of overnight reports, looking for anything out of place, any sign of Finch's involvement that he might have overlooked. But the reports yielded nothing, no breadcrumb trail to follow, no hidden messages within the daily grind of police work.

With a heavy sigh, George leaned back in his chair, his eyes closing momentarily as he gathered his thoughts. The absence of Finch's input was a gap in his defences, a breach in the walls he had carefully erected against the chaos of the Ripper's making.

The phone remained silent, an ominous totem to the uncertainty that clouded George's mind. Where was Mark Finch? And more importantly, why was he silent now when George needed his counsel the most?

The office had an oppressive feel, the walls closing in as George sat across from his old mentor, Detective Sergeant Mason. There was a sense of sanctuary here in the past, but now, it was a stage for confessions and catharsis. George's head hung heavy, weighed down by responsibility and the scent of fear that seemed to cling to the very air.

"I can feel it, Luke," George's voice broke the silence, a raw whisper. "It's like the blood of the next victims is already on my hands."

Mason leaned forward, his eyes sharp and piercing, yet not without empathy. "George, you've been doing this long enough to know that's not how it works. The only blood on your hands is the kind that comes from fighting back, not from giving up."

George's eyes met Mason's, the connection a lifeline thrown across the turbulent sea of his doubt. "But it's like I'm fighting shadows. I swing, and he's not there. He's always one step ahead."

"Then you keep swinging," Mason said, his voice firm, the strength in it a reflection of years on the force and the wisdom earned through battles fought and won. "You keep going through the darkness. It's the only way we ever catch these bastards."

The resolve in Mason's words was a beacon, and George felt a spark of his old determination flicker to life. "It's this feeling, Luke... like I'm so close to him I can almost reach out and—"

"And you will," Mason cut in, his conviction unwavering.

George straightened up, the mantle of his role settling back onto his shoulders. Mason's belief in him was a powerful antidote to the poison of doubt. "I just need a break. One piece of solid evidence."

"And it'll come," Mason assured him. "Because he's human, and he'll make a mistake. They always do."

The room seemed a little less constricting, the air a bit easier to breathe. George stood, his posture more that of the detective that Leeds knew and respected. "Thanks, Luke. I needed that."

Mason also stood, his presence a testament to the old guard, the breed of detective that had trained men like George. "Go get him, George. And remember, this whole department is behind you, no matter what the papers say or how the whispers sound."

A few minutes after Mason left, George's phone rang.

"Are you OK, George?"

"Mark, I'm sorry I missed you today," George began, his voice heavy with fatigue. "We're spinning our wheels here. We're no closer to understanding this... this bastard's motives."

Finch's voice was steady and calm, a counterpoint to the turmoil in George's mind. "It's a marathon, not a sprint, George. You've got to maintain faith in your abilities."

George leaned back in his chair, his gaze fixed on the wall. "Faith feels like a luxury I can't afford right now. Every dead end feels like a victory for him."

"The moment you lose faith in yourself, that's when he truly wins," Finch replied. "This is exactly when your determination matters most."

George ran a hand over his face, the stubble scratching at

his palm, a tactile reminder of the days that had blended into one long, sleepless night. "Determination's all well and good, but it doesn't bring back the dead, Mark."

There was a pause on the line, a breath of silence that held more weight than words. "No, it doesn't. But it can save the living. You know this."

George's eyes didn't waver from the wall; the faces there were a mosaic of the Ripper's making. Guilt gnawed at him, each new victim a personal affront, a life he had failed to save.

"I can't shake the feeling that there's something I've missed, something staring me right in the face," George confessed, his voice a murmur barely louder than a whisper.

"You're only human, George. And this killer... he's counting on you to feel this way. To feel overwhelmed, guilty."

"Isn't guilt part of the job description?" The attempt at humour was hollow, and George knew it.

"Only if it fuels you to push harder, to dig deeper," Finch encouraged. "You've been in tough spots before. Think back. What did you do then?"

George's eyes flickered over the photos, each one a life, a story cut short. "I kept going," he said, almost surprised at his own resilience. "I kept looking until I found something that cracked the case wide open."

"And you will this time, too," Finch affirmed. "Because that's who you are, George. You're the man who finds the light in the darkest of places."

The call ended, but George remained seated, Finch's words echoing in the stillness. His eyes moved from one photo to the next, from one victim to another, their silent pleas for justice fuelling the fire Finch had stoked.

* * *

Detective Chief Inspector Atkinson and Detective Superintendent Smith, figures of unyielding authority, entered the Incident Room with purpose. They were Moses and the police officers the sea, parting as they made their way to George Beaumont.

Atkinson's voice cut across the room, a blade sharp enough to slice through the tense air. "Beaumont, a word." It wasn't a request but a summons. The room fell into a hush, every officer present feeling the gravity of the moment.

George straightened to his full height, his gaze fixed on his superiors as they approached. The murmurs ceased, and the clack of keyboards faded into silence. All eyes were on them, the undercurrent of whispers now a palpable tension that clung to the walls.

"Sir?" George's voice was a controlled calm, but his eyes betrayed the storm raging beneath.

Atkinson didn't hesitate, his words deliberate and heavy. "Allegations have been made, George. You're being accused of being... the Ripper."

The accusation hung in the air, a toxic fog that threatened to choke the truth from the room. George's colleagues shifted uncomfortably, the room a tableau of shock and disbelief.

"That's absurd." George's voice was a thunderclap of defiance. He turned to Smith with pleading in his eyes. "You know me, sir."

Smith stepped forward, his voice a scalpel dissecting the trust built over the years. "We need to consider every possibility, George. Your recent behaviour, the evidence—"

"What evidence?" George's rebuttal was swift, the disbelief

in his tone edged with anger. "Because I'm dedicated? Because I'm thorough?"

Atkinson's face was a mask of official regret, his words the hammer of judgment. "You've been too close to this case. We've found evidence at the scenes that could be linked to you."

George felt the room spin, the faces of his colleagues blurring into a tableau of doubt and suspicion. "I explained the hair. I'm innocent." His voice cracked like ice underfoot, the sound of his world fracturing.

Smith interjected, "It's protocol, George. We have to follow—"

"Protocol?" George spat the word as if it were poison. "My life's work has been dedicated to stopping monsters like the Ripper, and this is how you repay that dedication?"

The intensity of the exchange held the room hostage, the emotional interactions a storm that left no one untouched. George's hands trembled, not with fear, but with the force of the injustice being thrust upon him.

"Look at me," George implored his plea, a command that resonated in every corner of the room. "Look at me and tell me you honestly believe I could do this."

Silence was his only answer, a void where once would have been an immediate dismissal of such an outlandish claim. The trust he had built over decades seemed to crumble before his eyes.

"I will not stand here and be accused," George declared, his voice a fortress of resolve amidst the ruins of doubt. "I demand a formal investigation. Let the evidence speak for itself."

Smith nodded at Atkinson, who said, "Fine, but until this matter is resolved, you're suspended."

The declaration was a gavel striking the bench, and the sound seemed to echo off the walls. George stood, a man alone against the tide, as the room slowly came back to life around him, the machinery of justice grinding forward, indifferent to the wreckage in its gears.

As he walked out of the Incident Room, his head held high, the whispers resumed, the stares lingered. But George Beaumont's determination remained unbroken; the truth would be his vindication.

Chapter Forty-one

It was freezing in the interview room at Wakefield HQ. Detective Chief Superintendent Harry Ramsdale sat with an air of detached professionalism. Across from him, George Beaumont bore the look of a man waging an internal war; his hands clasped tightly before him on the table.

Ramsdale's voice was even, betraying none of the tension that thrummed beneath the surface. "Detective Inspector Beaumont, can you tell me what motivated you to commit these murders?" The question, though expected, was a blade, and its edge cut deep into the silence.

George's response was immediate, a fierce rebuttal that left no room for doubt. "I didn't commit any murders. I'm innocent." His voice, usually a bastion of control, now carried the strain of anger and disbelief.

Beside George, his solicitor's hand was a sudden weight on his arm, a silent command that spoke volumes. The solicitor's head shook almost imperceptibly, a reminder of the 'no comment' strategy they had agreed upon. But in the face of such a vile accusation, silence was a cage, and George's words had flown in the face of restraint.

Ramsdale observed George with a clinical eye, his demeanour unchanging. "Your fingerprints were found at the crime scenes, Inspector Beaumont. How do you explain that?"

George's solicitor leaned in, his voice a whisper that carried the force of law. "No comment," he interjected before George could speak again.

The room felt colder, the air thinner, as if the very atmosphere had been tainted by the proceedings. Through the one-way mirror, Smith and Atkinson watched, their expressions unreadable, their thoughts obscured by the reflective glass that separated them from the theatre of interrogation.

Ramsdale continued, unfazed by the solicitor's intervention. "And what about the evidence found in your home? The photos of the victims, the detailed notes?"

Again, the solicitor's voice, a shield raised against the barrage of implication. "No comment."

George sat back, the muscles in his jaw clenching and unclenching as he fought against the instinct to defend himself with words, with truth. Each 'no comment' felt like an admission, each question a condemnation, and yet the alternative was to play into the narrative that had been crafted to ensnare him.

Ramsdale's gaze never wavered, his questions a relentless tide that sought to erode George's composure, to break through the barricades of 'no comment' and extract the confession that would seal the narrative.

But George was a fortress, his innocence the foundation upon which he stood unbroken. The questions continued each one a hammer blow, each 'no comment' a reinforcement of his walls.

"Your hair was found on Carolyn Carson," Ramsdale stated, his tone insinuating more than it asked. "And why didn't you disclose that you knew the victim?"

George's response was resolute, his voice firm with the ring of truth. "Because I knew Atkinson would sideline me from the case. And Isabella is my alibi; I was with her."

"And the hair?" Ramsdale prodded further, leaning forward with a predator's focus.

"I was at the scene as the Senior Investigating Officer. It's protocol for us to be there." George's answer was a bulwark against the tide of insinuation. "Cross-contamination."

Ramsdale's eyes narrowed slightly, a silent acknowledgement of George's rebuttal. He moved on, relentless. "Then explain why you were identified as the suspect in the digital identity parade?"

George's jaw tightened, a visible sign of his frustration. "Because I was at the scene. If witnesses saw me from their windows, it's because I was doing my job."

Ramsdale paused, considering George's words, before sliding a folder across the table. "Then how do you explain this?"

George opened the folder, his eyes quickly scanning the contents. His heart rate spiked as he read the statement of a fourth witness—a witness claiming to have seen George acting strangely, fleeing the scene in East Ardsley where Ellie had been found.

"That's impossible," George stated, his voice edged with incredulity. "He must have seen the actual killer."

Ramsdale shook his head, a slow, deliberate motion. "The witness was adamant. He identified you, George Beaumont, the detective from the news, the one leading the Ripper investigation."

George's mind raced his thoughts a storm of confusion and denial. "He's mistaken. I wasn't there. He could have seen anyone—it was dark, it was—"

"But he didn't see just anyone," Ramsdale cut in, his voice quiet but heavy with implication. "He saw you."

The words hung in the air, a verdict delivered without a trial. George felt the walls close in, the room shrink. The weight of the accusation was suffocating, a noose tightening around his neck.

He met Ramsdale's gaze, his own eyes a tumult of emotion. "I'm being framed," he said, the words a quiet declaration, a vow spoken before the gods of truth and justice.

The accusation clung to the air in the sterile interview room, a tangible shroud that seemed to mute the usual sounds of the station outside. Detective Chief Superintendent Ramsdale regarded George with an expression that was both stern and regretful, as if he, too, felt the weight of the moment.

"Isabella can alibi me for the times of the murders," George insisted, his voice steady despite the maelstrom of betrayal and confusion brewing within him.

Ramsdale folded his hands atop the cold metal table, his gaze never leaving George's. "We've spoken with her, George. She mentioned that she's often asleep well before you. She can't provide a solid alibi for any of the times in question."

The words hit George like a physical blow, a breach in the last bastion of his defence. He had expected Isabella's unwavering support, her testimony to be his shield. To hear of her inability to vouch for his whereabouts felt like an unforeseen stab in the dark.

Ramsdale's expression softened minutely, a silent acknowledgement of the pain his words had caused. "You're free to go, Beaumont. There's not enough evidence to hold you. But you're suspended from duty, effective immediately. And you'll be released on bail. The desk sergeant will explain the conditions."

* * *

Home was no sanctuary. The silence between George and Isabella was a chasm, wide and deep. She reached out to him, her words a lifeline he wasn't ready to grasp. "George, let's talk—"

But he couldn't face her, not yet. Not with the bitter taste of betrayal still fresh on his tongue. The sofa in his home office became his refuge, a makeshift bed in a room that had witnessed his dedication—and now his downfall.

He found solace in the burn of whiskey, each sip a dulling of the sharp edges of reality. The liquid fire was a companion in his solitude, the only one he allowed himself as the darkness of the room closed in around him.

Isabella's silhouette appeared in the doorway, her form backlit by the dim hallway light, a silent question in her posture. George turned away, the shadows shielded against the pleading in her eyes. The click of the door closing was a soft punctuation to the distance between them.

The alcohol wove its numbing spell, and George succumbed to a fitful slumber, his dreams a chaotic tapestry of accusation and innocence.

Chapter Forty-two

Sunlight seeped through the blinds, casting a cruel illumination on the figure sprawled on the sofa. George Beaumont's sleep was shallow and restless, marred by the ghostly afterimages of dreams he'd rather forget. The ring of his mobile phone cut through the silence like a siren, its shrill tone an assault on the remnants of peace he clung to. He groaned his hand, a heavy, clumsy creature as it fumbled for the device.

"Beaumont," he managed to grunt, his voice gravelly with the remnants of sleep and whiskey.

"George, it's Luke. You need to hear this," came the voice of Luke Mason, urgent and edged with an excitement that felt out of place in George's murky reality.

He sat up, the movement sending a sharp protest through his skull. "Are you sure you should be ringing me, Luke?"

"Probably not; but there's been a breakthrough. It's time to pick the fruits of your labour, son."

"What?"

Mason laughed. "I've been digging through old records, and I've found something—documents about a child raised in Scotland by an adopted family, the child's parents a man named Peter William Sutcliffe and a woman named Annie Jones." He paused, then added, "The birth certificate I got from Scotland's Adoption Register states Sutcliffe's occupation was a truck driver, and Annie's address is in Chapeltown."

"Could be a coincidence."

"It's not, son," Mason said. "Sutcliffe had an illegitimate son, given up for adoption in secret. As you thought."

George's hangover was momentarily forgotten, his mind suddenly razor-sharp. "Are you sure?"

"As certain as I can be without DNA. George, this could be our link. The copycat could be Sutcliffe's son, as you said."

The implications of Luke's discovery spread through George's thoughts like wildfire. A son, a living legacy of the original Ripper, hidden from the world, his heritage a possible catalyst for this new wave of terror.

"Luke, that's... that's incredible. You're brilliant," George said, the words an inadequate vessel for the gratitude he felt. "We need to follow this up immediately."

"I'm on it, but George, be careful. This information is volatile. If it's true, the Ripper might not be done yet."

George stood, the floor a stable ground after days of feeling adrift. "Keep me posted on every development, Luke."

He ended the call, a newfound determination coursing through him. This was the break they needed, the key to understanding the mind behind the madness. The son of the Ripper, a man shaped by a legacy of darkness—could he truly be the one?

The hangover was now a dull background noise, and George's mind raced with the possibilities. He showered quickly, the cold water a shock to his system, a baptism into the new day and the revelations it brought.

As he dressed, his movements were methodical, the actions of a man who had been given a second chance. He had been lost, but now there was a path before him, and he would follow it to the end.

* * *

At his home office, Beaumont sat frozen before his computer, the glow of the screen casting him in a ghostly pallor. The words on the display blurred before his eyes, the name 'FINCH' a stark, unyielding beacon amidst the sea of information. The boy adopted by a family with that name—could it really be Mark?

George's mind rebelled against the idea, every rational instinct within him screaming that it was impossible. Mark Finch, his friend, his confidant, the man who had been by his side through the darkest of cases. The idea that Mark could be the son of Peter Sutcliffe and that he could be carrying on the Ripper's gruesome legacy was repulsive.

But as the shock wore off, replaced by the cold, analytical detachment that had served him so well as a detective, George knew he had to follow the evidence, no matter where it led. Mark had vanished right when they were closing in on the truth, his absence a void that now screamed of guilt.

George leaned back in his chair, his mind racing as he pieced together the puzzle with a new, horrifying perspective. Mark's intimate knowledge of the case, of George's old cases, and of George himself—it all fit together with a chilling precision. Once seen as strokes of genius, the profiler's insights now took on a more sinister cast—the insights of a man crafting his own narrative.

The realisation hit George with the force of a physical blow. Everything did make sense—Mark's strategic disappearances, his uncanny ability to predict the copycat Ripper's moves and his deep understanding of the original crimes. It was all too convenient, too close.

George's hands trembled as he gathered the evidence, the reports, the timelines. Each piece slotted into place with a damning finality. Mark Finch, the man he had trusted above all others, was the prime suspect. The son of a monster, perhaps seeking to outdo his father's infamy or to forge his own dark destiny.

The room seemed to close in on George, the walls whispering of betrayal. He stood abruptly, a man propelled by a need to act. The night was deep and dark outside, a mirror to the turmoil within him.

He had to find Mark, had to confront him, had to know the truth. The thought of arresting his friend was churned his stomach, but the thought of letting the Ripper continue his bloody work was even worse. And so, with a heavy heart, George grabbed his coat and keys.

* * *

The afternoon air was crisp, carrying a chill that seemed to cut straight to the bone, but George Beaumont barely felt it as he stood outside Mark Finch's house in the affluent suburb of Roundhay. The street was silent, the Finch residence dark and seemingly empty, an outward reflection of the void George felt within.

With methodical precision, George donned gloves and shoe covers, the ritual familiar yet foreign in the context of his purpose. He retrieved the spare key from beneath the garden gnome, an act that felt like betrayal cloaked in necessity. As the DI keyed in the alarm code, the digits that spelt out the birth date of Mark's youngest daughter, a pang of sadness struck him. This wasn't just a house—it was the home of a man he had considered a brother.

The interior of the house was still; the only sound was the soft ticking of a grandfather clock. George crept in the halls of a life he thought he knew. Room by room, he searched, the silence his only companion. The familiarity of the space clashed with the dissonance of his mission, each memory that surfaced a sharp jab of conflict.

Finally, in the study, George found what he hadn't known he was looking for. Mark's laptop sat on the desk, its screen dark but inviting. With a sense of inevitability, George powered it on, his fingers moving with a practised ease that belied the turmoil in his gut.

The desktop was neat and organised, a digital reflection of Mark's methodical mind. But it was the encrypted folder that drew George's attention, its label nondescript, yet screaming of secrets held within. It took time, more time than George was comfortable with, but he eventually broke through the encryption, shaking his head at the fact the code was, again, Mark's youngest daughter's date of birth, his heart pounding a relentless beat against his ribs.

The digital contents of the folder spilt out before him, a Pandora's box of documents, research on Sutcliffe, and the adoption that had remained a secret for decades. There, in stark black and white, was the confirmation of the lineage that tied Mark to the original Ripper, the bloodline that suggested a legacy of darkness passed from father to son.

George sat back, the chair creaking under his weight, his breath coming in shallow gasps. The moral and emotional implications of the findings were a maelstrom that threatened to engulf him. This was his friend, his confidant, and yet, the evidence was irrefutable.

The betrayal bit deep, deeper than the cold that seeped through the walls. Mark Finch, the man he had trusted with his life, was now the prime suspect in a case that had consumed George's very being. The knowledge was a weight, a millstone around his neck that promised to drag him down into an abyss from which there was no return.

He had to make a decision and had to act, but the path forward was murky, clouded by a fog of doubt and hurt. The laptop before him held the answers, but it also held the end of a friendship, the demise of a bond that George had thought unbreakable.

With heavy hands, George closed the laptop, the click of the lid sounding like the final note of a requiem. He stood, the room suddenly claustrophobic, the house a mausoleum to the death of trust. He left as silently as he had arrived, the darkness outside now a welcome veil as he grappled with the next steps.

The drive home was automatic, his mind elsewhere, wrestling with what had been and of what needed to be done.

* * *

George's call to DCI Atkinson pierced the stillness of the afternoon like a distress flare launched into a dark sky. His voice, once the epitome of confidence and authority, now carried an urgent tremor that betrayed his inner turmoil.

"DCI Atkinson, it's George. I've found something you need to see," George said, his words rushing out as he paced the confines of his living room.

There was a pause on the line, a hesitation that spoke volumes. "Beaumont, you're on thin ice as it is," Atkinson's voice was a blend of scepticism and warning. "Your bail conditions—"

"This isn't about my bail conditions," George interjected, the desperation clear in his voice. "It's about Finch. Mark Finch. He's Sutcliffe's son, Alistair. He's the one we've been looking for."

The silence that followed was loaded, the unspoken disbelief from Atkinson almost palpable through the phone. "That's a serious accusation, George. And coming from you, under these circumstances... it sounds like the ramblings of a desperate man."

George stopped pacing, his fists clenching in frustration. "I'm telling you, it all adds up. He knew the cases, he knew the victims, he knew me. He's been orchestrating this from the start."

Atkinson's sigh was a gust of impatience. "Your claims are wild, Beaumont. And you're violating your bail by contacting me about the case, let alone breaking into Finch's house. You're not thinking clearly."

"I am thinking clearly! For fuck's sake!" George's shout was a sharp crack in the quiet of his home. "You have to listen to me. For once, just listen!"

There was a rustle on the line, the sound of Atkinson shifting in his seat. "Your obsession with this case is clouding your judgment. You're too emotionally involved. I should have taken you off the case sooner."

"Emotionally involved?" George's laugh was bitter, humourless. "I'm trying to stop a killer, Alistair. Isn't that the job? Isn't that what we're all trying to do?"

"Your job right now is to keep a low profile and let us handle the investigation," Atkinson's voice was firm, a commander regaining control of a rogue element.

George could almost see Atkinson's self-satisfied smirk, the predatory glint in his eye. "And George, between you and me," Atkinson's voice dropped, a whisper of malice threading through the words, "I would love nothing more than to put you away. It would be the cherry on top of this whole sorry mess."

The words were a cold slap, a reminder of the precarious ledge upon which George now found himself. His next move had to be calculated, or he'd fall into the abyss Atkinson so cheerfully described.

"Remember your conditions, Beaumont," Atkinson warned. "Stay away from anything related to this case. That's not a request."

With that, the line went dead, leaving George with a churning stomach and a head full of thunderous thoughts. The man he'd once respected now taunted him with the prospect of his downfall.

George's hand trembled as he placed the phone down, the device now an extension of the cage he found himself in. But the fire within him, the flame that had been fed by truth and justice, refused to be snuffed out.

He would have to move carefully, but he would not be deterred. The truth was a weapon, and George Beaumont was still a formidable adversary, with or without a warrant card. The game was far from over.

Chapter Forty-three

The sight that greeted George as he entered his home was both unexpected and strangely comforting. In his kitchen stood DS Mason, alongside DC Candy Nichols, both wearing expressions that were a mix of concern and determination. Isabella was with them, her eyes reflecting a mixture of relief and steadfast support upon seeing George.

"What's going on?" George's voice was weary but edged with the sharpness that came from too many hours spent in a storm of emotion and doubt.

"We believe you, George," Mason stated firmly, the words cutting through the fog that seemed to perpetually surround George now. "You're being framed, and we're here to help set it right."

Nichols nodded in agreement, her youthful face set in a frown of resolve. "We just need to go over everything you found at Mark's. Every detail could be crucial."

George's shoulders, which had been knotted with tension, seemed to ease slightly. He recounted the visit to Mark's house, each piece of evidence he had unearthed, and the damning implications of the encrypted files on Mark's laptop. Mason and Nichols listened intently, their expressions hardening with every word.

"We'll take it from here, George. We're going to dig into Mark Finch's background and follow up on your leads," Mason promised, his voice a low rumble of assurance. "Whatever it takes, we're going to uncover the truth."

Isabella reached out, her hand finding George's, her touch a lifeline back to the world he felt he was losing his grip on. "We're with you, George. All the way."

Mason checked his watch, his brow creasing slightly. "I have to head to Elland Road for the night shift," he said, pushing back his chair with a scrape. "Candy, you keep working on those files. George, try and get some rest."

With a nod to each of them, Mason departed, leaving George with the sense that he wasn't alone in this fight. The solidarity of his colleagues, the unspoken pact they had formed in the sanctity of his kitchen, fortified him.

Nichols gave George a reassuring smile. "We'll get to the bottom of this, sir. You have my word."

As they dispersed, George felt a semblance of control returning. His world had been upended, but there remained those who stood with him against the tide of accusation and doubt.

The house fell quiet as Nichols left, the night enveloping it in a shroud of silence. Isabella and George stood in the kitchen, the heart of their home, surrounded by the echoes of the allegiance that had been pledged there.

"Isabella," George began, his voice a whisper, "I—"

She silenced him with a finger to his lips. "No need to explain. I believe in you, George. I always have." She kissed him.

"I love you," he said.

"I love you more," she replied.

The simplicity of her faith in him was a relief. At that

moment, the kitchen became a haven against the chaos that raged outside.

* * *

The station was quiet, the kind of hush that only the night shift knew, punctuated by the soft clicking of keyboards and the occasional crackle of radio dispatch. DS Luke Mason sat at his desk, surrounded by towering stacks of case files and faded photographs, the dim glow of his desk lamp casting long shadows across the room.

His eyes were narrowed in concentration as he sifted through the newly uncovered evidence, pieces of a puzzle that were slowly merging into a horrifying picture. Each document, each snippet of information he unearthed about Mark Finch, seemed to weave an ever-tighter web of connection to the dark legacy of Peter Sutcliffe.

The pieces were disparate—forgotten witness statements, adoption records lost in bureaucratic labyrinths, cryptic notes in margins—but together, they sang a dirge of twisted lineage. Mason's hands were steady, but there was a tremor in his heart as he contemplated the implications of his findings.

It was late when he finally traced Mark to an address, a nondescript flat in Hunslet near the River Aire. The flat lay in a shadowy part of the city, where the water whispered secrets to those who dared listen. Mason grabbed his coat, the fabric whispering a soft assent as it slipped over his shoulders.

He dialled George's number with fingers that betrayed none of his inner turmoil. The ringtone cut through the silence, once, twice, then a click, and George's weary voice filled the void.

"George, it's Mason. I've got something. I've tracked Mark to a flat in Hunslet."

The pause on the line was pregnant with a mixture of hope and dread.

"Are you sure?" George's voice was thick with a cocktail of emotions.

"As sure as I can be without laying eyes on him. I need you to meet me here," Mason said, the weight of his words an unfortunate counterpoint to the urgency that propelled them.

There was a rustle, the sound of George moving, a man spurred into action by the ghosts of unsolved crimes. "Give me the address. I'm on my way."

The call ended, but the silence that followed was short-lived. Mason moved with purpose, his every step a declaration of intent. He would face whatever darkness awaited and stand firm against a monster's legacy. The night was his ally, the city his chessboard, and he was a knight moving to checkmate the shadow that had haunted Leeds for too long.

The drive to Hunslet was a blur, the city lights streaking past like falling stars. Mason's grip on the steering wheel was firm, his jaw set. He parked a discreet distance from the address, his eyes scanning the building, a nondescript edifice that could harbour any number of secrets.

He waited, the minutes stretching into eternities until George's familiar silhouette emerged from the darkness. Their eyes met, and a silent understanding passed between them. This was it—the culmination of all their fears and hopes, the nexus of past and present.

Together, they approached the flat.

* * *

The flat's door gave way with a reluctant groan, revealing a scene that halted both George and Luke in their tracks. The interior was dim, the only light spilling in from the street lamps outside, casting long, distorted shadows across the walls. And there, in the midst of the gloom, was the unmistakable outline of a body.

Mark Finch lay motionless, the grim display before them unmistakably reminiscent of the other Ripper victims. It was a scene that George had become all too familiar with, but seeing Mark at its centre tore through him like a blade.

Luke was the first to recover from the initial shock, his training kicking in as he stepped back outside to call for backup. His voice, as he relayed their grim discovery, was a distant buzz in George's ears, muffled by the pounding of blood in his head.

Left alone with the corpse of his friend, George felt the walls of the flat close in around him. He knelt beside Mark, his vision blurring as the reality of the situation sunk in. Tears, unbidden and unwelcome, streamed down his face, the grief a raw, open wound.

"Mark," George whispered the name, a prayer, a curse, an apology. His mind reeled, caught between the Mark he knew and the shadowy figure he had suspected him of being. The idea that Mark could have been the West Yorkshire Ripper had consumed him, and now, with Mark's lifeless body before him, that suspicion felt like a betrayal of the highest order.

Anger surged through him, hot and fierce, not just at the killer who had done this, but at himself for ever doubting his friend. George's fists clenched, the need for retribution burning in his chest.

He should have seen it, should have known. The Ripper had

been playing them all for fools, and now Mark had paid the price for George's blind determination.

"I'm sorry," he said, his voice breaking with the force of his regret. "I'm so damn sorry."

The revelation hit George with the force of a storm: Atkinson, the man who had been a thorn in his side, the insider with access to every detail of the investigation. It made sense, a twisted sort of sense that aligned with the chaos that had become George's reality. But as his mind raced to piece together the evidence pointing to Atkinson, the sound of a door quietly closing elsewhere in the flat shattered his train of thought.

He turned to see PC Andrew Finch, the officer who had stopped him from driving that fateful night, standing in the doorway. His arrival was too timely, his presence too convenient. Suspicion coiled within George like a spring.

"How did you get here so quickly, Finch?" George's voice was a growl, his body tensing as instinct screamed that he was in the presence of the predator they had been hunting.

Andrew's eyes held a glint of something dark and unreadable. Without a word, his hand moved to his belt, and the metallic flash of a knife blade caught the dim light.

Adrenaline surged through George, his training taking over. He'd been a decent boxer in his youth, and though years had passed, the muscle memory was etched deep. He sidestepped the first slash, the movement fluid despite the tight confines of the room and his injured leg.

"Think, Andrew! You don't want to do this," George tried to reason, even as he prepared for the next attack.

But Andrew Finch was beyond reason, his movements fuelled by a madness that had been carefully concealed behind the badge of law. He lunged again, the knife arcing through the air with lethal intent.

George ducked, feeling the whoosh of the blade above his head, and countered with a swift jab to Andrew's midsection. The punch landed with a satisfying thud, but it only seemed to incense the man further.

They were locked in a deadly dance, each move choreographed by survival instinct and desperation. George dodged another swipe, the knife grazing his sleeve, a near miss that sent a shiver down his spine.

"Andrew, stop!" George shouted, but the man before him was no longer the composed officer he had known. This was the face of the West Yorkshire Ripper, unmasked at last.

The fight spilt across the room, a tangle of limbs and grim determination. George's fists were his weapons, his defence a series of blocks and feints that kept the blade at bay. He aimed for Andrew's hand, trying to knock the weapon free, but Finch was relentless.

With a burst of effort, George seized an opening, delivering a powerful uppercut that connected with Andrew's jaw. The impact sent the older man reeling, the knife clattering to the floor.

Luke Mason's arrival with Candy Nichols and Jay Scott was like cavalry to George's one-man stand-off. They rushed into the flat, their training kicking in as they assessed the situation, their collective presence a brief respite in the chaos.

Andrew Finch's eyes darted between the newcomers, calculating his dwindling options. His momentary distraction allowed them to close in, and together, they wrestled him into submission. But Andrew was desperation incarnate, his actions wild and unrestrained. With a sudden, brutal movement, he drove his elbow into Candy's head, the impact sending her reeling.

Jay instinctively went to her aid, his concern for his lover momentarily overriding the danger at hand. This left Luke, his years showing only in the lines of experience on his face, grappling with Andrew. Despite his age, Luke's grip was that of someone who had spent a lifetime upholding the law, but Andrew's younger body proved overwhelming. He shoved Luke aside with a force that spoke of a deep-seated need to escape to continue his twisted mission.

George, who had momentarily been a bystander, now saw Andrew turn to face him. The knife, which had skittered across the floor earlier, was now in George's hand, its cold steel a stark reminder of the stakes at play.

"Enough, Andrew!" George bellowed, his voice echoing with the authority that had been momentarily shaken but never shattered.

Andrew charged like a bull, his earlier finesse replaced by the raw energy of survival. George's mind was clear, his resolve steeled by the knowledge that he could not let this killer escape. He held the knife defensively, his body language not of aggression but of preparedness.

Andrew barrelled towards him, and George had no time to sidestep.

Chapter Forty-four

The two men clashed, brief but intense, a clash of wills where only one could prevail. And when backup finally arrived, flooding the flat with the sounds of authority and the promise of justice, it was George who stood unyielding, bloodied knife in his hand, Andrew finally subdued at his feet.

The revelation fell upon the room, a confession that churned the already tumultuous atmosphere into a whirlpool. Andrew Finch lay subdued, the life draining from him with the admission of his bloodline. His breaths came in ragged gasps, his eyes meeting George's with a clarity that seemed incongruent with the chaos he had wrought.

George knelt beside him, the knife long since discarded, his gaze never wavering from the broken figure before him. "Why, Andrew? Why all this slaughter?"

Andrew's laugh was devoid of humour, a hollow sound that echoed off the bare walls. "I didn't kill those women," he spat the truth, a venom on his tongue. "That was Mark. Mark was the Ripper, not me."

The room seemed to still, the implications of his words settling like dust after an explosion. George's mind raced, the pieces of the puzzle clicking into place with a sickening certainty.

"Mark... he was like him, like our father," Andrew continued, his voice a bitter whisper. "Killing... he couldn't stop. It was in his blood. In our blood. But I wouldn't let it be me. I couldn't."

"And your mother?" George prompted, though he wasn't sure he wanted to hear more of the tragic tale.

Andrew's face contorted with the memory, a pain that ran deeper than the physical wounds he had sustained. "She killed herself. Couldn't bear the shame of birthing Sutcliffe's spawn. But I had to live with it, live with being the son of that monster."

George felt a pang of sympathy for Andrew despite everything. "And Mark?"

A darkness passed over Andrew's features, a shadow that seemed to swallow the light. "I killed him. He had to be stopped. I had to clean the stain he was spreading, the stain our father spread."

The confession hung between them, a grim testament to the legacy of Peter Sutcliffe that continued to haunt Leeds. George stood slowly, his body aching from the fight, his heart heavy with the night's toll.

"So you took justice into your own hands," George said, the statement not a question but a sad acknowledgement.

Andrew's gaze was unfocused, lost in the depths of his own fractured psyche. "Justice? No. It was... purification. Erasing the curse of our lineage."

The room was still, save for the soft, insistent hum of Candy Nichols' recorder, which had captured every word of Andrew Finch's chilling confession. The device lay on the table, a silent guardian of the truth that had just unravelled in the sparsely furnished room.

George stood motionless, his eyes fixed on Andrew, who

lay slumped, the life ebbing from his body with each laboured breath. It was a sombre vigil, the final moments of a man whose existence had been a maelstrom of inherited hatred and self-loathing. Then he stood back as the backup officers moved in, their steps methodical, their faces sombre. They had come expecting to aid in the capture of the West Yorkshire Ripper, only to find a tragedy of Shakespearean proportions.

As Andrew was placed on a gurney and wheeled away, George watched the end of a saga that had terrorised the city for too long. The sons of Sutcliffe, each carrying the burden of their lineage in different, destructive ways.

The drive to the station that night was the longest of George's life, each mile a stretch of introspection and exhaustion. The city of Leeds would sleep a little easier now, but for those who had been touched by the darkness of the Ripper's legacy, sleep would be long in coming.

George knew the story would be sensationalised, twisted into headlines and soundbites. But behind the media frenzy were real lives, real pain, and a tale of two brothers ensnared by a past they never asked for.

* * *

Back at Elland Road station, George turned to face his team, the weight of his duty etched into the lines of his face. His voice, when he spoke, was laced with the fatigue of countless sleepless nights and the gravity of the story he was about to unfold.

"Andrew Finch has given a full confession," he began, his tone steady despite the tumult within. "He wasn't the Ripper... not the one who's been killing all these women."

A collective intake of breath rippled through the room, a wave of shock that crested against the walls.

"He killed Mark... his half-brother, who was... who was the actual Ripper. They were both Sutcliffe's sons by different mothers, both adopted into Finch families. Mark in Scotland, Andrew here in England."

The task force was silent, their eyes wide as they struggled to assimilate the harrowing narrative.

"Mark's mother died giving birth, and Andrew's mother... she took her own life." George's voice cracked on the words, the tragedy of the Finch brothers' lives a palpable thing that seemed to hang in the air.

"Why did he do it?" a voice asked, breaking the silence—a question on all their minds.

"He wanted to cleanse the family name," George replied, looking at Tashan, who had asked the question. "He couldn't bear the legacy, the stain that his father and brother had left on the world. He saw himself as a purifier, not a perpetrator."

The room was steeped in a grim contemplation as George's team absorbed the implications. They had chased shadows and sifted through lies, only to find that the truth was more twisted than any fiction they could have conceived.

The confession, now a permanent record thanks to Candy's foresight, was the key that would vindicate George. It would clear his name, restore his honour, and close a chapter that had been written in blood. George saw the respect and relief in their eyes, the silent acknowledgement of battles fought and won.

They had arrived minutes too late to save Andrew Finch, but just in time to witness the closing of a case that would be etched into the annals of criminal history.

In the days to come, there would be reports to file, press conferences to hold, and wounds to heal. But for now, in the quiet aftermath of revelation and death, there was only the task force, George Beaumont, and the tape that had captured a dying man's last words—a testament to the truth that had almost been buried in lies.

Chapter Forty-five

In the Incident Room the following morning, the undercurrent of relief that always followed the resolution of a case was obvious. Detective Inspector George Beaumont stood before the Big Board, the epicentre of the investigation that had consumed his life. His hands, steady and sure, began the process of dismantling the tapestry of photos and notes, each piece a fragment of the narrative that had terrorised Leeds.

As he removed the pins, his movements were methodical, a ritual of closure. The faces of victims stared back at him, their eyes a silent chorus of the pain and fear they had endured. One by one, he took them down, each photograph a life cut brutally short, each name a reminder of the duty he bore to seek justice for the fallen.

The room around him was quiet; the usual hustle of activity stilled. His colleagues gave him space, understanding that for George, this was not just the end of an investigation but the closing of a personal chapter fraught with anguish and betrayal.

George's fingers paused on a photo of Mark Finch, the man he had called a friend, the man he had mourned. The image was a candid one, Mark's smile frozen in time, a stark contrast to the legacy of darkness he had inherited. A wave of sorrow washed over George, a mix of grief for the friend he had lost and the bitter taste of the truth that had come too late.

The pang of loss was sharp, a reminder that the lines between friend and foe had blurred into a grey that George still struggled to navigate. He placed the photo gently into a file, a silent epitaph for a life that had been as complicated as the case itself.

With the Big Board cleared, George turned to the files that littered the tables, the physical accumulation of weeks of work. He began to pack them away, each folder a chapter in the twisted saga that had unfolded. His hands were efficient, but his heart was heavy, the weight of the investigation a mantle he would carry long after the files were boxed and stored.

He lingered on the photo of Mark again, allowing himself a moment to remember the man, not the monster. In that snapshot, Mark was just a man with a smile and a life ahead of him, not the son of a notorious killer, not a brother twisted by a shared bloodline.

"Goodbye, Mark," George murmured, the words a benediction, a release.

He snapped the lid on the last box, the sound final and resolute. The Incident Room, once a hive of frenetic energy, was now a tomb of silence. George took one last look around, the memories of the case etched into the very walls.

In his office, George sat contemplating the void left by the case's end. The knock on the door was an intrusion, unexpected yet not unwelcome. DSU Jim Smith entered, a man who had always been a silhouette against the backdrop of the investigation, bearing something new—a USB stick that gleamed dully in the fluorescent light.

George received it with a nod, his curiosity piqued as he

inserted the device into his laptop. The screen flickered to life, revealing a video file. He clicked play, and an interview room materialised before him.

The witness, a man whose face was etched with lines of strain, sat rigid in the chair. As Smith began the questioning, the man's eyes darted around, his body language screaming discomfort. The words spilt from him, halting and pained, as he recounted the horror of being confronted by the masked figure known as the West Yorkshire Ripper.

George's fingers tightened around the mouse, his knuckles whitening. The witness detailed the threats made against his family, the cold, hard edge in the Ripper's voice as he forced a false testimony. This testimony had pointed its accusing finger squarely at George.

Frustration boiled up inside George, a roiling tempest that threatened to spill over. The depth of the betrayal was a chasm that yawned wide and dark. Mark Finch, his best mate, the man he had trusted, had been behind this orchestrated charade all along.

"Why, Mark?" The question was a whisper, a breath of disbelief that dissipated into the stillness of the office. "What did I do to deserve this?"

George leaned back in his chair, the creak of the leather a counterpoint to the chaos in his mind. Sadness washed over him in waves, a tide that eroded the foundations of his understanding. The man he had known, the friend he had laughed with, shared secrets with, had become a secret shrouded in shadows.

The video continued to play, the witness' voice a low murmur of fear. George's eyes never left the screen, but his thoughts were adrift, navigating the treacherous waters of doubt and confusion. He had been a pawn in Mark's sick game, a scapegoat for the sins of a man consumed by his father's legacy.

They should have looked at Mark immediately, especially considering he had dark hair and a dark full beard. George remembered the lecture he watched Mark give and scolded himself as he should have known then. He even remembered the glint in Mark's eye as he held Sutcliffe's letter to Crystal Smithies.

George should have seen all of this, but the truth blind sided him.

As the interrogation concluded, George sat in the aftermath, the silence deafening. He pulled out the USB with a mechanical motion, his movements numb. He would need to process this to understand the why of it all, but for now, he allowed himself to feel the sting of the betrayal, the raw wound that would take time to heal.

George stood, his office suddenly a prison of memories and what-ifs. He needed air, space to breathe, to think. With heavy steps, he left the room and left the video and its revelations behind.

* * *

The garden of Isabella's Morley home was a display of domestic tranquillity, a stark contrast to the cacophony of the station.

George, with sleeves rolled up and a tenderness in his actions, was the central figure in this serene landscape, a father transformed by the simple joys of playing with his children.

Jack, with the boundless energy of youth, chased after a ball, his laughter a melody that played counterpoint to the darker notes of George's recent past. George joined in the chase, a smile on his face, his movements unburdened by the weight of the case that had so recently consumed him.

On a blanket on the grass, with the innocence of infancy, Olivia watched her brother and father, her tiny, gloved hands reaching for the daisies that peppered the lawn. George would occasionally swoop in, lifting her gently into the air, eliciting gurgles of delight that warmed his heart.

Here, in the sanctuary of his garden, George found a semblance of peace. The laughter of his children, the soft rustle of the leaves in the gentle breeze, and the comforting presence of home began to soften the sharp edges of the memories that had etched themselves into his mind.

Hope, a fragile seed, began to take root. The future, once obscured by the fog of the Ripper's legacy, now seemed to spread out before him, filled with the possibility of healing and growth. The shadows of the past, while not forgotten, were held at bay by the light of the present moment, by the infectious joy of his children, and by the love that bound them.

George tossed the ball to Jack, who caught it with a triumphant whoop. The simple act was a comfort to George's soul, a reminder that life was a tapestry of moments, some dark, some bright, but all woven together into the fabric of one's existence.

As Olivia clapped her hands, her delight untarnished by the complexities of the world beyond the garden, George felt the tightness in his chest ease. The horrors he had witnessed, the darkness he had confronted, would always be a part of him, but they would not define him. Not when he had so much to live for, so much to cherish.

The afternoon waned, the sun's descent painting the sky in hues of orange and purple. George picked up Olivia, her tiny body nestling against his chest, and took Jack's hand, leading him back towards the house. Their silhouettes, a father and his children, were a testament to the resilience of the human spirit.

Inside, the scent of tea wafted from the kitchen, where Isabella was putting the final touches on the meal.

The garden, with its scattered toys and the echo of laughter, stood as a reminder of the day's simple joys. George looked back one last time before closing the door behind him, a silent vow made always to remember the healing power of love and the promise of new beginnings.

Later that evening, once the kids had been put to bed, Isabella sat on the sofa, the soft glow of the lamp lending a gentle halo to her figure, her arms outstretched. She was the lighthouse in his storm, her presence a beacon of steadfast love and support.

Wordlessly, George crossed the room and wrapped his arms around her, pulling her into an embrace that spoke volumes where words fell short. He inhaled the scent of her hair, a fragrance that spoke of home and heart, and let out a shuddering breath, the tension seeping from his bones.

Isabella's arms tightened around him, her own breath warm against his neck. "Welcome back," she whispered, the words a lifeline.

In that embrace, George found clarity. He had bristled at her honesty during the investigation, her inability to provide the alibi he so desperately needed. But as he held her, he understood the unyielding nature of her integrity. Isabella, a

Detective Sergeant in her own right, was bound by the same code that governed his life. She might have been on maternity leave, but the oath she had taken to uphold the law knew no pause for personal life.

"I'm so sorry," he murmured into her hair, the words muffled but fervent. "For expecting you to lie for me."

She pulled back just enough to meet his eyes, her own shining with unshed tears. "I forgive you."

In that moment, George realised that her steadfastness was not a betrayal, but a testament to the strength of her character. It was one of the countless reasons he loved her, why he had vowed to share his life with her.

"Thank you," he said, a simple phrase that encapsulated his gratitude not just for her support but for her unwavering commitment to the truth. "For being my rock."

She smiled, a soft curving of lips that held the promise of brighter days. "Always."

They stood together in the quiet of their home, two souls entwined by love and shared duty. The world outside could wait; the echoes of the case would fade, but the bond they shared was unbreakable.

As Isabella leaned into him, her body a comforting weight against his, George felt the last of the day's shadows recede. The case had consumed him, but it had not devoured his spirit. And with Isabella by his side, he knew there was nothing they couldn't face together.

The night stretched out before them, not as a chasm of darkness to be feared but as a canvas of possibility. Tomorrow, the sun would rise on a new chapter, and they would greet it together as partners in life and in justice. For now, they had this moment, a sanctuary of peace in the aftermath of the storm.

And for George, it was everything.

334

Epilogue

Elland Road Police Station buzzed with the undercurrent of routine chaos, the ebb and flow of cases and paperwork, of crimes and resolutions. Yet amidst this constant tumult, there was a sense of celebration, a momentary bright spot that drew people together in the usually stark environment of the precinct.

George leaned against the door frame of his former deputy's new office, arms folded, a smile tugging at the corners of his mouth. Inside, Luke Mason sat behind the desk that signified his new rank, the title of Detective Inspector now attached to his name. The office still smelled faintly of fresh paint and anticipation.

"Congratulations, Luke," George said, the words filled with genuine pride. "Detective Inspector Mason. Has a nice ring to it, doesn't it?"

Luke looked up, his face creased with a smile that matched the twinkle in his eye. "Thanks, George. It's going to take some getting used to, but I'm ready for the challenge."

George entered the room, his gait relaxed, but his eyes surveyed the space with an appraising gaze. "I have no doubt you'll handle it with the same tenacity you've shown all these years."

There was a beat of comfortable silence between them, a mutual respect that had been forged in the fires of countless investigations.

"You know, I'm going to miss having you on my team," George admitted, his voice carrying a tinge of nostalgia. "But this is a well-deserved step up."

Luke nodded, leaning back in his chair, the leather creaking under his weight. "Thank you, George, you've always been a good friend."

The word 'friend' hung in the air, weighted with significance. They had been through the wringer together and had seen the best and worst of humanity side by side. The mentorship had grown into a partnership, one that had weathered storms few could understand.

George's smile widened as he stepped forward, extending his hand. "Just make sure you don't forget us little people when you're running the show."

Luke's laugh was hearty as he stood to shake George's hand, a firm grip that spoke of solidarity. "Never," he promised. "How could I forget the team that's been like family?"

George felt a swell of pride at Luke's words, at the acknowledgement of the bond they shared. "You'll do great things, Luke. I expect nothing less."

The handshake lingered for a moment longer before they released, a silent pact that no promotion or change in rank could sever the ties that bound them.

As George turned to leave, he paused at the door, looking back at Luke, who was already sifting through the paperwork that came with the new position. "And Luke," George added, "if you ever need anything, you know where to find me."

Luke glanced up, his expression earnest. "Thanks, George. That means a lot."

With a final nod, George stepped out of the office, the door closing softly behind him. He walked down the corridor, the sounds of the station and a familiar symphony that accompanied his thoughts.

* * *

The therapist's office was a quiet haven, insulated from the clamour of the outside world, its decor intentionally neutral, the air tinged with a professional calm. George sat in an armchair that felt too soft, his posture rigid, an island of tension in a sea designed for tranquillity.

Dr Helen Saunders, a woman with a face that had learned to display concern without crossing into pity, sat across from him. Her notepad was open, a pen poised, but mostly, she offered her attention, a silent invitation for George to unpack the tumult within.

George's gaze, however, was fixed on a spot just beyond the window, where the sky was a murky shade of grey, mirroring the turmoil he felt. He took a breath, a deep one, trying to tether himself to the present, away from the ghosts that lingered on the periphery of his consciousness.

"Mark and I, we were like brothers," George began, his voice a controlled baritone that belied the confusion churning inside him. "I trusted him with my life, and yet..." His words trailed off, the sentence unfinished, the betrayal too raw to voice fully.

Dr Saunders nodded, her expression encouraging. "And now you're grappling with a reality that contradicts everything you knew," she prompted gently.

"Yes," George affirmed, a rush of words spilling forth. "He was The West Yorkshire Ripper, Helen. The man who stood by my side, who I laughed and argued with, who I—" A pained pause. "He was a monster, and I never saw it. How could I not have seen it?"

The question hung between them, heavy with the weight of the unanswerable. George's fists clenched involuntarily, a physical manifestation of his internal struggle. He was a detective trained to see beneath the surface, yet the truth had eluded him until it was too late.

"And you feel you can't reconcile the man you knew with the actions he took," Dr Saunders said, not a question, but a statement that laid bare his inner conflict.

George's jaw tightened, a muscle twitching as he fought against the swell of emotions. "I want to confront him, ask him 'why.' But I can't. He's gone, and all I have are questions that will never be answered."

The silence that followed was filled with empathy, Dr Saunders allowing the space for George's admission to resonate. There were no easy answers, no platitudes that could bridge the gap in his understanding.

"You're mourning, George," she finally said. "Not just for the friendship that was lost, but for the trust that was broken. It's a profound loss, the effects of which are not easily resolved."

George's eyes met hers, and for a moment, they shared a connection, one human to another, beyond the roles of therapist and patient. The acknowledgement in her gaze was a validation of the depth of his pain.

The session continued with a dance of words and silences, of shared insights and solitary reflections. George spoke of his doubts, his anger, his sense of betrayal. Dr Saunders listened, guided, and occasionally challenged, her presence a steady constant.

As the hour waned, George stood to leave, feeling marginally lighter, though the burden he carried was one he knew would not lift easily. The door to the therapist's office closed softly behind him, the click of the latch a punctuation mark on another step in his journey toward understanding.

* * *

The cemetery was a landscape of melancholy beauty, an expanse of verdant lawns punctuated by headstones that stood like silent sentinels, guarding the memories of those who rested beneath. It was a place where the living came to commune with the dead, where silence was a language and grief was the air one breathed.

George stood apart from Mark's grave, his presence unobtrusive, his respect for the family's grief paramount. From a respectful distance, he watched as Mark's wife and daughters clustered around the fresh mound of earth that marked the final resting place of a husband and father. Their figures were bowed, not just by the wind that swept through the trees but by the weight of the loss they carried.

He waited, patience borne of understanding, until the family's slow, reluctant departure left the grave alone, save for the offerings of flowers and the occasional flutter of a bird overhead. Only then did George approach, his footsteps muffled by the grass, his heart heavy with a sorrow that was both personal and profound.

In his hands, he carried a simple bouquet, the blooms a vibrant contrast to the muted tones of the graveyard. Carefully, he laid them at the base of the headstone, a splash of colour against the grey. Beside the flowers, he placed a photograph, its edges slightly curled with age.

The image was a snapshot of a time long past, of two boys with bright eyes and smiles unburdened by the shadows that would later claim them. They stood side by side, the promise of youth etched into their features, the future a canvas yet untouched by the dark brush of the Ripper's legacy.

George stepped back, his eyes fixed on the photograph. There they were, two lads, Mark older and taller than the younger George, full of dreams and mischief, unaware of the twisted path one would walk. How could such innocence be the prelude to such horror? The question churned within him, a tide that ebbed and flowed with the rhythm of his own conflicted emotions.

He felt the pull of the past, the what-ifs and the whys that haunted the corridors of his mind. Yet, standing there amidst the silence of the cemetery, George felt a shift within him—a subtle lifting of the burden he had carried since the case's end.

The wind whispered through the trees, a hushed chorus that seemed to carry with it the echoes of laughter and the remnants of a friendship that had been more brotherhood than bond. For a moment, George allowed himself to remember Mark as he had been, not as the man he had become.

A solitary figure amidst the graves, George paid his respects not just to Mark but to the memory of what had been. In the quiet that surrounded him, he whispered a goodbye, not just to his friend, but to the part of himself that had been lost in the unravelling of the Ripper's tale.

As he turned to leave, the sun broke through the clouds, its rays a benediction, a gentle touch that seemed to say that while the past could not be changed, the future still held the possibility of redemption and healing. George walked away from the grave, from the cemetery, with the photograph's image imprinted not just on the paper but on his heart— a reminder of hope before the darkness and the light that persisted beyond it.

Also by Lee Brook

Book 1: THE MISS MURDERER

Book 2: THE BONE SAW RIPPER

Book 3: THE BLONDE DELILAH

Book 4: THE CROSS FLATTS SNATCHER

Book 5: THE MIDDLETON WOODS STALKER

Book 7: THE FOOTBALLER AND THE WIFE

Book 8: THE NEW FOREST VILLAGE BOOK CLUB

Novella 1: MISSING: MICHELLE CROMACK

Book 9: THE KILLER IN THE FAMILY

Book 10: THE STOURTON STONE CIRCLE

Novella 2: A HALLOWEEN TO REMEMBER: THE LEEDS VAM-
PIRE

Novella 3: ECHOES OF THE RIPPER: THE LONG SHADOW

Book 11: THE WEST YORKSHIRE RIPPER

Book 12: THE SHADOWS OF YULETIDE

Book 13: THE SHADOWS OF THE PAST

343

Book 14: THE ECHOES OF SILENCE

Book 15: BENEATH THE SURFACE

More coming in 2024

9 781917 228107